Lor...

A season of secr...

A darkly dangerous stranger is out for revenge, delivering a silken rope as his calling card. Through him, a long-forgotten scandal is reawakened. The notorious events of 1794, which saw one man murdered and another hanged for the crime, are ripe gossip in the ton. Was the right culprit brought to justice or is there a treacherous murderer still at large?

As the murky waters of the past are disturbed, so servants find love with roguish lords, and proper ladies fall for rebellious outcasts until, finally, the true murderer and spy is revealed.

Regency Silk & Scandal

From glittering ballrooms to a Cornish smuggler's cove; from the wilds of Scotland to a Romany camp— join the highest and lowest in society as they find love in this thrilling new eight-book miniseries!

Praise for award-winning author Christine Merrill

Paying the Virgin's Price
Second in the Regency Silk & Scandal miniseries
"Merrill quickly draws readers into this dark tale of
vengeance and redemption. The mystery carries the
readers onward, as do the finely drawn characters."
—*RT Book Reviews*

Seducing a Stranger
"Lushly sensual."
—*Chicago Tribune*

A Wicked Liaison
"Humor, suspense and a hot romance."
—*RT Book Reviews*

The Mistletoe Wager
"The perfect book to pick up at the beginning of the
holiday season for a strong dose of Christmas spirit."
—*RT Book Reviews*

The Inconvenient Duchess
"A well-crafted, potent and passionate story."
—*RT Book Reviews*

Christine Merrill

TAKEN BY THE WICKED RAKE

HARLEQUIN®

TORONTO • NEW YORK • LONDON
AMSTERDAM • PARIS • SYDNEY • HAMBURG
STOCKHOLM • ATHENS • TOKYO • MILAN • MADRID
PRAGUE • WARSAW • BUDAPEST • AUCKLAND

If you purchased this book without a cover you should be aware that this book is stolen property. It was reported as "unsold and destroyed" to the publisher, and neither the author nor the publisher has received any payment for this "stripped book."

Recycling programs
for this product may
not exist in your area.

ISBN-13: 978-0-373-29624-8

TAKEN BY THE WICKED RAKE

Copyright © 2010 by Christine Merrill

First North American Publication 2011

All rights reserved. Except for use in any review, the reproduction or utilization of this work in whole or in part in any form by any electronic, mechanical or other means, now known or hereafter invented, including xerography, photocopying and recording, or in any information storage or retrieval system, is forbidden without the written permission of the publisher, Harlequin Enterprises Limited, 225 Duncan Mill Road, Don Mills, Ontario, Canada M3B 3K9.

This is a work of fiction. Names, characters, places and incidents are either the product of the author's imagination or are used fictitiously, and any resemblance to actual persons, living or dead, business establishments, events or locales is entirely coincidental.

This edition published by arrangement with Harlequin Books S.A.

For questions and comments about the quality of this book please contact us at Customer_eCare@Harlequin.ca.

® and TM are trademarks of the publisher. Trademarks indicated with ® are registered in the United States Patent and Trademark Office, the Canadian Trade Marks Office and in other countries.

www.eHarlequin.com

Printed in U.S.A.

Dear Reader,

What a long and amazing journey it has been to get to this, the last book of the Regency Silk & Scandal series. My fellow authors and I started out in the summer of 2008, with little more than a few suggestions from editor Jo Grant at Harlequin Mills & Boon that we create a story line and series with a varied cast of characters, and some kind of scandal.

Between us, we have planned weddings, funerals and a hanging. We've cursed, spied and refought the battle of Waterloo. After two years, the people we created have become like an extended and rather dysfunctional family to my fellow writers and me, or, as Louise Allen dubbed us, The Continuistas.

We've had some interesting discussions in the course of writing these books. Where can you go if you want to make out in Hyde Park? And what kind of trees were there in 1814? How many times has Stephano been shot, stabbed or drowned? And where are the scars?

And how, exactly, do you cook a hedgehog?

At the end of it, I think we all are standing back, a bit surprised at what a good time we had. I hope that it has been as much fun for you, the reader, as it was for us.

Happy reading,

Christine Merrill

To Annie, Gayle, Julia, Louise and Margaret, again.
And always. What a wild ride it's been.

Look for these novels in the Regency miniseries

SILK & SCANDAL

The Lord and the Wayward Lady by Louise Allen

Paying the Virgin's Price by Christine Merrill

The Smuggler and the Society Bride by Julia Justiss

Claiming the Forbidden Bride by Gayle Wilson

The Viscount and the Virgin by Annie Burrows

Unlacing the Innocent Miss by Margaret McPhee

The Officer and the Proper Lady by Louise Allen

Taken by the Wicked Rake by Christine Merrill

**Did you know these novels are also
available as ebooks?
Visit www.eHarlequin.com**

Chapter One

August, 1915, Warrenford Park

'Are you enjoying the party, my dear?' Robert Veryan, Viscount Keddinton, rocked back on his heels, as though proud of the job he had done in entertaining his only goddaughter. His wife, Felicity, stood on her other side, equally satisfied with their efforts.

Verity Carlow looked around the ballroom at Warrenford Park. The walls were a pristine white, the accents gold, the design classic and without the fussy Rococo that she had seen in some houses. The music playing in the background was sedate, and as clean and expertly rendered as the white walls. The dancers on the polished marble floor moved to the tune like clockwork figures, and the observers kept their chatter to a polite and unobtrusive level.

It was well-ordered perfection.

The sight of it made her head ache. She gave her host a brave smile that did not suit her mood and said, 'It is

a lovely evening. Thank you so much, Uncle Robert.'
He was no more her real uncle than this ball was a true
entertainment. But if he wished to think himself so, it
would be unkind to disappoint him or to complain that
throwing her this party was little better than putting cur-
tains over the bars of a cage.

She could not, for one minute, fool herself into thinking that this was a pleasant trip to the country. Her brother, Marcus, had made it clear that she was being sent to
Keddinton's country estate so that the family could more
easily control her acquaintances and associations.

It was more than a little unfair of Marc to treat her so.
In her twenty-one years, she had done nothing to give
her family cause to worry. Her past was devoid of even
the smallest misstep. But it did not matter to anyone
what she had or had not done. When they had sent her
into exile, her brothers cited unnamed predators and
vague 'risks to the family' and promised that it was done
for her own safety. But when she had asked for details,
they had been unwilling to clarify their statements so
that she might do anything to protect herself.

How could she know what to guard against, if no one
would tell her the truth? When she asked who or what
she needed to avoid, the best they would manage was
a rueful shake of their heads, and the answer, 'Everything.' They had packed her off to the country, where
she would be bored but safe. And there would be no
getting 'round Keddinton on the details of the trouble,
or when it might be safe for her to return to London.
Uncle Robert was the biggest spymaster in England.
She might as well have tried to coax secrets out of the
ballroom walls.

He was smiling at her now. And though his expression seemed harmless and friendly, she was sure his sharp grey eyes were as ever-watchful as a jailer's. As if to confirm the fact, he said, 'I promised your father that I would keep you safe. And so I shall. It is an honour and a privilege to do so. But it must have been difficult for you to leave your friends in town.'

'It was no hardship to come here,' she lied. 'You know that I always enjoy our visits.' Although she was not sure why he felt the need to watch over her so closely. If there were evil people who wished to harm her, did it not make more sense to find and cage them, instead of standing guard on her as though they expected her to instigate the problem through her own foolishness?

Lady Keddinton added her thoughts to her husband's. 'We want to make sure that you are not feeling blue. And we will give you opportunity to continue to socialize. For I know your family had hoped that, by now, you would have made a match.'

Verity looked at her hostess more closely. Was this an honest comment or just another quiet prod to make her choose from among the carefully vetted candidates in this room? She would think it was the latter, had not Aunt Felicity two unmarried daughters to dispose of.

Not that she wished to poach suitors from the Veryan girls. Verity had hoped that she might be free for a time from making any choice at all. She gave a firm nod of thanks and said, 'There have been three weddings in the family within twelve months. We have had quite enough excitement, even without my help. I think it is probably better that I wait another Season to marry, if only to avoid further stress upon father.'

'But it would not stress him at all,' Uncle Robert said. 'I know for a fact that he is most eager to see you settled.'

Before he dies. Why would he not just say the words aloud, for he was clearly thinking them?

Verity wished that she were allowed to curse, even in the silence of her own mind. To do it aloud would be even better. There were times when it would be most satisfying to tell everyone what she was really thinking. She would say that there was not a single man in London or the country that had raised in her the least desire for an association longer than a single dance. But everyone expected her to make a choice that would set the course of her entire life, so that her father could pass on, believing she was happy and settled.

Uncle Robert was still smiling. 'Now that Alexander is home, you need not fear loneliness.'

'I am sure you will find him good company. You played together quite charmingly when children.' Aunt Felicity was smiling as if there was little left to arrange but a suitable date and the menu for a wedding breakfast.

Although she worked very hard to retain control of her emotions, Verity could not marshal the small sigh that escaped her, on the mention of the Veryans' son. She remembered him not as a good playfellow, but as a miserable little toad. Their recent meetings had done nothing to change her opinion of him. If the true reason for this visit was to isolate her from London Society to put the good character of Alexander Veryan in sharper relief, then she would make her brothers pay dearly for the trick.

Especially since, once they chose to marry, everyone around her had paired off in record time with people that would be considered far too unsuitable for her. Though his bride, Nell, was the sweetest girl in the world, Marcus had married beneath his station. Her sister, Honoria, had admitted in a particularly unguarded letter, that her new husband had only recently stopped smuggling and found honest trade. Even Diana Price, who had been a paragon of virtue while she had chaperoned the Carlow girls, had thrown propriety aside to marry the gambler Nathan Wardale.

Of course, brother Hal's wife, Julia, was beyond reproach. But since Hal himself was incorrigible, his choosing such a worthy bride had been as surprising as the others' selections.

It was clear that each of the matches had been made on the basis of an almost overpowering attraction. The parties involved had been swept away by their feelings, and had given over to actions that were most unlike their usual behaviour.

Then they had all turned to Verity, thinking that for her it would be different. She was to be the sensible one and listen to the wise counsel of people who were happy enough to ignore their own advice. She was expected to barter herself away to someone like Alexander Veryan, making a minimum of bother to her family. Everyone could then go back to their adoring spouses, secure in the knowledge that it was someone else's job to worry about little Verity's future happiness.

'And here is Alexander, now.' Lady Keddinton smiled with such pride at the approach of her son that he might as well have been Lord Wellington in full dress uniform.

But all Verity saw was a young man graced with deficiencies in height and colouring, whose grey Veryan eyes seemed watery and cold in his pale face.

'Verity.' He bowed to her and reached for her hand before she could offer it. His own was soft and damp.

'Alexander.' Why could she not stop smiling, even when cool indifference was needed? Mother's obsessive insistence that she be graceful and charming in all situations was no aid in putting off this most persistent of young men.

'Are you free for the next dance?'

She glanced at the musicians, who were running through the first notes of a quadrille. Saying yes now would allow her to beg off later, should the dance master call for a waltz, or some other dance that required prolonged physical contact with her partner. She smiled again. 'Of course, Alexander.' She allowed him to keep her hand as he led her to the floor, hoping that he did not equate simple courtesy with a desire on her part for increased intimacy.

They formed up with three other couples to begin the intricate steps of the dance. And immediately, her pulse quickened and her fears of a sensible future with Alexander dissolved. She was looking across the square into the eyes of the most fascinating man she'd ever seen. The eyes in question were large and dark, liquid and bottomless, fringed with long black lashes, and set in an olive-skinned face. The man's nose was straight, and his full lips curved in the faintest of smiles as he looked across at her, returning her admiration.

She walked around him, following the dance. It gave her an opportunity to admire the cut of his coat. He was almost too well dressed, his clothes narrowly missing foppishness, just as his face on another man might have been feminine. The darkness of his skin made his cravat and shirt seem blindingly white, and his deep blue coat was as soft and dark as the night.

There was a glint of silver at his wrist, when he reached for her hand, as though his shirt cuff concealed some bit of jewellery. What an unusual thing it was, to see a man ornamented in such a way. If she had truly seen a bracelet, there must be some story attached to it. Looking at the man, she was sure that the tale would be both exciting and romantic, and that she would very much enjoy hearing it.

The touch of his hand was warm and dry, and full of interesting roughness. She wondered just what he had been doing to cause those imperfections. Riding? Duelling? Or was he adept at some art or science that she knew nothing of? In any case, he was gentle to her, and the friction of skin against skin was delicate and exciting.

She returned with reluctance to her own partner, and he caught her hand again in his disappointingly moist grip.

So went the dance, with a series of brief and inviting touches from the gentleman opposite her that made poor Alexander suffer by comparison.

Through it all, the dark stranger smiled at her. There was no mistaking his interest. He was looking at her with curiosity and a bit of sympathy, as though he wondered how she came to be matched with the man beside her. And was she mistaking it, or was there longing there, as well? If she read the truth on his face, he wished he had been partnering her instead of the woman at his side. That woman was receiving only polite attention from him, much to her obvious chagrin.

Verity smiled back at him, wishing she had a fan to hide her blush and covertly signal her interest. If Lady Keddinton would allow an introduction, she was sure that he would turn out to be a horrible rake. He looked like just the sort of man that Diana would have singled out as the worst in the room.

And the hint of a sparkle in his eyes told her that he could see how he was affecting her. For all her previous and undesired poise, she could find no way to disguise her reaction to the stranger.

Verity felt another pang of loneliness. She needed the guidance of Diana and Honoria. Either of them would have prevented her from doing what she longed to do right now. Diana would have cautioned her against it. And Honoria would have very likely done it in her stead. But as Verity looked at the dark man, she felt the undeniable tug of curiosity. She wanted to talk to him.

When the dance ended, she asked Alexander to return her to Aunt Felicity, and go to fetch a lemonade. Once he was out of earshot, she asked Lady Keddinton, 'Who is that man, standing there, by the musicians?' She held her breath, taken by the sudden fear that he was an uninvited guest. Suppose he was the stranger she had been warned about, and his interest in her sprung from a desire to do her harm?

Lady Keddinton, who was many years married and far too sensible to do such a thing, blushed like a schoolgirl. 'That is Lord Salterton. He is…' She paused for a moment, as though trying to remember how she had come to invite someone more interesting than Alexander to Verity's party. 'A friend of my husband's, I believe.' She glanced around, seeking Uncle Robert's agreement, but he was deep in conversation on the other side of the room. She returned her attention to the man they had been discussing. 'He is recently returned to London, having travelled in the Orient.' She gave the smallest sigh. 'A most fascinating gentleman.'

Verity's fears subsided. He could have no part in the family's recent troubles, if he had been in the Orient when they happened. She gave a small, envious sigh. If she asked, would he share stories of his adventures? After looking into his eyes, she was sure that he had seen things that were wonderful, horrible and far more exciting than anything found in her limited experience. 'It must be very educational to be so widely travelled. May I...' Verity paused, trying not to appear too eager. '...May I be introduced to him? Or would that be too forward?'

Her hostess hesitated, as though trying to find a logical reason to separate the guest of honour from one of the guests brought to honour her.

But the gentleman in question settled the matter for them. He was making his way across the room towards them, moving with a dancer's grace as though he was walking in time to the music. He bowed slightly to his hostess, and favoured her with a smile that made the old lady's face turn an even more shocking shade of pink. 'Lady Keddinton, such a lovely evening. It is good to be warmly welcomed, after such a long time away from England.'

His voice was low and smooth, and as captivating as

his person. He spoke precisely and with a faint unidenti-
fiable accent, as though English was his second language
and not his first. Verity drank in each word. She studied
the man as minutely as courtesy would allow, fearing
that she would not get another chance. Once Aunt Felicity noticed her interest, she would be sure to send Lord
Salterton away. And then Verity would never know if
the small scar upon the lobe of his ear was because it
had been pierced to hold a ring.

Now he was turning to look at Verity again. She
dropped her eyes quickly so that he would not catch
her staring. 'And I must say the company is charming,
as well. I beg you, do me the honour of presenting me
to your friend, for I have few acquaintances here and
wish that were not the case.'

He wished to meet her? Now it took all her control
to maintain the thin veneer of polite interest that hid
her true desires from Aunt Felicity. It would be a bitter
disappointment if her instant attraction to the gentleman
prevented his invitation to future gatherings.

Lady Keddinton's smile turned frosty. She could not
very well cut the man, when he was being so perfectly
civil. 'Lady Verity Carlow, may I present Lord Stephen
Salterton.'

When the turn came for her to speak, her poise failed
her and Verity stammered as though she were just out
of the schoolroom.

And Lord Salterton was polite enough to pretend he
did not notice the fact. He said, 'Would you do me the
honour of another dance, Lady Verity?'

She thought again of her brother's warning, and felt
quite ridiculous for it. It was not even a waltz, and she

was in a public place with a man that her hostess knew well enough to introduce. Dancing with Lord Salterton hardly fell under the class of associating with strangers. It would be no more forward than dancing with Alexander had been, and considerably more pleasant. 'Certainly, sir.'

He offered her his arm, and led her out onto the floor. It was amazing that something so simple could be so affecting. She had walked thus with him in the quadrille. But not as his partner. Now it was as if he had claimed her for his own. As they moved through the form of the dance, she was barely aware of the others in the room with her, only the man at her side. Perhaps it was because he did not speak. In a less skilled dancer, she would have suspected that he required full attention for counting the steps. But this man seemed to be focusing solely upon her, watching her as she moved, gazing into her eyes as they met and turned. And he sighed ever so slightly, each time they parted. Was he too shy to speak? She did not think so. There had been nothing in his gaze to indicate the fact, as she had watched him.

But his reticence made her want to draw nearer.

'It is a lovely evening, is it not?' She spoke to fill the silence between them, and felt incredibly gauche for it. Could she not have come up with something more interesting to say to a man that had been everywhere? Although what about her could possibly entertain a man so worldly, she had no—

'Yes. Delightful.' He looked straight at her as he said it, so she was sure that the comment was intended as a compliment to her and had nothing at all to do with the dance.

'Thank you.' And that had been a remarkably stupid response. If he'd meant anything other than what she assumed, it would have made no sense at all.

His lips twitched a little. He knew exactly what she'd thought, and her answer amused him. 'You're most welcome.'

Welcome to do what? His response had proved her perceptions were correct. And now, though he appeared to answer her in kind, he had included an invitation to something, she was sure. He wanted something from her. Or wanted her to want something from him. Or he meant something else entirely that she did not understand.

Oh, how she wished Diana was here to explain. Although it was probably best that she was not. Diana would have glared from across the room, dismissed him with a snap of her fan, and packed Verity off to home before either of them could manage another cryptic exchange.

He gave another smile and an exasperated sigh, as if to say, 'You are not particularly skilled at flirtation, so I shall be forced to help you.'

And then, he said aloud, 'It is a lovely night. But it is most oppressive in the ballroom. Perhaps a turn around the garden would be pleasant.' He spoke the words with such deliberate slowness, that she was sure he meant…

Where I mean to kiss you senseless, as soon as we are out of sight of the house.

'No,' she said, suddenly and firmly. 'I do not think that would be wise at all. I do not like gardens.' Which was not only untrue, but another exceptionally odd statement.

'You do not like gardens?' He smiled again, as though her attempted set down were but another joke. 'Perhaps it is because you have not seen them in the moonlight.'

Or with the right company.

That was what he meant. She was sure of it. For all his good looks and attractively chosen words, he was the sort of man who expected a tryst in the garden after a single dance, and he was vain enough to assume she would throw off the strictures of Society for an opportunity to be alone with him.

'On the contrary. I am not so foolish as to think that what appeals to me in moonlight will have the same charm when the sun rises. Now, if you will excuse me.' And she walked away and left him on the dance floor.

She hurried to the ladies' retiring room, one hand to her face, feeling the growing warmth of her cheeks. She'd made a cake of herself in front of everyone by walking away from the most desirable man in the room, in the middle of a set.

Which was not to say she desired him, of course. Or that she secretly wished to go out in the garden and see if her suspicions about him were correct. Because, if conversation had turned immediately to horticulture, she would not have been able to contain her disappointment.

No. No. No. She was not to go off with strangers. And even if he was a friend, she did not wish a compromising situation in the garden with him. She was not even sure she wished to marry at all. Men were a bother, and it would be just as easy to go through life alone than to adjust one's habits to suit.

Of course, it was doubtful that what he was offering had anything to do with marriage. Merely the most pleasant type of dalliance. One might go out into the garden with one such as Lord Stephen Salterton, and come back a changed woman. And no one need be the wiser.

She put a hand to her temple, as though she could push the thoughts back out of her head. With a few words and half a dance, the man had put ideas there that she could have gone a lifetime without thinking. It was a very good thing that she had not gone outside with him, for it would have been the first step on the road to ruin.

She glanced around herself, relieved to see that she was alone in the room. It was early in the evening, and there was little need for the other female guests to be hiding away with fatigue, either real or pretended. She would take a few moments to compose herself, and then return to the party. Another turn around the dance floor with Alexander would chill any romantic notions in her head. And she would never again speak to the upsetting Lord Salterton.

But just to be on the safe side, she would stay away from the garden doors.

She glanced in the mirror, straightening hair that did not need straightening, and smoothing skirts that were already in place. If one took sufficient care with one's appearance—and did not get overheated by a few simple dances—it was hardly necessary to fuss further. It was not as if a brief conversation with a man was as strenuous as a tussle in the bushes.

And now, she was thinking of tussling, and bushes and gardens. And Lord Stephen Salterton. And her cheeks were growing pink again.

Diana had warned her of the dangers of feelings such as these, and of the need to repress them at all costs. While men might think such things about even the gentlest of young ladies, it did not do for young ladies to emulate their coarse behaviour.

She took a few deep breaths and made her mind a blank so that she might return herself to something akin to normal. And then she stepped from the room.

As soon as she was clear of the door, arms seized her from behind, and a hand covered her mouth, stuffing a rag between her teeth to muffle her attempt at a scream.

Chapter Two

Her assailant wrapped her round about with a piece of rope, firmly pinning her arms to her sides until it was difficult to stand without his help. Then he began to push her toward the back door of the house, and into the very gardens she had planned to avoid.

She stumbled and kicked against him, trying to bump into walls in an effort to shake free of him and stop his progress. But her struggles had no effect. He had a firm grip on the ropes around her body and kept her upright, pivoting easily as she fought to throw him off balance. When he spoke, his voice was barely winded, as though the effort to contain her were no more difficult than walking alone. 'This would have been simpler if you had gone into the garden when I asked. But you are not as easy to gull as the rest of your family. Now, we must do it the hard way. Cease your fighting, for it will accomplish nothing. I am much stronger, and I have no wish to prove that fact by striking you.'

She had imagined that the man who grabbed her must

be some ruffian or stranger who had wandered into the house through an open back door. But the man whispering into her ear made no effort to hide the exotic cadence of his voice. It was Lord Stephen Salterton who held her. To be so used by an apparent gentleman was the last thing she had expected. Could *he* have been the one that had been the reason for all of Marc's vague and dreadful warnings, after all?

She responded by fighting harder, her hands forming claws where they were trapped at her sides. But Salterton continued propelling her forward and out of the house. Why was there not a servant, a footman, someone or anyone who could stop this progress with a scream or a shout? The way before them was clear; it seemed that her abductor had known it would be so. He had planned his assault for a time when he would not be interrupted. He had known where she would go when he angered her. He had hidden a rope and the gag, so that he might quickly render her helpless. He knew how to get her out of the house and away.

There was nothing random or careless in the actions of this man. If he could slip under the guard of Robert Veryan to accomplish what he had, he must be even more dangerous than Marc had imagined.

Once clear of the house, he hoisted her off the ground and carried her into the night, running easily through the trees as though he could see in the darkness as well as in the light. Then he stopped and released her. And although she could barely stand unsupported, he was spinning her round and round on her feet until she was dizzy. When he stopped, she was no longer sure which way she should run to regain the safety of the house, even if she could manage it. Before she could find her balance again, he had gotten a sack from a hiding place behind a nearby tree and pulled it over her upper body. She could feel him binding it with more rope, tangling it around her skirts until her legs were trapped, immobile.

Then he scooped her up in his arms again, and went further into the trees. She could hear the crunch of leaves under his feet and feel branches slapping and tugging at her body as he ran. And then, she heard the sound of a horse snorting impatiently, and the creak of leather harnesses and wooden wheels. He lifted her further from the ground, and then dropped her none too gently onto the floor of a wagon or carriage. She felt the body tip as he leapt into the driver's seat, and heard him snapping the reins and murmuring to the horse in a foreign language, which made it start forward at a brisk pace.

For a moment, she was frozen with the fear of what had happened. And then, she struggled to master her mind. Even though she could not use her eyes or her voice, she still had her ears. What else could she learn from them?

She was alone with this man. She'd heard no other voice offering to help him as he had loaded her into the wagon, nor had it seemed that there was anyone else involved in her capture, other than Salterton himself. No matter what his intent towards her person, as long as they were moving, he was busy driving. Nothing worse was likely to happen to her than had already. It was only when the wagon stopped that she would have anything to fear.

This fact provided some comfort and made it easier to control her panic. She had time in which to form a plan to thwart him. If he truly was a gentleman, then perhaps this abduction was something more than the coarse violation she had at first expected. Perhaps he only wanted ransom, for she could not think what she might have done to offend the man that would drive him to violence.

She tested her bonds and was sure, from the feel of them, that she was not strong enough to break them. But either he had overestimated her size in the voluminous gown, or had spared some small feeling to her femininity. The ropes were not as tight as she would have made them, had she been trying to subdue him. She wiggled her arm inside the sleeve of the dress.

She could manage only a small movement, but it was better than nothing. She smiled to herself, and set to work pressing her hand tight to her side, and wiggling it out from under first one loop, and then the next, working the coils of rope down her body. As her first arm came free, the bonds became looser still, and she found she could move the other arm. If both were untied, then perhaps her legs…

She shifted and stretched against the bonds. Their increasing slackness let her grip the inside of the sack, and work the fabric of it up and out of her way. If she could move it to a place where she might throw it off along with the rest of the ropes, when the wagon stopped she would kick free of the bonds and run. Who knew what he might do if he caught her? But she doubted it would be worse than what would happen if she went passively to her fate.

At last, she felt the horse stop, and heard the driver get out. But instead of coming to pull her out, he had gone to the other side of the wagon, as though he had forgotten her existence.

As soon as she was sure he was out of arm's length, she wiggled free of the last of the ropes and tried to throw herself out of the carriage. There was a loud, ripping noise as her dress caught on a rough bit of wood. Then her petticoat tore from hem to waist, and she tumbled out and into the mud of the road. She scrabbled for purchase, slipping, falling, and then standing to run a few unsteady paces as the feeling returned to her legs. After the darkness inside the sack, the night seemed as bright as day. The landscape was unfamiliar. She did not know if there would be rescue ahead. But anywhere might do, as long as it was far away from her captor.

She heard a curse from the other side of the wagon, and the sound of Salterton coming after her. The ground was wet from a recent rain, and the heavy clay sucked one of the slippers from her feet, leaving her to run unsteadily in her stocking and remaining shoe. The puddles soaked her skirts, and the silk gown which had seemed so light on the dance floor, grew heavy and clung to her legs, making it even more difficult to run. She stepped on a flint, feeling the point of it rip through her stocking and poke into the soft flesh of her sole.

She had made it barely fifty feet when he caught her. He was annoyingly clean, having taken the time to pick his way slowly on the higher and drier ground, while she had blundered through the worst of the mud. He glanced down at her, where she had fallen again, wet and dejected at his feet. 'Are you quite through?'

Truth be told, she was. It was clear that she would not escape him shoeless and with no idea of her location or destination. But all the same, she made another lunge away from him.

He caught her by the last bit of rope still trailing from her waist, and pulled her back as easily as if he was controlling a dog on a lead.

She turned and struck out, scratching at his face.

He swore and gave a shove, pushing her down on her back in the mud. The impact jarred through her, causing more shock than damage. Then he yanked her upright, until her face was close to his own. 'I have no desire to do that again. But if you persist in that behaviour, I will take whatever steps are necessary to subdue you. Do you understand?'

She opened her mouth, trying to scream at him from around the gag, and reached to remove it. But he caught her hands to stop her, smiling at her efforts. 'A nod will be sufficient. I have no intention of unmuzzling you until I am sure that you will not bite. And as for screaming to attract attention? I have taken you to a place so remote that no one will hear you, even if you cry out.'

At his words, the reality of her situation struck her again. She was very much alone, in a strange place with a strange man. He was smiling at her, but there was no warmth or friendship in his face. His look said that he would stop at nothing to get what he wanted. And for whatever reason, he wanted *her*.

After her fall, the soft net of her evening gown was soaking wet, clinging to her skin in ways that revealed more than she would have liked. The cold night air cut through it, making her shiver. But Salterton stood close enough to her that she could feel the heat of his body, and his hands were warm and dry, just as she remembered them from the ballroom. His grip on her wrists was not gentle, but neither did it hurt her. And for a moment, her mind tricked her into thinking it was not for restraint, but out of possessiveness that he held her, as though this touch was a shared pleasure—the first of many. And then, she remembered it for what it was, and struggled against him.

It did her no good. He was so solid and still that it was like fighting against a statue. At last, he grew tired of it, and said, 'You strike me as being smart enough not to expend effort to no purpose. Your attempt at escape and your pitiful cat scratching is more amusing than anything else. Let me give you a word of advice. If you cooperate with me and give me no more trouble, you will be returned undamaged to the arms of your family. But if you resist, that may not be the case.'

She went still, as well, turning her rage inward to calm her body and her mind. As he had done before, he'd seemed to speak to her without words. He still smiled at her, but there was something, a hint in the darkness of his eyes that said, *I am not as unmoved by you as I appear. Do not tempt me. And do not try my patience.*

As if to confirm her fears, he raked her body with a slow, interested gaze, lingering in ways that no gentleman should linger. Then, he released her wrists and held out a hand, as if he were a gentleman, offering to help her back to the wagon.

She gave another little shiver, as though she could shake his eyes from off her form, and tried to loosen the wet cloth where it clung. Then she ignored his outstretched hand, walking with difficulty, for the torn fabric of her dress bunched and tangled around her legs.

He shrugged and grabbed the rope at her waist, giving a sharp tug on it as if to remind her who was in control. Then, with no further offers of help, he led her back to the wagon, returned to his place in the driver's seat and waited for her to climb in beside him.

She glared at him, for he must know that she could not get up onto the seat without his help.

'You seemed eager enough to manage before. I could help you. Or I could tie your leash to the backboard and let you run along behind. Or shall I leave you here, just as you are? You could congratulate yourself on the success of your escape. And if you are lucky, you might be found and rescued before you die of exposure.'

She dropped her gaze and waited for him to decide what he wished to do, unwilling to show any sign that he might take for weakness or cooperation. At last, he reached out and pulled her up to sit beside him. Then he retied the rope about her, binding her arms again and tying the other end to his wrist.

'This is much friendlier, is it not? And so much easier to prevent further attempts to leave me. He gave the rope around her waist a small tug to tighten the knot. 'You may struggle as you wish. It will not break. And it will not cut your tender English skin. It is silk. The same rope that hung the Earl of Leybourne, when your father let him die for a murder he did not commit.'

Was this what it was about? The Earl of Leybourne? Was Salterton some kin of his? She had met William Wardale's children, and none were anything like this man. She had meant to shower him in a tirade of abuse, behind the muffle of the gag in her mouth. But all she could manage was puzzled silence.

He was staring at her, awaiting a response. And then he laughed out loud. 'If you could see the look on your face. It is most amusing. I will remove the gag now, so that you may argue with me as you wish to. You will tell me that your father is innocent. That you think I am a villain. And that I shall pay dearly for this dishonour to you. I have had business with your family before, and I have come through it all with a whole skin. Though you rant and rail, it shall be the same again, I am sure.'

He reached over and yanked down her gag, pulling the handkerchief out of her mouth, and tossing it into her lap. She glanced down to see, in some relief, that the thing had been clean before he'd forced it upon her. And there, in the corner, the initials S and H.

He nudged her. 'Go ahead. What have you to say for yourself?'

'Stephen Hebden?' Despite her family's attempts to keep her in the dark, she had heard his name.

She knew she had guessed correctly, for he started a little as she called him by his real name. And then, he collected himself and returned to taunting her. 'Some call me that. You may think of me as Stephano Beshaley, bastard son of Kit Hebden and Jaelle the Gypsy.'

So this was the man that her brothers had been warning her about. And she had fallen easily into his clutches, just as they had feared. It annoyed her that she had proved herself to be the naïve girl everyone thought her to be. If she had any wit at all, she would need to use it to escape from this situation, for the man at her side was smarter than she had given him credit. She stared at him, trying to divine his true character and wondering how she might separate reality from facade. 'Your half sister Imogen told me of you. You are the Gypsy child that Amanda Hebden raised as her own.'

He rocked back in his seat as though a simple statement of fact bothered him more than the abuse he was expecting. 'I am no longer a child. And I do not consider a few years of room and board to indicate any maternal devotion on the part of Hebden's *gadji* wife.' Hebden's eyes blazed with a cold merciless light. 'After my father was no longer alive to protect me, my stepmother and her family could not get rid of me fast enough.'

Was that pride in his voice, that his father's family could not hold him? Or had their rejection hurt him? Because she could not believe that the feud between the families was all the result of a little boy's injured feelings. She hazarded a guess. 'If you did not like them, and they did not like you, then it was probably for the best that they sent you back to your mother and her people.'

'Sent me to my mother's people?' He snorted. 'They sent me to a foundling home and forgot all about me. When the Gypsies offered me a place, I returned to them with pride. And the Rom are not—' his sneer deepened '—my *mother's* people. They are *my* people, now. And they accepted me, even though I was a half-breed *gaujo*, whose mother was not alive to plead for my admittance to the tribe.'

'Your mother had died, as well?' she asked.

'Of grief. Because the Hebden family did not want me, but neither would they return me to her.'

Sympathy blotted the anger she felt with him. 'I am sorry.'

For a moment, he seemed genuinely puzzled by her response. 'Sorry? Why should you be sorry?'

'Why should I not be? It is a sad story. You and your mother were both badly served. Because I am only a girl, I have no say in the actions of my family. There is little I can do for you, other than to offer my sympathy for your loss.'

She prayed that he understood the fact, and agreed with her. For by the way he had been staring at her, the fact that she was an innocent girl had everything to do with the reason he had taken her. And she feared that he would demand far more than an apology, before the evening was through. 'I am without value to you. Truly. But my father is rich, and powerful,' she blurted.

'I know who your father is.' He smiled as though he had been waiting for the chance to reveal the extent of his knowledge. 'George Carlow. Earl of Narborough. Betrayer of William Wardale. And true murderer of my father, Christopher Hebden.'

'My father a murderer? You are insane!' Any plan to reason her way to freedom was destroyed. But she could not let such an outrageous lie stand unchallenged.

'Ha!' he shouted back, as though he was satisfied with the revelation of her true nature, and twitched the reins to speed the horse. 'My mother died with a curse on her lips for both the Carlows and the Wardales. Twenty years later, the Wardale children are thriving, and George Carlow sickens and dies.'

'He sickens because he is old. Your continual harassment of my family is what weakens him. And he is not dying,' she said, feeling the rising panic that had come so often in these past months. Because he could not be dying. Not now, when she was far from home and unable to be with him. 'But you are trying to drive him into the grave, even though he has done nothing wrong.'

'At best, your father was a meddling fool with no love for me or my family. At worst, he was a murderer. Soon, I will know the truth. Then the man who really killed my father will pay for his crime.' He wrapped the rope around his hand and tugged it tight. 'I will not bother with silk, or take the time to be gentle.' And in that moment, he looked capable of murder.

'But I had nothing to do with this. I was a baby when it happened. Let me go, and I will tell him what you said.' Her voice sounded weak, pitiful. She struggled to control it so that he would not hear her fear and use it against her.

'The children will pay for the sins of their fathers,' he intoned, as though reciting scripture. 'By my mother's curse, you bear the guilt of your family. If your father wishes to stay my hand against you, he will admit what he did.'

She wished that she could raise her arms, so that she could put her hands to her ears and block out the man's madness. If a twenty-year-old grievance and a dead woman's curse had driven him to take her, then what hope did she have that he would be satisfied and release her, even if her father told him the lie he wished to hear?

She looked ahead of the wagon, trying to guess where they might be going. The road had narrowed before them. And now, there were overarching trees to block out the stars. She wished she knew enough about such things to guess which direction they had gone. Although she suspected that the glow on her left might be the first light of dawn. They had been travelling for hours, and she had not seen so much as a cottage.

Then, in front of her, another faint glow. She sniffed the wind. Wood fires. A horse gave a welcoming whinny as they drew near. They passed another bend in the road. And there before them, in a clearing surrounded by beeches, was a Gypsy camp.

She had never seen such a place before, but it must be that. There was a circle of tents, some of them big enough for a whole family, and also several curved roofed wagons that looked like small houses on wheels. But it was too early for the people to be awake. No lanterns were lit, and the cooking fires were banked. If she cried out, would anyone wake to help her? Or would they lie still in the dark, pretending that they did not hear?

The man who called himself Stephano Beshaley had driven close to the largest of the wagons, this one painted in green and gold. He slid out of the seat beside her, still holding the rope that bound her waist and hands. He tugged until she followed him to the ground, catching her as she almost fell. And then, he was pulling her towards the brightly painted wagon.

She set her feet in the ground and wrapped her hands on the rope, pulling back to free herself. 'No.'

He laughed, and tugged back until she stumbled forward, into his arms. He held her, wrapping his arms about her waist, until there was no space left between them. 'You will say yes to me, until I say otherwise.'

'I will not,' she shouted. But his touch made her feel so strange that suddenly she was not sure what would happen if he did not release her. 'Let me go!' She squirmed and pushed at his arms, trying to get away, but only succeeded in tearing a hole in her bodice when the net caught on the buttons of his coat. 'Help me! Someone! Please!'

There was a grumbling from one of the tents, followed by laughter from another, and a child's murmuring of questions, which were quickly silenced. But no one appeared, neither to aid her, nor to be curious about the goings on.

Her shouts made him hold her all the tighter, as though he meant to squeeze the air from her lungs. Perhaps that was what was happening, for she felt light-headed, almost to the point of faintness. The contact of their bodies was more terrifyingly intimate than anything she'd experienced. But the fear she felt was not for the man who held her, but of the other more pleasant sensations he evoked. With a final shudder, she forced herself to stop fighting and lie still in his arms. For when she moved her body against the hardness of his, she could not remember why she wished to escape.

He must have felt it, as well, for he stood very still, and his eyes seemed to go even darker. He was staring at her lips as though he could know the taste of them, just by looking. And for a moment, she thought the same. For though he had not moved, she could imagine the feel of his mouth on hers, kissing her with such force that she would beg to surrender to him.

He moved suddenly, scooping her legs out from under her and carrying her up the little wooden steps of the wagon. He fumbled with the latch for a moment, then took her through and kicked the door shut behind them. It was too dark to see, but he had dropped her onto something soft that felt like a mattress.

She lay still, sure that any movement would draw dangerous attention from him. She should have thrown herself out of the wagon—to her death if necessary— instead of listening to his bitter childhood stories. Now, he was standing between her and the door, fumbling to light a candle. If she tried to push past him, she could not help but touch him. And if she touched him…

She was shaking, now. She told herself that it was only because she was cold and wet from her struggles in the bog. But she knew it was more than that. He was reaching for her.

And she closed her eyes and trembled with anticipation.

She felt his hands at her waist, untying the rope that was still attached there, drawing it out from under her body, and casting it away.

When she looked up at him, he was staring down at her, his own face devoid of emotion. 'Strip.'

'I beg your pardon?' She scooted away from him on the bed.

'Remove your clothing. To the last stitch. And then wash yourself.'

'I will do no such thing.'

'You will do as I say.' He rubbed his thumb across his own dark skin, and then held it out to show her that is was clean. 'You think me a dirty Gypsy? This does not wash off. But you?'

He reached for her, and she flinched away from him.

But he caught her under the jaw and held her face still, running his other thumb slowly along her cheek. Then he held it out to show her the mud. 'You are filthy. And you are sitting on my bed. Your fancy dress is ruined, and as useless in a Gypsy camp as the woman it covers. Remove your clothing and wash yourself, or I will do it for you.'

Then he turned away from her, going to a trunk in the corner. He began removing his own clothes, stripping off coat and waistcoat, cravat and shirt, brushing away the dried mud from them and folding each piece and putting it on a chair in front of him. When he stood bare to the waist, he splashed himself with water from the basin, and towelled dry.

Although she tried not to stare, it was almost impossible to look away. His body was lithe and his dark skin marked with a crisscross of scars. His shoulders were wide and strong, and she shivered as she saw the sinewy arms that had held her. The silver bracelet on his wrist almost seemed to glow against the darkness of his skin.

Then he pulled off his boots and trousers, and continued to wash. She could see the long line of his well-muscled flank. The curves and planes of his body were as well defined as a Greek statue—and every bit as bare. And he was as casual in his nakedness as the statue might have been, for he paid no more attention to her, as if he was alone in the room.

As she watched him, her insides gave a funny lurch and her heart beat unsteadily in her chest. It must be the result of too much fear and not enough food or sleep, and the stress of not knowing what might happen to her in the coming hours. If he was not watching, and she could not manage the strength to escape, she should at least gather the energy to protest this most recent threat to her honour. She should not be sitting on the bed in a daze, thinking things that did not match with what she ought to be feeling, in her current and extremely precarious condition.

She should not be staring.

Perhaps it was the disinterest he was showing her, at the moment when she expected him to be the most threatening. But she was overcome with a languor, and the desire to lie back on the bed and continue to gaze upon him. For he was beautiful in his nakedness, and totally alien from anything or anyone she had known.

He began to dress again, pulling on a pair of loose wool trousers, low boots, and a shirt of striped silk. Then he reached into a pouch at his waist and removed a gold hoop, fixing it in the hole in his ear. When he turned back to her, the English gentleman she had danced with might as well have never existed. This man was every bit a Gypsy.

As he stared at her, his cold expression was softening into a seductive smile. Though he had not been bothered by it, he must have known that she had been watching him change, and known the affect the sight of him would have on her. 'Well? Do not sit gawking at me, woman. Do as I say. Give me your clothing.'

And for a moment, the idea beckoned to her. To be wild and carefree, and cast off her old life as easily as she had her clothes. Then the truth of the situation rushed back like cold rain, and she found her voice again. 'Certainly not. Perhaps you have no shame and no sense. But I have no intention of removing my clothes for your entertainment.'

'My entertainment?' He laughed. 'If I wished a naked woman in my vardo, I could have a new one every night, each more beautiful than the last. I do not need to take by force what will be freely given if I but ask. I have need of your clothing, and considerably less interest in the sight of your body than you had in mine.'

Not only had he known she was watching, but there was something in his smile that made her believe he had taken more time than he'd needed to change, to pique her interest. If so, then his shamelessness knew no bounds. She shuddered in disgust. 'Your desires in the matter are of little concern to me. I am here against my will. You may think and say and do what you will, but I do not intend to cooperate in your plans for me.'

He stared at her, with the relaxed, almost lazy smile that a cat might give to a mouse. 'Very well, then. If you will not remove your clothes, I must resort to force after all.' He took a single step in her direction before she lost her nerve.

'Leave me alone in the wagon, and I will do what you ask,' she said hurriedly. 'But if you remain…'

What would she do? She had best not offer any suggestions, or he might remain and take the clothing himself.

After what seemed like an infinity, he said, 'I will wait outside. When you are finished, you will knock on the door and place your clothing on the step.'

She nodded, and watched as he took himself out of her presence. As the door shut, she stared at it. She was rid of the Gypsy, for now, at least. And with his absence, sanity returned, and with it, her desire to escape.

She glanced around the little room. The windows were too small for her to pass through. The only way out was through the door in front of her, and Stephano stood just on the other side. She reached for the handle and opened the door a crack.

He stood facing her, just as she had suspected, arms folded across his chest. 'I am waiting.'

She shut the door in defeat. To disobey him might mean disaster. And he was right in one thing, at least. She was tired and dirty, and her clothing was cold and wet. The beautiful gown of white net that she had worn to the ball was little better than a rag. She was even more miserable than she might be if she removed it.

She glanced around the wagon. What was she to wear instead? Did he mean to bring her replacements? Or was it just an elaborate ruse to make her bare herself? She was shivering as she fumbled with the closures on her ball gown. She dropped it and the muddy, torn petticoats into a heap on the floor, and then bundled them up, and opened the door a crack, pushing them out toward the Gypsy.

His hand appeared in the crack in the door, and he opened it wider, but did not look in. 'The rest, as well.'

'Most certainly not.'

'The stays, the shift. Stockings and shoes—' he paused '—shoe, rather. You left one behind already. Remove them, or I shall.'

She slammed the door, and shouted through the

wood. 'Bastard!' And was surprised by the sound of her own voice.

He laughed in response. 'An accurate assessment of my parentage. But unusual to hear it from such ladylike lips. Perhaps it was the gown alone that gave you the air of gentility. Who knows what you shall be like, when you wear nothing but skin?'

'*You* certainly shall not.'

He laughed again. 'You are right in that. I must leave you alone for the day. And I will not have you thinking that, when I am gone, you can turn my people against me, or make a daring escape cross country. You will find it difficult to do, if you must walk through the camp dressed as nature intended, with not even shoes for protection.'

'You mean to leave me…' She swallowed.

'Better than not leaving you alone, while in that condition. Unless you prefer…'

For the second time in her life, she cursed aloud.

He laughed again. 'I thought not. You will be perfectly safe, shut up in the wagon. No one will trouble you. No one would dare.' There was a darkness in his tone that made her sure of the truth. And then, the smile was back in his voice. 'And if you are good, and behave yourself in my absence? Then I shall return some of your clothing to you this evening.'

'You will return my own things to me as a reward?' She cursed him again.

He laughed again. 'Not if you act in that way. Now, remove the rest. Or…' He let the last word hang in the air, and she reached for the laces. When she had another small pile of clothes before her, she hid herself behind the door, opened it a crack and forced the things out of the wagon, then quickly slammed the door again.

There was a moment of silence, and then the Gypsy said, 'All seems to be in order. My bed might not be to your liking, but it is the best I mean to offer. I suggest you avail yourself of it. I will return later in the day.'

And then, she heard no more.

Chapter Three

Stephano stood perfectly still in the bedroom of his London home on Bloomsbury Square, undergoing the transformation from Gypsy back to gentleman. His valet, Munch, cast aside a wrinkled strip of linen and started with a fresh cravat. 'If you insist on starting again…' Stephano muttered, eager to be getting on to his appointment. He had wasted hours in the night, traipsing around the countryside to befuddle the Carlow girl as to their location. And now, the delivery of the ransom demand had been complicated by Robert Veryan's unexpected flight to London.

'If you are going to Keddinton's office, then the knot must be perfect.' Munch's flat voice came out of an equally flat face, and often left people expecting a man of limited dexterity or intelligence. But his thick fingers did not fumble as he tied the fresh knot, nor did his perception of the situation. 'You cannot expect the man to take you seriously, if you treat him otherwise. And you cannot afford to show weakness, even something as small as a wilted cravat.'

'True, I suppose. But damn the man for spoiling my morning. I had hoped to be done with this business before breakfast, so that I might have a decent meal and a little sleep. Now, it will take the better part of the day. It is easier to appear strong when I am rested.'

His friend and butler, Akshat, waited patiently at his right hand. 'How are you feeling this morning, Stephen Sahib?'

In truth, he felt better than he had expected, after a sleepless night and several hours in the saddle. 'The headache is not so bad today. After a cup of your special tea, I shall feel almost normal.'

Akshat had anticipated his request, and was stirring the special herbs that were the closest thing to a remedy for the incessant pounding in his skull. If it could keep him clear-headed for just a few more days, he had hopes that the curse would be ended, and the headache would go with it.

He drank the proffered tea, and looked at himself in the mirror. He was a new man. Or his old self, perhaps. He was no longer sure. But he knew it was Stephen Hebden the jewel merchant who was reflected in the cheval glass, as he brushed at an imaginary speck of lint on the flawless black wool. When a member of the gentry needed someone to dispose of the family diamonds, or find a jeweller to produce a paste copy of something that had been lost at hazard—or forgotten in a mistress's bed—there was none better than Mr Hebden to handle the thing. He was discreet, scrupulously honest, and always seemed to be where he was needed, when he was needed. It said much to his knowledge of the lives of his customers.

He grinned at himself in the mirror. And if one had business of a less scrupulous nature, Mr Hebden could always count on Salterton. And then, of course, there was the Gypsy, Beshaley. Robert Veryan had dealt with all three, at one time or another. And while the servants at Bloomsbury Square were quite used to Mr Stephen's unusual ways, Veryan found it quite upsetting to get visits from a man who could not be filed easily for future reference. Today, he would use the old man's unease to good advantage.

Stephano glanced again at the cut of his coat. What do you think, Munch? Sombre enough to visit a viscount?'

The Indian grinned at him, and Munch said, 'Sombre enough to attend the funeral of one.'

'Very good. When one means to be as serious as death, one might as well dress the part.' And the severity of the tailoring did much to clear his head of distractions for the difficult day ahead. Although he had not expected to make a trip to London for his interview with Keddinton, he would almost have deemed the kidnap a success. But he had underestimated his captive, and his reaction to her.

He resisted the urge to pull apart Munch's carefully tied cravat while attempting to cool the heat in his blood. He had been watching the girl from a distance for weeks, convinced she was no different from a dozen other Society misses. She was lovely, of course. But a trifle less outgoing than her peers. And more malleable of opinion, if her reaction to the people around her was any indication. She seemed to follow more than she led, and she did it with so little complaint that he wondered if she was perhaps a bit slow of wit.

A deficiency of that sort would explain her tepid reaction to the gentlemen who courted her. When the men she had spurned were away from female company and felt ungentlemanly enough to comment on her, they shook their heads in disgust and announced that, although her pedigree was excellent, the girl was not quite right. Though their suits had met with approval from her father, Earl of Narborough, and her brother, Viscount Stanegate, they had been received by the lady with blank disinterest and a polite 'No, thank you.' It was almost as if the girl did not understand the need to marry, or the obligation to marry well.

When he had planned her abduction, Stephano had expected to have little trouble with her. Either she would go willingly into the garden because she lacked the sense not to, or she would retreat to the retiring room and he would take her in the back hall.

But he had imagined her frightened to passivity, not fighting him each step of the way. He had not expected her to work free of her bonds, nor thought her capable of tearing her virginal white ball gown to shreds in her attempt to escape.

Nor had he expected the lusciousness of the body that the dress had hidden. Or how her eyes had turned from green to golden brown as he'd held her. Or the way those changeable eyes had watched him undress. When he had planned the abduction, he had not expected to want her.

He looked again at his sober reflection in the mirror,

and put aside his thoughts of sins of the flesh. While the lust that she inspired in him might have been a pleasant surprise, he did not have the time or inclination to act on it. It was an unnecessary complication if the plan was to hold her honour hostage to gain her family's cooperation.

When he arrived at Lord Keddinton's London home a short time later, he pushed his way past the butler, assuring the poor man that an appointment was unnecessary: Robert Veryan was always at home to him.

Keddinton sat at the desk in his office, a look of alarm on his pasty face. 'Hebden. Is it wise to visit in daylight?'

Stephano stared down at the cowardly little man. 'Was it wise to run back to London so soon after the disappearance of your guest? You should have taken the time to look for the girl, before declaring her irretrievable.'

'I—I—I felt that the family must be told, in person, of what had occurred.' The man's eyes shifted nervously along with his story.

'You thought to outrun me, more like. By coming here, you deviated from the instructions I set out for you. You were to await my message to you, and then you were to deliver it. It was most inconvenient for me to have to follow you here. Inconvenient, but by no means difficult.'

When Keddinton offered no further explanation, Stephano dropped the package he had brought onto the desk in front of him. 'You will take this to Carlow.'

The man ignored his order and said, 'The girl. Is she still safe? Because you took her from my house.'

'Exactly as you knew I would,' Stephano reminded him calmly. 'We agreed on the method and location, before I took any action.'

Keddinton's breathing was shallow, as though now that the deed was done, he was a scant inch from panic. 'She was supposed to be in my care. And if the Carlows realize that it was I who recommended Lord Salterton to my wife…'

'You will tell them you had no idea that the man was a problem, and that you are not even sure he was the one who took her. Her absence was not discovered until late in the evening, was it? And others had departed by that time, as well. I took care that no one saw me leaving. The corridor and the grounds were empty, as you'd promised they would be.'

'But still…' Keddinton seemed to be searching for a problem where none existed.

'Thinking of your own skin, are you?' Stephen wondered who the bigger villain might be, George Carlow, or Veryan for his easy betrayal of his old friend.

And worse, that it would happen at the expense of an innocent girl… It had been difficult for Stephano to reconcile himself to his own part in the crime. He had not stuck at kidnapping women before. But it had never ended well for him. He was almost guaranteed a headache so strong that he would be too sick to move for several days. His late mother might still want her vengeance, but it was as though she punished him for the dishonourable acts she pushed him to commit.

But though his head might feel better today, it turned his stomach at how easy it had been to persuade Verity Carlow's godfather to help in her abduction.

Keddinton opened the package in front of him, and went even paler when he recognized the contents. It was a chemise, embroidered at the throat with the initials V C, and tied tightly about the waist with red silk rope. He looked up at Stephen with alarm. 'My God, Hebden. You didn't…'

'Touch the girl?' Stephano laughed in response. 'Certainly not. She is worth more to me as a virgin hostage, than she is as some temporary plaything.' But the image of the girl sprang to his mind, sprawled upon his bed with her skirts ripped near to the waist to give a tantalizing glimpse of her silk-covered legs. 'Since you are so quick to search the package I intended for another, then you had best read the attached note.' He quoted from memory. 'Your daughter is safe, for now. If you wish her to return the same, then admit in public what you have done.'

'But is this—' he poked at the chemise and shuddered in distaste '—is this necessary? Surely you did not need to be quite so theatrical.'

'Theatrical?' He laughed again. 'I have made both the Carlows and the Wardales shake in their beds for months, each one worrying that they would get a bit of rope in the mail. All because of a curse that would have no hold over them, if they did not secretly believe that they were deserving of punishment. And now, because I have sent you a lady's undergarment, you think that I am developing a taste for the theatrical?' He could still feel the softness of the garment, as he'd tied it up, and the softness of the girl that had worn it. He felt the pounding in his head begin again, as he thought of the girl, naked in the wagon, waiting for his return. If he truly wanted revenge, it would be so very easy. And so very pleasurable. He laughed louder. But the sound did nothing to stop the lurid thoughts in his head or the agony they brought with them.

Then, as if one pain would stop another, he grabbed the letter opener from Keddinton's desk, and dragged the blade of it along his palm until a line of red appeared there. He held his hand out over the shift, watching the drops of crimson fall onto the muslin. He made a fist, and squeezed it shut, until his mind cared about nothing but its own pain and the sharp sting of the open cut.

Then he looked up at Robert Veryan, as the blood continued to drip from his hand. 'This, you snivelling coward, is what a taste for the dramatic looks like. Tell your friend, the murderer Carlow, that for now it is my own blood that was spilled. But if he does not accede to my demands, then the next package will be soaked in his daughter's blood. Can you manage that, without running away again?' He leaned over the desk and watched the older man shrink away from him. It was as easy as it had ever been to intimidate him into obedience.

Keddinton gave a shaky nod. 'If they agree to your demands, how shall I reach you?'

Stephano reached into his pocket for a handkerchief to bandage his still-bleeding hand. 'You do not reach me, Veryan. I am unreachable. Invisible. Unfindable. As is the girl, until this is over.'

In fact, she was hidden on Veryan's own property, less than six miles from his house. If the man had been the expert spy catcher everyone thought him, such a simple deception should have been impossible. But the profound ignorance he displayed over small things was more than a match for the intelligence he displayed in others. 'I will return to you in a week's time, and expect to hear George Carlow's answer. Should you, through disobedience or incompetence, give me reason to come back here before then, it will go hard for you. Do not run, for I will have no trouble finding you, no matter where you might hide. And I will punish you. Is that understood?'

He gave Veryan a moment to remember their first meeting. He had recognized the man as a weak link in the chain that would lead him to his father's killer. He had broken into Veryan's private rooms, in the night. And then he had shaken the man once, as a terrier might shake a rat, and left him weeping on the floor. It had not taken a single blow to convince him to turn traitor to his friends and serve as Stephano's right hand in vengeance.

It was just one more proof of the falseness of the honour that supposed English gentlemen held so high.

'As long as there is nothing to lead them back to me in this,' Veryan muttered.

'Is that all that concerns you?' Stephano sneered. 'This will be over soon, Veryan, and you will be safe. Now that I have the girl, it will not take long for Carlow to reveal his part in the murder.' Because he could not imagine the man would be so casual with the safety of his youngest daughter. 'But it does my heart good to see your very belated care for Verity Carlow's safety.'

'When you asked me to help you, you promised you would not hurt her,' Veryan said the words with a whine, as though they were a defence of his betrayal.

So Stephano leered at him and said, 'Perhaps I regret

my promise. She is a most lovely girl, and as a Gypsy, I have no honour, and am used to taking whatever I desire.' The headache grew. And for a moment, his sight dimmed as though the pain behind his eyes was an impenetrable fog.

When his vision cleared, Veryan was gaping like a fish, eyes goggling with shock as though he were sharing an office with a fiend from hell.

Stephano sighed and took a moment to compose his features, hiding his weakness from the spymaster. Then he said, 'If they do not tell the world of her disappearance, then no one shall know of it. Once they give me what I want, I will bring her back as quickly and secretly as I took her. She will be back in her home before anyone knows that she is missing, reputation intact and none the worse for the experience.' And with that vaguely honourable promise, the agony diminished.

Veryan grinned at him, the sweat beading on his forehead. 'That is good. And they will never know it was me.'

Again, back to the man's only true fear. 'I will certainly not tell them, Veryan. And once Carlow's involvement in my father's death is uncovered, no one will care how it came about.'

'And we will be heroes,' Keddinton said.

'Because justice will have been done.' Stephano repeated it as he had, several times before, to buck up the spirits of the oily little man. It was the carrot to match the stick. Keddinton had gotten it into his head that catching a traitor and murderer, after all this time, would be the thing to propel him to greater heights in government and another title. Perhaps it would. Stephano had little interest in the details. But if they helped to keep the man in line, he could think what he liked.

Now that the headache was receding, he could feel the pain in his hand again. As he flexed his fingers, he was annoyed to see blood seeping through the makeshift bandage. He glared at Keddinton. 'Deliver the package and my message. Tell Stanegate I accosted you in the street and was gone before you could follow. He will take this to his father. I will return in a week.' And he turned and left the proud Viscount Keddinton shaking behind his desk.

When she could no longer hear the Gypsy taunting her from outside the vardo wagon, Verity shouted a brief tirade of curses and pleas into the silence on the other side of the door. Then she fell silent herself, as she suspected that further shouting served no purpose. No one had come to help her when Stephen Hebden had brought her into the camp. If anyone wished to help her now, there could be no doubt of her location, nor the fact that she was held against her will. And since she had seen none of the other Gypsies, she did not even know if she wanted their help. Perhaps the tribe was full of men even more brutal than her captor. If that was the case, she would gain nothing by calling attention to herself. She had no proof that the person that might come to her aid was any better than the one who had taken her.

She glanced around the little room that would be her prison for the day. There was a basin with fresh water, and a small mirror on the wall. She went to it, and looked at her reflection. It was as he had said. Her face was streaked with dirt, and mud was caked under her nails. Even her feet were dirty, for the muddy water of the roadway had soaked through her stockings. Carefully, she began to wash herself. Then she took down her hair, combing the leaves out of it with her fingers, then reaching hesitantly for the set of silver brushes that sat on the small shelf below the mirror. They were beautiful things, as was the silver handle of his razor, ornamented with a pattern of leaves and vines. The metal was smooth from use, but well cared for.

And the blade of the razor was sharp. He'd left her alone with access to a weapon. What did it say about the man, that he would do such a thing? He had not seemed foolish. But if he made such a blunder, then he was underestimating her. She glanced wildly around the room, looking for a place to conceal it. If she hid the thing, it should be where she could get to it, should she need to use it. He had seen to it that there was no way for her to secrete it on her person. Her only option might be to lie in wait for him, and strike quickly when he opened the door. But for now, she returned the razor to where she'd found it.

She looked in the mirror again. At least now, she felt clean, although still just as vulnerable as she had. But it was good that she was alone, she reminded herself. The last thing she needed, in her current state, was company. She glanced around the room. In another life, she'd have found it cheerful. The wood of the bed frame and the little table and chair were carved and painted with bright designs of flowers and birds. She wondered if her captor had done the work himself, or it had been decorated by another. The chest in the corner had the name 'Magda' carved carefully into the top. Was the woman a wife or a lover? It was impossible to tell.

She hesitated only a moment, before opening it. It was not locked. But if he'd wanted privacy, then he'd have been better to leave her where she was, and not to lock her up here. The trunk was full of neatly folded men's clothes, just as she had expected. Here was the suit that she had admired on him in the civilized setting of the Keddinton ballroom. Her hand was resting on the fine linen of his shirt, and she imagined slipping it over herself.

Would it be more decent or less, she wondered, for a woman to cover her nakedness with men's clothing? To go without stays and feel the cloth of the shirt rubbing against one's breasts, the unfamiliar sensations of trousers, covering while they revealed. And to have the whole of the ensemble bearing the faint smell of the man she had danced with. Wood smoke and brandy with an underlay of exotic spice. It would be as intimate as a touch.

The thought made her dizzy. She hoped it was the strangeness of her surroundings and her helplessness in them that was making her feel so odd. But in some part, it was because of the way she'd felt about the false Lord Salterton, right up to the moment when he had ruined it all by taking her. Although she should be terrified of him, she was more angry than frightened. For to suddenly have the fluttery feelings towards a man that she had been waiting and hoping to have, only to have them for someone so villainous, so cruel, and so clearly unworthy... She was disappointed in herself, and in him, for not being the man she wished him to be.

She pressed her hands to her temples. She must be losing her mind. She thrust the clothing back into the chest. She did not want to get any closer to her kidnapper than was necessary. There had to be a better way to solve her predicament than to put on his shirt, even if it was the most sensible course of action.

The door behind her opened.

She slammed the chest shut and jumped away from it, grabbing a blanket from the bed to hide her body and the razor from the shelf, ready to strike at the first hand that touched her.

When she turned to confront the person who had entered, she was surprised to see an old woman holding a cloth bundle in her arms. Her visitor was eyeing her with disdain, although she gave a faint nod of approval at the sight of the bare blade in her hand.

The whole tribe was as mad as Stephano, if threatening a stranger with a makeshift weapon was seen as an acceptable greeting. God only knew what he had said to the people in his camp. Despite all her screaming, Verity could guess how it must look to the old woman, if she was hiding in the man's wagon, without a stitch on. She put on her most innocent expression, set the razor aside, and held out a hand in supplication. 'I am held against my will,' she whispered. 'Can you help me?' The blanket slipped alarmingly, and she pulled her hand back to catch it.

The bundle that the old Gypsy had brought turned out to be an armload of women's clothing, which she tossed down on the bed at Verity's side. Then she spoke to her in a torrent of alien language, to which Verity could only shake her head in confusion. Whatever the crone had said, it sounded more disgusted than sympathetic. She finished with a nod that seemed to indicate this was all the help Verity was likely to receive, and perhaps more than she deserved. Then, she held out a hand.

Did the woman expect payment for the clothing? Because she must know it was quite impossible. Verity shook her head again, and said slowly, 'I have nothing to give you. He took it all.'

The woman gave her another frustrated look that said she must be an idiot, and then responded in equally slow English. 'Give me your palm.'

Timidly, Verity held out a hand.

The old Gypsy turned it palm up, then shifted it back and forth in the light, muttering and responding with a curse before pushing Verity's hand away. Then, she left the wagon as suddenly as she had come, slamming the door behind her.

Verity stared at the pile of clothing on the bed, then picked up a dress and examined it. It was clearly used, but in good condition, and a bright green that would complement her eyes. Perhaps she was as foolish as the woman thought, if she was concerned with her appearance at a time like this. The accompanying petticoats were heavy, and the stays were light to allow easy movement. The stockings were thick, but well cared for, and the shoes sensible.

It was a suitable garment for life in a Gypsy camp, allowing for comfort, freedom and protection from the elements. Attractive, yet sensible. If she ever meant to escape and return to her old life, she would need such garments to travel in, and it would do her no good to baulk at wearing someone else's hand-me-downs. She dressed hurriedly. And then she tried the door.

She had imagined she would find it locked, but it opened easily under her hand. Had her kidnapper left it unlocked, sure that her nakedness would hold her inside? Or had the old woman left it so when she had departed? And had she done it on purpose, or by accident? What might happen to her, should Verity decide to exit?

She took a deep breath, and turned the handle. It was like looking out into another world. The camp had been dark and quiet when she entered, and she had taken little note of it, other than to know that she did not wish to be there. But in daylight, it was very different indeed. All around were beech trees, and light filtered through the green and yellow leaves, making the sunlight seem soft and golden, and the sound of birds and the rustle of the wind in the trees made a constant background to the activity around her.

The camp itself was made mostly of willow bender tents. She counted six large canvas structures that looked almost as permanent as cottages, and several smaller tents, each with a cooking fire in front. There were only two or three of the wagons she had come to associate with Gypsies, and the one she had exited was by far the grandest. It was large and sturdy, and the green paint was fresh and clean. Something about it gave her the impression of power, as well as wealth. She was sure that the man who owned it was the leader of this tribe. If that was true, how much help could she expect from the people around her?

And there were many. Men sat on benches beside the fires, carving or mending shoes or pots; women bustled over the meals they were cooking; and several small children darted in and out amongst the tents, playing at tag or ball.

She went down the little wooden steps to the ground. She could feel a shifting of awareness, although few were brazen enough to stare directly back at her. To test her theory, she strode purposefully toward the edge of the camp to see how they would respond. There were ponies and carts behind some of the tents. If she borrowed one, she could find a road and leave. A road would lead her somewhere, eventually.

But before she could reach the trees, a man stepped into her path. He was shorter than Stephano, but no less intimidating. He smiled at her, showing a gold tooth, and crossed his arms over his chest. Then he took a menacing step toward her, and she scurried back into the clearing.

She could hear his laughter behind her and his call to another man, who responded with laughter of his own. She wondered had the threat been real or merely a test. If so, she had proven herself easily frightened, and for little reason.

She turned back to the camp, and looked across it at the old woman who had given her the clothing, who stood beside her fire, stirring something in a large cast-iron pot. If she had a friend here, this woman might be it. She was the only person who had shown her kindness. She stepped toward the woman's tent and said, 'Excuse me?'

She might not have existed, for all the attention that was returned to her.

She tried again. 'I wished to thank you for the clothing. It was very kind of you, and I appreciate it.'

The woman looked up at her with a barely raised eyebrow. She paused for a moment, as though thinking. Then she removed a scarf from her pocket, and spread it over a nearby bench. 'Sit.' It was more a command than a request.

All the same, Verity said, 'Thank you,' as she took the seat. She wondered if the woman spoke enough English for her to be understood. Or was it only her stubbornness that made her silent? Just in case, she said, 'This is a most unexpected turn of events. Last night, I was attending a ball at the house of my godfather. And this morning finds me in a Gypsy camp, surrounded by strangers. The man who brought me here is not friend to me, nor my family.'

She paused, hoping that the woman might supply some opinion on this, but none was forthcoming.

She continued. 'I am afraid that he might mean me harm. He brought me here against my will. But it will not matter for long, I am sure. I am the Earl of Narborough's daughter. My family will be looking for me, and they will be most angry with whoever has taken me, and will see that justice is done.'

She said it loud enough so that all around might hear, and left another gap in the conversation, hoping that any eavesdroppers would consider the possibility of retribution. Counting the hours since her abduction, there had been barely enough time for Uncle Robert to notice her absence and send for her brothers. But if she could keep safe for another day, or maybe two, they would find her and bring her home.

It would not even take that long, if she could persuade someone in the camp to bring them a message. 'They will also be most grateful to whoever might help me return to them. And most generous. My family is very wealthy.' And that should influence anyone who might be bribable.

Then she stated her greatest fear, more softly, so that only the old woman could hear. 'I am concerned for what will happen to me, when my captor returns. I doubt that his plans for me are those of a gentleman. If you should hear any noises coming from the wagon… If I should be forced to scream for help…'

The woman turned to her and gave her another cold stare, which caused her to fall silent. Then the old Gypsy went to the fire and removed the kettle, pulled a chipped mug from the table beside the fire, filled it and handed it to Verity. She went to a basket beside the tent, cut a thick crust from a loaf of bread, and handed her that, as well.

'Thank you,' Verity said loudly. And then she whispered, 'Does this mean you will help me?'

The woman said back in English, 'It means that, if your mouth is full, you will not talk so much.' And she walked away, returning to her tent and pulling the flap closed behind her.

Verity sat alone by the fire, chewing upon the crust of bread, waiting to see what would happen next. Whatever she had expected of a Gypsy camp, it was not what she was seeing. After the half-hearted threat when she had tried to leave, the people were showing her no interest, too caught up in the work of the day to care about a stranger in their midst. There was the regular clink, clink of someone hammering a patch onto a pot, and another man worked the bellows over a small, portable forge.

A few men worked together over a lathe, turning what appeared to be chair legs, or spindles for a banister. While they worked, they chatted in the strange language that the old woman spoke, sometimes resorting to a phrase or two of English before someone nodded in her direction and put a stop to it. Women tended fires and children, hung washing or swept debris from the floors of their tents. Everywhere she looked, people seemed busy.

All except her.

And she could not help the creeping feeling that she got on the back of her neck sometimes, that she was meant to be doing something, or being something, or going somewhere. Last night, Stephen Hebden had called her useless. She feared it was true. If the future had plans for her, she must hope that it would require nothing more taxing than watercolour drawing and excellent table manners. And playing the harp, of course.

Uncle Robert had insisted that she continue her lessons during her visit with him. As she played, the ethereal sound of the instrument made her feel even less content than before. When people heard her practice, they made what they thought were flattering comments about her angelic nature. But from the way their attention seemed to drift as they talked to her, she suspected that, while they might claim to like angels very much, the company of them was sought in moderation and tempered with that of much more earthly women.

She watched the angle of the light passing through the leaves, changing as the sun moved through the sky.

And she wondered again at her location. Perhaps now that the people around her were too busy to notice, she should try again to slip away. But if she did escape, where would she go?

Home, of course. She would find someone to escort her back to London. But of late, with Father sick and everyone else grown busy with their new lives, home did not really feel like home to her.

She glanced around the camp again. But neither did this place, with its distant inhabitants and glowing sunlight. She had not slept since the Gypsy had kidnapped her, and now that she had opportunity, she was too tired to run away. Thanks to the old woman, she was neither as hungry nor as cold as she had been. Perhaps, after a nap, she would be better able to think of a way out of this dilemma. She closed her eyes and let her head loll.

Chapter Four

❧

It took longer than expected for Stephano to return to camp that night. He was not used to the new location, after the recent move. His family had chosen wisely, for the spot was so subtle and well disguised that he had needed to stop and observe the *patrin* that had been left to mark the way. A broken twig here, a torn leaf there, a bundle of flowers tied to a branch. All served as indicators that he must go left or right through the trees to find the camp again, on ways so small it was almost as great a challenge to ride his horse as it had been to steer the gig when he had taken Verity Carlow.

It told him something of her cleverness, that his captive had turned his momentary confusion on the previous night into an escape attempt. If she was as sharp today, he would be hard-pressed to keep track of her. The trip to London and back had left him dull witted. His head hurt, and the cut on his hand pained him more than it should.

They must be growing near, for his big black stallion,

Zor, pricked up his ears, and fought to set his own pace. It was not worth struggling for control, so he gave the beast its head, and in no time, the journey was done.

As he fed and groomed his horse, from every corner of the camp he heard cries of 'Stephano! *Sastimos*, Stephano!' And felt an answering surge of joy at the warmth of their greetings. Children crowded around him, begging for the bag of sweets they knew he would bring. The sun was dropping towards the horizon, and he could smell the evening meals cooking on the fires inside the circle of tents. The women shouted warnings to their offspring about ruined suppers and gave him half-hearted scolds about sweets before a meal. But they smiled as they did it, and he knew that there would be a plate of food waiting for him at any campfire he chose.

For a moment, the warmth and friendship overcame the headache which was rising again as he prepared for the angry confrontation that awaited him on the other side of his vardo door. By now, Verity Carlow would be hungry, as well as cold. And since it was unlikely that she had missed a meal in twenty-one years, she would be overcome by the hardship. Her temper would be somewhere between merely foul and completely hysterical. And he would be forced to bear the brunt of it, without response. He had promised Keddinton that he would not hurt her, nor did he wish to.

But life would be much easier if he gave over the last of his scruples and settled violence with violence. To follow the way of his mother's curse, guided by fate and the pain in his head, made life far too complicated. If he wished revenge against any of the Carlow men, it would have been so much easier to catch them unawares and knife them in the ribs. Or meet them on the field of honour, as his father would have wanted. He was proficient with a variety of weapons, and sure of success because right was on his side.

And as for the girl?

Her golden brown hair was the colour of wild honey, and she had skin like fresh milk. It made him hungry, in so many ways, to think of her. And the look in her huge eyes when they'd danced had been a mixture of innocence and curiosity, just as the colour of them had blended green and brown. Although she had been by far the most cautious member of her family, he had seen the way she'd looked at him, last night in the vardo. She would put up a token resistance to his advances, before offering her maidenhead. And when he'd had his fill of milk and honey, he could have laughed at her disgrace and sent her home to break her father's heart.

As his own father had done to his mother. The thought set his head to hammering again. He suspected that the spirit of his mother would have more sympathy for the girl than she would for her own son, and would make him suffer greatly should he abuse her.

If only to save himself a headache, he would treat Verity Carlow with respect, if not with kindness. She could have her ragged dress back and a bowl of stew for supper. And she would sleep alone in his bed, which was the softest in the camp. He would turn a deaf ear to her complaints. In a week or less, her father would be begging to get her back, and Stephano would be glad to be rid of her.

He glanced over at his grandmother's tent, and at the

trim Romany girl that sat on the bench beside it. Soon he would settle the Beshaley curse. And if he survived the experience, he would spend his evenings by the fire in camp, flirting with a pretty girl like that. He would have a happy wife, and a vardo full of children.

And then, the last rays of sun touched the honey-blond hair of the girl by the fire. His anger at his own mistake made his head ring with pain as sharp and clear as ever he'd felt. He handed the last of the candy from his pocket to the nearest child, and stalked across the camp to confront his escaped prisoner. 'What are you doing, out of the wagon?'

'I'm sorry?' Lady Verity Carlow gave him a frigid smile. 'Did you mean for me to remain there? You did not say.'

'I thought the message was clear enough.'

'I assumed that you had come to your senses, and sent the old lady to feed and clothe me, as an apology.' She lifted her chin and gathered her dignity. With a little toss of her head, she made the borrowed dress look like the height of London fashion. 'Unless she came to me without your permission. Perhaps your followers are not as obedient as you think.'

Which was true enough, if they were talking of his grandmother. 'Magda!' He bellowed her name, and the old crone came out of her tent—slowly, to show him that his desire for her immediate presence was not likely to hurry her steps.

She glanced up at him in mock surprise and said in Romany. 'You have returned, grandson?'

He answered her in the same language, knowing she would only pretend ignorance if he talked English for the benefit of his prisoner. 'Old woman, who let the girl out of my vardo?'

'I did, of course. She was squalling like a baby goat.' She turned to the girl and made a rude, bleating noise that made Verity jump back in alarm. 'I looked in through the window and saw that you had left her bare. And with not a thing to eat. You had given no word when you might return. Did you mean to starve her?'

'I was not gone a day, as you can see. Missing a meal would do her no harm.'

Magda shrugged. 'How was I to know? So I gave her some clothes so that she would not shame herself, and brought her out to feed her. What do you mean, bringing this *gadji* into the camp to sleep in my wagon?'

'I built the wagon for you. I use it because you refuse to sleep there.'

Magda made a face. 'The soft bed hurts my back. And a true Rom does not need such luxury. To sleep on the ground as Devla intended—'

'Why is it that you only wish to sleep on Devla's earth, when I offer to make you comfortable by giving you a bed?'

'I do not want your bed, if you mean to pollute it with a *gadji*.'

'She is here as a hostage, to gain control of her father. And where she sleeps is none of your business, old woman.' Magda was glaring at him, again, and he flashed the ward against the evil eye because he knew it would annoy her.

'Evil?' She laughed. 'It is high time you worried about such things. Bringing an English girl here is bringing the curse back to our home.'

'I never meant for her to leave the vardo.'

'Even worse.' Magda moaned. 'Is she a *gadji* whore, that you must keep her naked in your bed? Your mother would roll in her grave, to see that you have learned nothing from her mistakes.'

'Do not mention my mother, *chivani*.'

'I will do as I like.' She looked at the girl and cried, 'Whore!' But since she was still speaking Romany, the girl merely looked puzzled by the outburst.

'She is not a whore, and I do not mean to bed her. I took her clothing to make it impossible for her to run. In a few days she will be gone.'

'A few days, a few minutes, a few years. It does not matter.' Magda moaned. 'What decent Rom will give his daughter to you, if this is the way you behave?'

'I do not seek a bride, Rom or otherwise.'

'Just a whore. Perhaps her family will not mind what she has been to you. But you, at least, should have enough pride not to flaunt your lewd behaviour in front of your grandmother.'

'And now, you are a frail old granny, and shocked to death by this slip of a girl. Ayyy!' He threw his hands in the air and then reached for the loaf of bread. 'Perhaps you will treat her better, if she is my wife.'

'You would not.' His grandmother looked sincerely horrified by the idea.

'I would.' He walked over to Verity Carlow and offered the bread to her.

She looked at it with suspicion, and made no move to take it, so he forced it into her hands. 'You are hungry. Eat.'

She looked to Magda, trying to understand the cause of her distress. 'Never.'

'It is not poison. Here.' He held out his hand for the loaf, and she gave it back to him, just as he had known she would. He took the bread, and held it out to the old woman. 'Salt the bread, Magda.'

'No.'

'Such disagreeable women. You are no better than she. Now salt the bread.'

His grandmother reached into the pouch at her side, took a pinch of salt and she sprinkled it on his bit of bread. He ate. 'There,' he said in Romany. 'The girl has given me bread. And I have eaten it.'

'She does not know what she is doing.'

'Neither do you, if you mean to stop me. Now salt the bread for her.'

Magda offered another pinch of salt, as the girl watched in curiosity.

'What is she doing?' she whispered to Stephano.

He spoke clearly in English, and made his voice calm so as not to frighten her. 'It is only salt. We sometimes eat it this way, in ceremony. It is a form of protection, and a public proof of my pledge not to harm you.' He held up the loaf so that others could see what he was doing, and a murmur of surprise travelled through the camp. Then he offered the bread to Verity again. 'Eat.'

She looked at it, and he could see her mouth begin to water. Even if Magda had fed her, he doubted she had eaten much. And then she looked at him, as though gauging whether she could trust him. He could see the moment that she decided it would be better to accept his peace offering than to fight him on small things. At last, she took the bread from his hand and ate.

He looked at Magda and switched back to Romany. 'There. Are you satisfied now? Bread and salt, from my hand to hers, and hers to mine. *Gadji* she may be, but she is my wife. And no one has the right to question me.'

'You mock me.'

'I show respect to you, and to her.' He looked back to the girl, still eating her bread, unsuspecting of what had occurred. He touched her hair, and she froze as he loosened the last of the pins that held it, until it was free. Then he pulled a scarf from around his throat and offered it to her. 'Cover your hair.'

He had pushed her to rebellion. She shook free of his touch, and put a hand to her own hair, as though to guard it from him. 'You have no right to tell me what to do.'

'I have every right. While you are in my world, I will offer you what protection I am able. But you would do well not to incite comment from the other men here. Now cover your hair.'

'As a disguise. Are you trying to make it harder for my family to find me?'

He smiled. 'It is not necessary to disguise you. No one will find you here. But look around. In my world, a modest woman keeps her hair covered. And I do not wish the others to think that you are less than modest.'

'That I…' She glanced around the crowd, and he could see the fear returning to her face. She was imagining rape at the hands of the dirty Gypsies again. His stomach knotted at the insult. But if fear made her obey him? Then very well, let her continue to think his people were animals. She snatched the scarf from his hand and tied it about her head, as the other married women did.

He nodded. 'While you are here, you will do as I say. With any luck, your visit will be short.'

After the unusual argument between her captor and the old lady, the camp settled down to enjoy their evening meal. Verity was wondering if it was appropriate to request more than the piece of bread she had been given, when the old woman appeared with a small bowl of stew and a bent fork. She thanked her, and tasted. It was a truly delicious hodgepodge of strange meats and vegetables that she suspected varied greatly according to what could be shot or scavenged in the vicinity of camp.

Stephen Hebden, or Stephano as he preferred to be called, ate in silence on the opposite side of the fire. And when she offered an impersonal thanks to their cook, he muttered, 'Magda.'

She looked up at him. 'I am sorry. Were you speaking to me?'

'Her name is Magda. She is my mother's mother.'

Verity nodded, for it explained much. 'If she lost your mother, she must have been glad to have you back.'

'Not really,' he said, forking up another bite of stew. She called me half caste. Not a true Rom, because of my father.' He continued, without looking up. 'And my *gadje* family thought much the same of me.' He used a bit of bread to wipe the gravy out of the bottom of his bowl.

Without his asking, Magda rose to refill it for him. She did not smile, and her ladle rapped sharply against the side of the bowl in disapproval.

But Verity suspected that the woman's stubborn indifference masked a genuine affection for him. Despite his thoughts on the subject, the women in his life had loved him more than he knew. 'It was not always thus,' she reminded him. 'Imogen said that Amanda Hebden treated you as her own son, while you were in her house. And it broke her heart to lose you.'

'So I have been told,' he said, without emotion. 'But she did not—she sent her own son to the foundling home when his father was gone. She buried her true son when he died, and she mourned over the grave. But when the place they sent me burned to the ground, she did not even come to claim my body.' The look in his eyes grew distant. 'I remember the flames licking the walls, and the thick, black smoke. I could not see. I could not breathe. And all around me, the crying of children. And then, the screaming.' And for a moment, it was fear Verity saw on his face, as he stared into the campfire.

Without thinking, she reached out a hand to comfort him, for the picture was so vivid that she could imagine the screams of the dying children.

He ignored her gesture and gave a short, sharp laugh, as though to break the spell. 'I called, and no one came. Death was all around. I crawled along the wall until I came to a window, and then I climbed out of it and dropped to the ground. My nightshirt was on fire, so I rolled in the muck until the flame died. People were running about, crying and wringing their hands, but none was doing a bit of good.'

It was an amazing tale, and every bit as exciting as she had expected from the well-travelled Lord Salterton. 'Perhaps they did come for you. But they arrived too late.'

He looked at her as though he thought her the world's greatest fool. 'My family did not look for me after the fire, because it was easier not to. It was easier for me to die tragically, than to admit their mistake. But no matter. I was not alone for long. There are always those who have a use for hungry strays.'

If she had been harbouring an illusion about a happy ending to the story, he quickly put it to rest. 'Children are easier to boost through the back windows of closed stores, when one wishes to steal. They can run unnoticed through crowds, picking pockets and cutting purses, because they are small. If they are kept underfed, all the better. It is harder to run with a full belly. If they are caught? What does it matter to the thief master? If the child returns, beat him, and he will run faster next time. And if he does not? Then there are always other children.'

This was even worse than the last. To have escaped from the fire, only to be starved and beaten and forced to steal. She leaned closer, eager to hear more. 'But you got away, did you not? And came to live with Magda and the others?' For strangely, it mattered very much to her. It was as though the little boy were a character in a horrible, sad story, and not the vile kidnapper by the fire. She wanted to know that his grandmother had found him and that all was well.

'You wish to know what happened? One day, I tried to pick the wrong pocket. Thom Argentari was my mother's Rom husband. Or had been, until she hung herself, after my father died. Thom grabbed me by the ear, and would have beaten me for a thief. But he recognized me. And though he had every reason to hate me for being my father's son, he brought me home.' Then, his smile turned cruel. 'Good fortune for me. But bad for you. The sweet old lady who fed you today is the same one who taught me the curse that my mother laid upon your people. She says that I survived the fire so that I might carry it out.'

Verity stared down into the bowl of stew in front of her, wishing that she could afford to throw it back in the old woman's face. But if she wished to survive this ordeal, she needed to take nourishment when she was able. Perhaps Magda was her true enemy. For at times, Stephano sounded no happier with his role in this than she was with being treated as his pawn. If there was something she might do, to turn him against his family...

'It is late,' he said, interrupting her thoughts. 'And time for bed.' His eyes flicked to the wagon.

In truth, she was exhausted, having slept little other than her nap by the fire. She could use a real night's sleep in a real bed. But the prospects available were daunting. 'Where...' she began cautiously.

'In the vardo. With me.' There was a chuckle of appreciation from a man at a nearby fire.

She stood up and the bowl in her lap fell to the ground, spilling the remainder of her dinner into the dirt. 'I most certainly will not.'

His glance shifted from her face to the food on the ground, and back, and his frown became a glare.

'Perhaps you do not understand your situation, *Lady* Verity. You are my prisoner. If you do not do as I say, I will force your cooperation. If you mean to waste the food that Magda gives you, I will not allow her to feed you at all. Pick up the mess you have made.'

She could feel herself colouring with shame at the carelessness. The stew had been good, but it was humble fare. It was possible that the old woman could barely afford to feed herself, and Verity had dropped her share of it into the dirt as though it was nothing. She picked up the bowl and scooped the spoiled meat into the fire, then whispered an apology to Magda. And then she remembered the reason for the accident and said, 'In your tent, is there space for me? I would not need much. A rug upon the ground, perhaps...'

And for a moment, she suspected the woman might accept her.

'No.' Stephano's voice cut through the silence. 'I forbid it. I have offered you my hospitality. You will learn to be grateful for it.' And without warning, he seized her by the wrist, pulled her into his arms and kissed her.

For a moment, she was too shocked even for outrage. Her mouth had been open, ready to protest when he had grabbed her. And now, he was inside it. Certainly, this was a mistake. In a moment, he would push her away in disgust. Or perhaps this was how all Gypsies kissed, because he did not seem to be the least surprised by what was happening. His tongue was stroking hers with an almost lazy possessiveness, as though he had known all along that they would end up, just like this. His one hand was still on her wrist, but his other hand twined in her hair, and his thumb was moving back and forth against her neck as though urging her to respond.

And Lord help her, she wanted to. This was wonderful. The night air was cool, but his body was warm and the scent of it was an elusive combination of fruit and spice that made her think of the sunlight and the heat of summer. His touch was a perfect blend of rough and gentle, and she felt the movement of his mouth on hers, and deep within her. It was as though he had found a way to become part of her, to share his soul with a single kiss. She had nothing to fear from him, for he offered pleasure beyond anything she could imagine. She had but to go with him to the vardo, and give him her body, as she had her lips.

Someone laughed, and there was a shout of approval. The sounds brought her back to reality: she remembered where she was, and who she was, and who she was kissing. And she began to fight him, turning her head from side to side to escape his mouth, and beating his chest with her free arm.

He stepped away and released her as quickly as he'd grabbed her. But his angry expression was gone, replaced by momentary surprise and then a satisfied grin. He stared at her and reached up to touch his own lips protectively, as though she had been the aggressor and he the innocent victim of her lust.

Her fists balled at her sides, rage towards him mingling with the shame of knowing that they had been observed. She looked at the people gathered in groups around her, longing to see a friendly face. If there was someone who was at least willing to speak English in her presence, then maybe they could talk reason to the dark man in front of her. But there was nothing but curiosity in the faces of the onlookers.

'We will go to the vardo, now.' Her captor's smile had changed. It was a knowing look, the smirk of a conqueror.

The crowd around them stilled, as though she were nothing more than a player on a stage and they were as eager to see what would happen next. There was no indication that they would help her if she asked, or intervene in any cruelty that the Gypsy might inflict on her. Her struggles would be further amusement for the tribe, and would take from her what last bit of dignity she might possess. So she looked at the man in front of her, and said clearly, so that all might hear, 'You will be sorry for this. I swear.'

And her few words seemed to be more than enough to satisfy them. Although her enemy was unmoved, the others looked away, fearing to meet her gaze. She saw a flurry of hand signals, as some people around her threw up wards against her, while others fumbled in pockets and at throats, reaching for talismans or lucky pieces.

And then, the fearsome Stephano Beshaley flinched. She was sure that his reaction was involuntary, and so swift that he did not realize he had done it. But for a moment, he looked as shocked and as pained as if she had slapped him hard upon the face. Then he blinked, and formed his hand into a fist, before flexing the fingers.

She thought for a moment that he meant to strike her for her impudence. But then she noticed the bandage wrapping the hand, and it seemed that his movements had more to do with the injury than any threat to her.

It made her smile to think that she could turn their Gypsy superstitions so easily against them. And so it would be with the curse against her family. She would find a weakness and exploit it, giving him more reason to fear and obey her than to follow the mad ravings of his long-dead mother.

If she lost her honour tonight, so be it. She would keep her self-respect, and do nothing to jeopardize her immediate safety. And she would survive to make this man pay for what he had done to her. She turned and walked ahead of Stephano Beshaley, toward the vardo.

When they entered the wagon, he reached behind her to shut the door, and she heard a bolt slide into place. Did he find it necessary to protect himself against his own people? More like, he knew that she could not open the door while he slept without his hearing the click of the lock. He could easily stop any escape attempts.

He had gone to the other side of the wagon and pulled off his jacket, draping it over a nearby chair. Then he turned to her and stared.

A shiver went through her as she looked at him. She could see the muscles beneath his thin shirt, the easy panther's grace, the line of his mouth as he observed her. He moved towards her, closing the distance until she could feel the heat of his skin on hers. Then he was reaching past her, to take a blanket off the bed. He pointed.

'You will sleep there.' He dropped his own blanket on the floor, arranging a place for himself there. Then he reached to loosen the cloth at his neck, and turned his back on her, readying himself for bed.

'I don't understand.' She hoped that he did not take her statement for disappointment. But after what had happened by the fire, his behaviour was most unexpected.

He glanced over his shoulder. 'Would you prefer the floor? Or do you wish me to join you?'

'No.' She backed away from him, until her shoulders bumped against the curved wall of the wagon.

He shrugged. 'After the way you behaved just now, I thought, perhaps…'

'You had no right to kiss me.'

'I had every right. I do as I please. It pleased me to kiss you.' He looked her up and down. 'And now, it pleases me to leave you alone.' He returned to his preparations for sleep.

Then he truly did not mean to touch her? Yesterday, he had said that he would release her unharmed. Perhaps he had told the truth. The kiss by the fire had been shocking, but it had done no permanent damage to her. If he did not attempt to duplicate it, then she would forget it on her return to her family.

If only she could ignore the strange feeling of intimacy, as she watched him undress, and the feeling that things were neither as simple nor as complicated as they seemed. It was as though they had already been lovers in some distant past and had no need to be coy. She was to be allowed into his life, completely and without fear or reservation. He was quite literally naked before her.

And yet, he showed no vulnerability. But then, what did he have to fear from her? Her words by the fire had bothered him more than any of her actions could. She thought of the razor, on the other side of the little room, and wondered if she would have the courage to use it. Perhaps, if he was moving against her in some way, forcing himself upon her in the night. But would she have the nerve to cut the man as he slept at her feet, just so she could get away from him?

It was wrong of him to keep her here. But it seemed wrong, as well, to respond violently, without further provocation.

She let her eyes drift away, to the bed behind her. It was piled with decadent layers of eiderdown that would keep out the night's chill. And though it was large enough for two, he was going to sleep on the floor. Then she looked down at her own clothing.

He did not look up. 'Prepare for bed.' It was a command.

'I have no nightclothes.' Even as she said it, it seemed foolish, for she could see glimpses of his bare skin that his blanket did not hide.

'Sleep in your clothes. Or your shift. Or nothing at all. It does not matter. Be quiet and lie down.'

She glanced back at the door again.

'And do not think you can run away in the night. I am a very light sleeper.'

He was between her and the door. She would have to step over him if she meant to get anywhere. And the thought of getting close, only to feel his hand grab for her ankle…

She sat suddenly down on the edge of the bed, overcome with a strange trembling, as though his fingers had actually touched her.

She had to admit, the bed she sat on was comfortable. It was almost softer than her mattress at home.

She reached down and slipped out of her shoes, stretching her toes and tucking her feet up under her, pulling a coverlet to her chin. It was too warm to sleep fully dressed. So with the blanket and the darkness hiding her from the man on the floor, she began to undo her clothing, wiggling out of dress, petticoats and stockings, and piling them neatly at the foot of the bed. When she had nothing left but the borrowed chemise, she crawled down beneath the rest of the covers and allowed herself a small sigh of relief.

There was no response from the man on the floor. He had turned from her, and not moved since she had begun to undress. Although they would be sleeping in close proximity, he was taking great pains to show no interest in her body. She wondered if that was the way of people forced to share a room, who did not wish to be intimate. They tended to their own business, and pretended not to see what was right before their eyes.

If so, it had been very rude of her to stare at him while he undressed. Perhaps she should apologize. But that would call even more attention… She would know better in the future.

But she had done it again, just now. He had stood on the other side of the room with his back turned to her, and stripped out of his clothes. And with lowered lashes, she had observed him. This time, she had noticed a pucker of skin at his hip that looked like an old scar. From the foundling fire, no doubt. That was where he had been burned as he escaped. It must have been quite large, when he was young. If she reached out to touch it, she could barely have covered it with her hand.

And now, she imagined doing just that. He was lying

on the floor, with his back to her. But if he were on the bed beside her, in that same position, she would place her hand on his hip just where the burn was, press her body tight to his and lay her cheek against his scarred back. The idea of him lying impassively beside her was strangely comforting; it made her feel less alone. Perhaps because he was the only link she had to the world she knew.

As she let her mind wander, she could imagine the warmth of him and the smoothness of his body where it was not broken by the marks of old injuries. And as she drifted into sleep, she swore she could smell sandalwood and oranges on his skin.

Chapter Five

Stephano woke as the light of the rising sun reached his window, opening his eyes and finding himself fully alert. He did not move, savouring the moment.

He was pain free.

It was rare to greet a morning without even a twinge of the headache that was likely to come later in the day. He'd thought, after giving up his bed to lie on the rug that covered the wooden planks of the vardo floor, that the dawn would find him in worse shape than usual, not better.

He had expected some punishment for the kiss he'd stolen. He had promised himself that he would not take such a liberty. But with her presence by the fire and the sham of a marriage, the evening had turned into an increasing series of mistakes. Then she had tricked him into talking of his childhood, and feigning sympathy, only to refuse his bed.

For a moment, he had forgotten that it was the whole bed he'd meant to offer, and not half of it. A simple explanation of the sleeping arrangements would have prevented her response. But the sight of her with the firelight shining on her hair made him forget what was gentlemanly or sensible. Instead, he had done what he wanted.

And remembering the sweet taste of her, it had been worth the risk of pain. All the more surprising to find that there was none. He took a breath and checked again. No, his head was definitely better. His hand still stung after yesterday's cut. But his mind was as clear and peaceful as anyone else's. He almost feared to move, for any change in position might spoil everything. He turned his head slightly to see the woman lying on his bed.

As if she felt his return to consciousness, she started awake, as well. He closed his eyes to slits, so he might observe her. Apparently, she did not wake as easily as he. Her eyes were open, but she did not seem to see, or comprehend her surroundings. She reminded him very much of a startled fawn, a wild thing that did not yet know the need for fear. A fawn with eyes that seemed to change from smoky green to golden brown as he watched them.

It annoyed him that she seemed to grow lovelier with each moment he spent in her presence. He had known she was a beauty when he had danced with her at Keddinton's house. But that was to be expected. With the fine gown, the care she had taken with her hair and face, and the perfection of her manners and movement, it might have been merely artifice. Even a dull, plain woman could appear beautiful in the light of candles, when the observers had partaken of enough wine.

But last night, she had been even prettier. The simplicity of her borrowed dress seemed to suit her, and her manner had been so relaxed that he had mistaken her from a distance for a Rom.

As they'd eaten, she'd a soft smile on her face. She was unaware the insults Magda had paid her by giving her the chipped mug and the smallest bowl, and covering the plain wood bench with a scarf to keep it clean from Lady Verity Carlow's *gadjikani* filth. Magda was sending a clear-enough message to everyone in the camp that she did not approve of Stephano's guest. So he had responded to his grandmother's scorn by marrying the girl in spite.

The whole camp had laughed at the display, making snide comments in Romany that she could not understand. And she had responded graciously to the meagre hospitality.

Now, in the morning light, there was no trace left of the woman he thought he had taken. Her hair was down, and hung around her shoulders in ripples of gold. Of the elaborate coiffure, only a few tiny braids remained, scattered amongst the loose waves. Her cheeks were pink from the touch of sun she had taken on the previous day, and her mouth needed no rouge to be a soft, kissable red.

She'd taken his advice and shed her garments under the blankets. As the sheet fell away, he saw her perfect white shoulders, the swell of her full breasts and just the hint of a rosy nipple, showing above the edge of the simple shift she wore.

He kept his breathing still and shallow, so she did not know he saw, but he felt his body stirring at the sight.

What might it be like to climb into that bed, touch those lips gently with his own and let first his hand, and then his mouth close over the tip of that perfect breast? To spend a carefree morning making love to her, as gently as the sun was rising.

Again, it was as though she had sensed his thought, for she woke fully to her surroundings. The look of sleepy peace on her face disappeared as she realized where she was, and her composure crumbled. Her shoulders slumped, and there was a hasty, fearful gathering as she brought the sheet to her chin and scrambled further back on the bed, her own back tight to the wall as though she expected that she would be beset from behind. She was staring at him, and he struggled to remain still and give no sign that he was awake, that he might have seen her body or be a threat to her safety.

It did not matter that she thought he was unconscious at her feet. She recoiled from him in terror and disgust. A shudder ran through her body, and she closed her beautiful eyes tight. For a moment, the lashes grew wet with the tears, and he heard a hitch in her breath like the beginning of a sob. And then she thrust her knuckles into her mouth, biting down and letting the pain drive away the weakness. She lifted her chin. When she removed her hand from her mouth, her breathing was steady, her face placid, her eyes scornful, and her terror of a moment before skilfully hidden.

The proud English beauty had returned, but dressed as a woman that looked as at home in his bed as a fair-skinned Rom girl. But hidden deep under it all was the truth. She was the frightened captive he had seen, and he could never be anything to her but the brute that had kidnapped her, her tormentor, the kind of animal that would force her to remove her clothing, then steal glimpses of her bared body and fantasize about joining with her.

The pain in his head returned then, a flash through his temples that brought with it a wave of nausea. He opened his eyes and rolled quickly away from her, almost retching before he could regain control of himself. Then he got up with his back to her, as though her presence in the wagon were no more important to him than a fly on the wall. He reached out for his trousers and pulled them on, and went to the basin, pouring water to wash. The cut on his hand was an angry red and screamed as the soap touched it. But he washed it carefully and rewrapped the wound. Then he ran a hand along his chin and reached for his razor.

He heard a quickly stifled gasp behind him as the blade glinted in the rising dawn.

He glanced into the mirror, meeting her eyes in the reflection, and brandished the razor. 'You think I mean to use this on you, I suppose. I would not bother to dull the blade. I am quite capable of controlling you without it.'

'If you dare to lay a hand on me...'

He laughed. 'You will scream for your brothers. And they will not hear you. If you do not give me cause to hurt you, as I promised, you will remain unharmed. Has your brother the soldier explained to you the concept of parole?'

She gave a small shake of her head.

'If you behave, you are free to do as you like while you are here. But if you try to leave the camp, you will not get far. And then I will find you, drag you back and tie you to the bed. Is that clear?'

'Clear or not, it does not matter. You have no right to keep me here. And no reason. I have done nothing to you. If you have a legitimate complaint with my family, you should behave as a gentleman and settle it rationally. Instead, you are threatening to tie me to a bed. I do not deserve punishment.'

'Neither did a little boy deserve to be separated from his mother, and then turned from the only home he ever knew when his new family tired of him. Crying and pleading for mercy will not change the facts.'

'I am not crying, and I have no intention of begging. If you wished to ruin my reputation, you have kept me more than long enough. I demand that you return me to London.'

She was not crying. It had been he who had cried for his mother, until the masters at the foundling home had beaten him into silence. He had managed to go for years without dwelling on that time. But now it seemed ever fresh in his pain-addled mind. 'Your reputation means nothing to me. If your family has any sense, they will not trumpet your disappearance about; and you will be returned to them, unharmed, once they have admitted to their part in my father's death.'

She tossed her head, doing her best to appear unconcerned. 'More likely, they will pretend to capitulate, and then hunt you like a dog. My brothers will kill you for this.'

'Perhaps they will. But it does not matter to me, as long as the truth is known and the curse is settled.'

'The curse again?' She sighed. 'Stephen Hebden, I cannot decide if you are mad, or just foolish.'

He closed his eyes, for the sound of his old name when it was used in the camp brought the pain to an unbearable level. 'If you expect me to answer you, then you will call me Stephano Beshaley.'

'Very well, Mr Beshaley. But in my opinion, such an assertion tips the scales towards madness. I understand the pains of your childhood, and that you might be angry with your own family for abandoning you, and mine for standing by and allowing it to happen. But can't you see that this talk of curses is nothing more than that— talk? Words spoken long ago, by a woman you never met, need have no bearing on your actions today.' Her words were rational and soothing, and he wished he could believe them.

He broke his gaze from her disquieting green-brown eyes, before the compassion in them led him astray from his destiny. 'It is not so easy as all that, Lady Verity. It brings me no pleasure to visit this upon any of you. Nor do I wish to see you ruined.'

'Then why will you not let me go?'

Stephano touched his temple with his unbandaged hand, and wondered if he dare tell her the truth? If he was doing wrong by his honesty, he would know soon enough. The pain would tell him. If he showed his weakness to her, it was likely to be worse than anything he had endured. But if he could not give her freedom, then she deserved some kind of an explanation.

He took a breath, leaned back against the wall of the vardo and prepared for the agony ahead. 'I did not come to this willingly. If I can offer you nothing else, know that I am sorry to have hurt you. But according to my grandmother, my fate was decided even before Kit Hebden died.' He stared down at the bandage on his hand. 'Magda has the ability to read the lines in a palm and know a man's destiny. And on mine, she sees two lines becoming one. She says that I was born two men. And two men cannot live in one body. If I am to survive, one of them must die.'

'Stephen Hebden?' she asked. And for a moment, he felt a pang of jealousy towards his other self. She sounded almost wistful as she said the name.

'An unhappy boy, and a man without family. Why do you care what happens to him?'

'Because I might like him, if I met him. Better than I like you. But this story has nothing to do with me and my family. You may be whoever you like, and it will not concern us.'

Her honesty stung him, but it was nothing like the pain he had expected. 'My mother's curse must be carried out. It is the Rom way.'

'And you are Rom,' she said, in a tired voice. 'And therefore you will not listen to reason.' She was staring at the floor, as though it exhausted her to speak to one so stubborn.

He turned his back upon her again, grabbing his shirt and stripping it over his head. 'I know it should not matter. It happened long ago, and you can see no reason for me to continue with it. I was raised by the *gadje*, just as you were. And at one time, were I told the nature of the man I would become, I would have laughed and sworn that it was not possible.'

He stopped to grip the washstand in front of him, and

then, he told her the rest of the truth. 'There is an ache in my head. It came to me on the day I first heard the curse. And it will not end until my mother and father are avenged. It guides me in my interactions with your family. And if I weaken or stray from what I know must be done, it punishes me.' If he had been expecting a thunderclap or some other thing that would mark the significance of the moment, he was disappointed. It felt no different to have spoken than it might have to remain silent.

'Have you seen a physician?' Her voice was so matter of fact and unimpressed by his suffering that he turned to face her again.

'It will do no good. My sister Nadya is a healer. She is much better than any *gadjikano* doctor. And she says there is nothing to be done for me. Sometimes the pain is so bad, I fear it will end me before I can finish what I am called to do.'

'So because you suffer and cannot trouble yourself to take some laudanum, we all must pay. That is not fair,' she said.

'I know it is not. But neither has it been fair for me, to know that my destiny is tied to words uttered by a woman I never met. Magda said it was out of love for me that my mother went mad.' He frowned. 'But what good was her love to me if this is all the life I am to have? I must be an arbiter of someone else's hatred. Jaelle laid a curse. If I do not deliver it, it will take me, as well. It is only when I follow the path set out for me that I have any peace at all. My head clears, and for a time, I am free of pain. If I do as fate bids me? My grandmother says I will survive. She has the sight. I have never known her to be wrong in such things.'

'Very well, then. Destroy my father and ruin me, for the sake of your head. If you believe the story you have just told me, then I will waste no more time in talking common sense to you.' He could see by the cold, flat look in her eyes that his revelation had angered her. Though she had shown understanding and pity at the tale of his childhood, his Rom life was as meaningless to her as it had been before. She pulled the blankets close about her shoulders. 'If you keep your bargain and do not harm me, I will abide by your parole. What is the point of running, if I do more harm to my reputation by wandering the countryside alone than by staying here? I would like to rise and dress. And I have no wish to share this wagon as I do it. Please, leave.' She pointed towards the door.

And he left, wondering what it meant that, in less than two days, his prisoner had grown brave enough to order him out of his home?

Chapter Six

Verity stomped around the small space of the vardo, wishing for a way to mitigate the anger she felt at her captor. Even if Stephano Beshaley was not a brute, he was still impossible. She had no desire to spend a week in his company, listening to his superstitious ramblings. She went to the mirror and took one of his silver-handled brushes and forced it through the tangles in her unmanageable hair. The combing seemed to make it even worse. It was as loose and disordered as her thoughts. She tied it back with the kerchief he had ordered her to wear, willing to allow that this particular restriction on her behaviour was a practical solution to her problems.

Now she was clean, dressed and groomed—a fat lot of good it would do her. By now, the family would be in an uproar and her brothers would have begun to search for her. Until they found her, or Stephano Beshaley decided to release her to them, she would have little to do but comb out her hair, and watch as her life fell apart because of the mad machinations of a megrim-addled Gypsy. There must be some way to get through to him, or some way to make herself feel less useless.

If she were in London, or at Warrenford Park with the Veryans, she would have been content to leave the difficulties to her father and brothers, preserving her own peace of mind through diversion. She could paint, walk sedately through the gardens, or even pluck on that blasted harp that everyone insisted she must enjoy, since she played so beautifully.

And for a moment, the memory of the previous night's kiss rose in her mind. He had said he would do as he wished, concerning her. There was obviously one activity that he must have considered, to pass her time in captivity. Judging by the night of uninterrupted sleep following the kiss he had pressed upon her, she had proven to him that she had no particular skills in that area. Now, he meant to leave her alone, just as he had originally planned.

The thought made her angry, although she was unsure why it would. She did not wish his attentions. But neither was it pleasant to feel deficient, when confronted with his rejection. She looked at the brush in her hand, and imagined the satisfying sound it would make, on contact with the mirror. And then, she put it down and picked up a straw broom from the corner of the wagon, using it with the vigour she had seen the Rom women use. She opened the vardo door and pushed the dust out onto the ground. There. That was some help, at least, for it had passed a few moments of her time.

She looked out the open door and saw no sign of Stephano, which was both a relief and strangely disappointing. While she did not really want another confrontation with him, it was annoying to think that he had gone off and left her again. What would become of her if he did not come back?

Someone would send for her family, she hoped. Across the circle of the camp, Magda worked over the open cook fire. Considering the way she had fostered Stephano's hatred of all things Carlow, the old woman was no friend to her. But her behaviour was hardly a personal insult. Magda seemed uniform in her hatred of Rom and *gadje*, equally annoyed by everyone. Verity went down the two wooden steps, and walked to the fire. When no food was offered, she helped herself to leftovers from the woman's breakfast.

Magda ignored her forwardness. But when Verity did not return to the vardo, Magda turned to stare at her and said, 'Ehh?' managing to put infinite meaning into something that was not even a word.

'I was wondering…' Stephano's grandmother was quite daunting, when one came close to her, and Verity's resolve almost faltered. But what had she to fear if her family was already cursed? She squared her shoulders and said, 'I was wondering if you had any tasks that I might do for you. Is there some way I could help, just to pass the time? It will be quite tiresome to do nothing all day. And it hardly seems right for me to sit, while everyone else works.'

'You live in a great house, with many servants, do you not? You have no trouble being idle when you are there.' This was more English than she had ever heard Magda use, and the clarity of meaning took Verity by surprise.

'That is different. The servants are paid for their duties. I am sure, if they were not serving my family, they would be serving someone else's. But the Rom do not seek to serve anyone, do they? So why should they serve me?'

'You are a guest here.' Magda gave her a glare of insulted hospitality.

'I am a captive. That makes me far less than a guest.'

Magda muttered something in Romany, under her breath, and stared at the girl for a moment. And then she reached out and pinched her arm. 'You are not strong enough for the work of a Rom woman. You cannot carry wood or water, with these arms. Can you cook?'

Verity thought about it. 'I do not know. I have never had reason to. Is it difficult?'

The old woman shrugged. 'Wash your hands. Take care with the nails. Then return to me.'

She did as she was bade, and with a strange sense of excitement. When she returned to Magda, the woman was mixing flour and water in a large wooden trough, and sprinkling it with yeast. She showed Verity how to knead the dough. Then she looked carefully at Verity, as though she could read her mood. 'Put your anger into the bread. It will soften the dough. Later, the heat of the fire will burn it away so that it does not taint the food.'

Verity worked the dough with her hands. 'For how long?'

Magda gave another shrug. 'You will know when you are done. Sometimes, a few minutes are enough. But when people around you are difficult?' She shrugged again. 'The bread takes much longer.'

She was right. Verity could feel the tension in her arms, her neck and her shoulders easing as she worked. All the frustrations of the morning, her captivity, and her captor. Her attractive captor, with his broad shoulders and big dark eyes.

She gave vent to her frustration and pounded savagely at the dough. Was she so horrible to him that he could not stand to look at her? It should not matter, really. The last thing she needed was excessive interest from Stephano Beshaley. She should be glad of his indifference.

And there was the problem. The knowledge that she would sleep alone in his bed was a comfort to her. But then, why did she look eagerly for him to return, whenever he left her? While she had not been particularly happy in her old life, she had not expected to leave it behind while tied in a sack and lying on the floor of a wagon. It was not as if she wished an assault upon her person.

But if Stephano had admitted that he had taken her because of a sudden and overpowering attraction, and that he had been willing to throw aside all propriety to woo her in solitude?

She punched the bread again. She would still have been furious with him, for his high-handed behaviour. But at least then, she would have felt some ownership of her predicament. In his explanation, he had talked of curses, and headaches, and a singular destiny that had little or nothing to do with the fate of Verity Carlow. And she had realized that she was less than a dumb beast to him. She might as well have been inanimate, for all he cared. His only interest in her was her last name and her connection to her father. She was no more than a pawn to him, just as she had been to her own family.

She tried to imagine any of the men she knew taking it upon themselves to capture her. Alexander Veryan?

She shuddered. It was impossible. There was no question in her mind that he lacked the resolve to take her anywhere. Even if he was capable of an attack, she doubted that he would risk something he could have gained legally with her father's blessing, because of an excess of passion for her. And even if he had, she would have told him not to be foolish, and he'd have released her immediately.

But she knew Stephano Beshaley to be capable of ruthlessly taking what he wanted. And while he had pretended interest to snare her, now that she was caught, he was showing none at all. She could not help wondering what it might be like if he cared. Suppose last night, he had closed the door of the wagon and finished what he had started…

Quite probably, it would have been horrible. She swallowed her frustration and hit the bread again.

Magda looked over her shoulder, startling her. She examined the dough and proclaimed it ready. Then she explained the setting aside, the rising, the punching down again, and how she would know when to place it in a pan on the fire. And when it would be ready to eat.

Verity remembered the smell of fresh bread. She might be a pawn in someone else's game, but at least she would not go hungry.

Then Magda gave her a large pile of unpeeled carrots, a bowl and a knife. Verity smiled. Apparently, she had found her destiny.

Stephen made his way back through the beeches with the brace of rabbits he had snared for the night's supper. And with each step nearer to camp, he could feel the pressure in his head begin to diminish. It was not until after he'd left the vardo that he had realized the truth. The only pain that had been with him, as he'd spoken to Verity Carlow, was the one in his hand. That had been as bad or worse as on the previous day. With Nadya gone off with Rhys Morgan, the *gaujo* she had married, the tribe was without a healer. Perhaps Magda could look at it, and see if there was anything to be done.

But though the cut might be infected, his head had been clear for most of the morning. There had been the one difficult moment, when he had first got up to dress. But the flash of pain had faded as he'd talked to her, dimming to nothing. It had been good to see the belief in her eyes when he had told her he did not mean to hurt her. She might not have liked his words, but she trusted him as much as someone in her position could.

And it had been good to tell her the truth of his life, no matter how mad it must sound to her. It raised the old desire in him to have a woman—not just to share a bed, but to share a confidence. Whether she liked it or not, he had shown her the contents of his soul. And for a moment, the burden on his mind had lifted and he had been free.

Then she had ordered him away and the pain had returned. Now that he was coming back to her, the pain was fading again. It would be a cruel jest indeed if he were to discover that the true path to peace led him directly to Verity Carlow. If that was the case, all hope was lost. Even if she could forgive the kidnapping, she would hate him for ever if he proved her father a murderer.

To test his theory, he walked towards camp with eyes on the ground, ignoring his surroundings and letting his head lead him. And like metal to a lodestone, he came directly to Magda's fire, where his hostage sat with a bowl of potatoes in her lap, peeling, slicing, and gossiping with the other married ladies. She looked up at him with her lovely hazel eyes, and frowned.

If the day had not gone wrong before, it was most assuredly so now. He reached absently into a nearby pan, and stole a hunk of bread, letting the scent and taste of a good food calm his nerves.

'You like?' Magda grinned at him.

'Good.' He nodded, frowning at the girl across the fire.

'A first effort, from the *bori*. She learns quickly.'

'*Bori*? You do not have a daughter-in-law.'

'You gave me one, yesterday. She made the bread you are eating.'

He choked on the crumbs still in his mouth. 'You are forcing an earl's daughter to work in your kitchen?'

'It makes no sense for an old woman to do for a healthy young one. And I did not force her. She offered. Her hands are too soft to be much help with drawing water or tending the fire. But she did well with the bread. And now, she helps with the stew. You chose wisely with this one, Stephano.' She gave him an approving nod.

'I did no such thing, mother of curses. She will return to her own people when I am done with her.'

Magda slapped him on the arm. 'And then, who will make your bread?'

It was such a strange question that he could not answer it. He had no wife. He had no plans to take one. And if he did, he could not even imagine what kind of woman it would be. He could have his pick of the Rom girls, and live in a tent or a wagon, or would he marry as Stephen Hebden, and have a *gadji* wife to live in Bloomsbury Square and preside over the servants in his kitchen?

He would have to choose one or the other, when the time came, for there was no way that he could have both. He looked at the crust in his hand, and tossed it into the fire. Which was a pity, for it had been very good. Then he gave his grandmother a roguish grin and a hug. 'You will make bread for me, *chivani* woman. You are so fond of my company that you will not let me go.' He laughed, hoping she would join him in the joke.

But instead, she cursed under her breath. 'I will not feed a man so foolish that he could not find the food if it were put under his very nose.' She pointed into the fire. 'And one who wastes that which he has been given. You may starve, for all I care.' She turned and stomped away from him, going back to her tent and letting the flap fall in such a way that told him she wanted a door, if only for the satisfaction of slamming it.

'At least you will not go hungry,' he called after her, and set the rabbits aside to be skinned and cooked. Magda was angry with him again, and he hardly knew why. Only yesterday, she had been furious with him for bringing Verity to the camp. Now it seemed they were the best of friends.

And without even turning to look, he could feel Magda's little *bori* coming to talk to him. The currents of pleasure and pain in his head shifted as though they were dust on the wind and she a fresh breeze. 'And what do you want from me?' he said, and turned quickly to see her startle.

But she stood her ground, and lifted her chin in defiance, holding the potatoes in front of her, as though she feared that he might come too close. 'I wish to know something.'

He held out his empty hands to her, and then pulled them back, for they were stained with the blood of the animals he had killed. 'What more could you want from me? I am already like an open book to you.'

'You claim you want justice for your mother and father. Is that correct?'

He nodded.

'But how is it just that I am to be tried and punished along with my family, without knowing the charge against us. You say we have been cursed by your mother. But I have never heard my family speak of it.'

'Never?' He had grown so used to hearing the words, and their fatal nature, that it had never occurred to him he might be alone in the knowledge.

'Why *should* we speak of it? Only the guilty would have something to fear from such a thing. If my father knew of the curse, he did not dwell on it, nor did he worry us children with it.' He could see the truth in the depths of her wide hazel eyes.

So the Carlow children did not think themselves

cursed. It made a strange sort of sense, when he thought of it. They had grown into happy, confident adults, no matter the stain their father had passed to them.

But the Wardale family had grown in a different way entirely. Nathan Wardale had known of the curse, even before Stephano. It had been at his father's hanging that Jaelle had said the words. And poor, innocent Nathan had grown into a superstitious man, convinced that his life was tainted by Gypsy magic.

'Mr Beshaley.' She said his name sharply, to break into his reverie. 'If my family is truly cursed by yours, I would like to hear the words, please.'

It was a reasonable demand. But why, now that he had the opportunity to deliver the curse in person, was it so hard to say the thing? The skin of his cut palm burned, as though pricked by hundreds of needles. He wrapped the fingers of his good hand around it, trying to numb the feeling long enough to think.

'Stephano, I am waiting.' Now, she put aside the bowl and stood before him, hands on hips, as though she would not let him pass without answering.

He closed his eyes and recited from memory. 'I call guilt to eat you alive and poison your hearts' blood. The children will pay for the sins of their fathers, till my justice destroys the wicked.'

She frowned. 'And you think that this refers to my family?'

He nodded. 'It refers to all who were involved in the death of my father.'

'But surely, it was meant for the Wardale family, if anyone. It was William Wardale that did the murder.'

'I have visited each of his children, in turn. Not only

have they survived, they have prospered. My attempts to lay the guilt and blame at their feet have left them happier and more prosperous than at any time since their father's death.'

She laughed. 'Then I suppose we Carlows should welcome your coming. How bad a curse can it be if it brings success?'

It annoyed him that she found amusement in something that had been the very bane of his existence for so many years. 'You will learn better than to mock this. If the curse is real, then the reason that the Wardales remain untouched is plain enough. If their father was innocent of the crime, then the Wardale children have suffered to no purpose. Since their previous misery was the result of your father's false accusation, it is a wonder they do not curse you, as well.'

Verity waved her hand. 'I know the Wardales. And while Nathan might have some of the same outlandish notions you do, they are far too sensible to curse us over this. If they have a serious grievance, or were in possession of evidence that would prove my father a murderer, they would have gone to the courts with it by now.' She smiled. 'Since they have not? Then we have nothing to fear.'

'Not all wrongs can be settled by law, Lady Verity. If your father deserves punishment, there is nothing he can do to escape the end my mother wished for him.'

'If you understand the curse correctly,' she added.

'And I do. I have lived with the words for most of my life.'

Verity Carlow's smile turned to one of triumph. 'Do you? Truly? For there is a family that you have not mentioned in this. A man who wronged your mother more than any other did, and whose children, by her own words, need to be punished.'

Had he missed someone, after all this time? If there was another, then he could set her free. If there was the slightest chance that her father was innocent, he would turn from the Carlows and not look back. For after staring into her strange green-brown eyes, he had lost the heart to persecute her. 'Another family? And who might there be that deserves this curse, more than you?'

'Why, you of course. You are the son of the man who seduced and abandoned your mother. It was his treachery in taking you that led to her madness and death. And if what you say is true, you have suffered more than any of us. I suggest, Stephano Beshaley, that before you come to my family with these threats, you listen to your own curses, and put your own house in order.'

Chapter Seven

After supper, she sat by the fire, enjoying the peace of the woodland changing to night around her, and the pleasant hum of conversation. More people were willing to speak English around her, since she had proved her worth. And now that they had stopped excluding her, she found Stephano's people to be good company.

They took great pains to impress upon her how lucky she was to have found favour with the great Stephano Beshaley. They could not say enough about his strength as a fighter, his wisdom as a leader, his shrewdness as a trader, and his travels to the Orient and India, from which he had returned with great wealth. And all this from one who had the misfortune to be born half *gaujo*. They spoke as though having a baron for a father was a disability that he had overcome. But they had forgiven him his parentage and assured her she was most fortunate to have captured his attention.

No matter how she tried, she could not seem to convince anyone that she was the captured and not the capturer. They could not fathom the idea that she had not come willingly to them, and did not wish to remain. In their eyes, nothing was better than the life of a Rom. They explained that, although she might not realize it, she did not need rescuing. She had, in fact, already been rescued from whatever unfortunate life she had been forced to lead.

It was annoying to think that they might be right. But for the problem of her captivity, and coming unwilling to it, she had to admit that she was enjoying her time in their camp. The everyday running of a household was quite different, when the house was a tent or a small wagon and one had to do all the work for it oneself. But the freedom to take one's shoes off and wade in the stream if one wished was a novelty that she was not likely to experience at home.

She frowned. It was very worrying to realize that she did not think of her home with the same longing as she had while with the Veryans. Another day had passed, and there was still no sign of her brothers. She had not thought of them at all since morning. And now that she had, it was only to worry that a sudden rescue would give her no time to say a proper goodbye to the Rom women she had met, or to arrange for further visits with them.

Once she returned home, she would never see Stephano Beshaley again. In a strange way, it was flattering to be the captive of a man who others held in such high esteem. She had to admit that, if the stories were true, he did seem to be most intelligent. And from the first, her own two eyes had shown her that he was the most handsome man she had seen, either in polite Society or in a Gypsy camp.

Considering the tragedy of his childhood, it was easy to see why he would be angry with people of her class. But beyond all the pain and anger, he must be a very resourceful and quick-witted man to have survived all that had happened to him. And then, there were his many travels and adventures. He had been everywhere, done everything, and moved easily amongst all types of people. She had been curious to hear his story, when she had thought him Lord Salterton. And her desire had not dimmed.

But no matter how intriguing she found him, she must not lose her head. There were a hundred reasons that she did not wish him to pay her court, to hold her hand, whisper affections or kiss her again. And she most definitely did not want him to come to her tonight, when they were alone together in the vardo, and do the sorts of things that she had feared from the first, but in gentleness instead of anger.

She put the thought firmly from her mind. A group of children had crowded around her feet, and watched in rapt attention as she began to draw the alphabet in the dirt. She offered the stick she had been using to each in turn, letting them trace what she had written. They mimicked her writing, and then smiled at her, fascinated by her teaching. She smiled back, gratified at how quickly they learned. When she looked into their dark eyes and happy faces, she was glad to have come here, whatever the reason had been.

The only person in camp who did not seem to be pleased with her was the man who had brought her to it.

Stephano stood a short ways off, leaning against a tree and glaring in her direction. After this morning, she was sure that he did not intend to hurt her, no matter what her father did. But there were times when he got that curious expression on his face, and her surety faltered. Perhaps he objected to the children learning to read English. Or reading at all. Although why he should wish his people to remain ignorant, she could not understand.

More likely it was something else that made him stare at her as though he wished her to be anywhere but where she was. He had taken the bread that she had made, tasted it and then thrown the rest uneaten into the fire. He must have known that it was safe to eat, for his own grandmother had watched her make it. She had eaten it herself, and knew that there was nothing wrong with the taste. But apparently, the touch of her hands was enough to render it inedible to him.

If he hated her so, then why could he not have taken someone else? Or why did he not just return her to her home? If he beat her, or shouted—behaved as a villain should—then she could hate him with impunity. But the hospitality of the camp, coupled with his cold courtesy and utter disgust of her, was more than a little upsetting.

And that led her to her greatest fear: that his dislike of her arose out of a weakness of her character more than from hatred of her family. She had followed the instructions of mother, nurse, sister and chaperone for years, until she could perform the rituals and courtesies of Society as easily as breathing. But at some point in all the instruction, she feared she had lost whatever wit and vitality she might have owned. And now there was nothing left to tempt the sort of man that might interest her. She had become an empty, vacuous shell.

One of the Rom, who had introduced himself to her as Valentine, came over to tease the children and comment on their lesson. She smiled up at him with relief. Val had made great effort, during the day, to make her laugh with tricks and stunts. She'd have found his attentions a trifle too warm had he not paid them equally to everyone around him. It seemed he was as naturally happy and outgoing as his kinsman was sullen and hostile.

He returned her smile and said, 'How are you getting along with our dear leader?' Val glanced in Stephano's direction, and then turned back to give her a brilliant, white smile.

She looked down at the ground and traced a few more letters in the dirt, pretending it did not matter. 'He hates me.' It felt better being able to voice the truth.

Val snorted. 'Hates what you do to him, more like.'

'Me?' She looked up in surprise. 'I do nothing to him, I swear.'

Val laughed again. 'And that is the heart of the problem, I am sure. But do not worry. For all his temper, he is a good man. If his attentions are unwelcome, you have but to tell him so, and you will have nothing to fear from him. Great though his pride might be, he is unlikely to die if you wound it.' And then, Val put his hands into his pockets and walked away.

She stood up, ready to follow him and argue that the problem was nothing of the sort. She had no reason to fear Stephano's attentions, since none appeared to be forthcoming. And if they were, she certainly would not have deemed them unwelcome—

She stopped in her tracks. Why was she thinking such foolishness? Stephano Beshaley was out to prove her father a murderer. Any animosity towards her was rooted there. She should not spin fancies about him, but should answer his hatred with her own. Although her father had many faults, she was sure that murder was not amongst them. The Gypsy's plans of vengeance would lead to nothing more than the ruin of her reputation.

Although she suspected that in her case, a ruined reputation might make for an easier life. If any word of this escapade leaked out, another Season would be impossible. No amount of explanation could persuade potential suitors that she was an acceptable choice. Mother would be destroyed; Father, enraged. Marc would blame himself, just as he had over Honoria.

And she would be packed off to Aunt Foxe to rusticate, and be for ever free of the obligation of husband hunting. The thought suited her well. She had no desire to wed the sort of older, more appropriate man that Diana Price had encouraged. Nor was she eager to accept Alexander Veryan, no matter how happy it might make the family. So far, none of the candidates who claimed to want her hand had shown any interest in the rest of her. They had been ready with a proposal before trying to steal even a chaste peck on the cheek.

Perhaps that was what attracted her to Stephano Beshaley. If and when he chose to marry, he would not base the decision solely on the prominence of the girl's family. He would choose the woman because he wanted

her. It would not matter to him who his father-in-law
might or might not be.

He only cared about the Carlow family because of
this silly curse. And even though she did not interest
him beyond that, he had at least bothered to kiss her
before making the decision. That was something, she
supposed. She frowned into the fire. If she had not been
so inexperienced at kissing, perhaps things might have
been different.

He had noticed her watching him. As the children
ran off to play, he pushed away from the tree he'd been
leaning on, and came slowly toward her. He paused a
few feet short of her, watching as she sat back down and
scrubbed the words out of the dirt with the end of her
stick, and then felt foolish for doing it. She was acting
as if she had something to hide. She must get hold of
herself immediately. 'Is there something the matter?'
She threw the stick into the fire and stared up at him,
waiting for his response.

He stared back at her. And she got the same light-
headed feeling she'd had when she'd first met him: as
though they were having some intimate and wordless
conversation. And now, it felt as if he were touching
her body, although he had made no move towards her.
Her breasts tingled as though his hands were upon them,
and her nipples went hard and achingly sensitive. She
wondered if he knew. For his breathing had changed,
growing slow and shallow. He seemed to be fighting to
keep control of his emotions.

He broke the gaze first, with a small shake of his
head as though it had taken effort to get free from her.
'Do not stare at me with those eyes. They cannot make

up their mind to be green or brown, any more than you can decide between *gadje* and Rom. You are a prisoner here. Do not forget it.'

'I was doing nothing objectionable. And as I remember, you had given me parole. But if you have changed your mind, and wish me to remain in the vardo, or to avoid the company of the children—'

'I said, it does not matter to me, what you do,' he barked back at her.

She stood up and prepared to walk away. 'Very well, then.'

'Nor does it matter what I do, apparently. It was all decided by Jaelle, years ago. I have no control over anything that is happening here.' And he dragged her into the shadow of a nearby wagon.

This time, she had a moment to prepare. She should have struggled or run from him. But she did not. She went willingly and waited for what she knew would come. And she shut her lips tight, to be ready.

But it did not seem to matter, for he forced them open again and thrust his tongue into her mouth. There had to be another word than *kiss* for what was happening to her. It was a claiming. A possession. One of his hands was twined in her hair, locking her mouth to his. And the other hand cupped her bottom, pressing her against his body so tight that she could feel him grow hard as he thrust into her mouth. There could be no doubt that he was teaching her about the physical act of love, in its most primal form. In the silent communion between them, he told her with his kiss, *This is how it will be when I take you.*

In response, she opened herself to him, and let him

do as he wished. She went limp in his arms, kept on her feet by the pressure of his hands and his lips. She imagined their bodies, joined as they could be, in the way that her body ached for. And she could feel the actual moment of surrender—passing through her in a shudder, and leaving her as a gasp—and the silent cry, *I am yours*.

He heard it. Or perhaps he felt it. But it was clear that he knew what had happened. For in the next moment, he pushed her away and wiped at his mouth with the back of his injured hand. 'And now, you try to bind me to you by lust? I do not want your body, *gadji* witch.' He spat upon the ground at her feet.

She could not decide what about his actions made her the most angry. Was it that he pretended to have no control over what had happened between them? That he blamed her for it? That he lied about wanting her? For it was quite obvious that he did. Or perhaps it was the way he spat, as though the taste of her was something vile that he could not wait to be rid of.

Without thinking, she spat in response, just as he had. 'If you do not want my body, then take my curse. That is all you seem to understand. This morning, you complained that your head hurt you. If it does, then I am glad of it, and I do not care if it kills you.' She pushed past him, and ran across the camp and into the vardo, slamming the door behind her so that he would not see the beginnings of her foolish tears.

With her sudden absence, he could feel the pain coming back into his head. And her fresh curse made his hand burn as though she had dropped a coal on it.

For a moment, he almost followed her, ready to beg her to take back the words. But it was foolish. What power did a *gadji* have to lay a curse upon him? Only a fool or an old woman would believe it possible. And Stephano Beshaley was no fool.

But something unnatural was afoot, and Verity Carlow was at the heart of it. Tonight, he had found the place on the opposite side of the camp that marked the border of her influence on him. To go farther was to risk pain. But to come too close created all manner of confused desires.

As he had watched her play with the children, it had occurred to him: if she liked Rom children so well, he should drag her back to the wagon and give her one of her own. Or several. He doubted that he would leave her alone after one. The picture of her, great with his child, smiling in welcome to him, was taking root in his mind, growing like a tree.

The delusion made him feel like the dirty Gypsy boy they'd called him, when they'd sent him to the foundling home. She was destined for a titled gentleman of some sort or other. At the very least, she would marry a legitimate son from a respectable family. Even the relatively unblemished Stephen Hebden would not be good enough for the likes of the Earl of Narborough's daughter. What chance did Stephano Beshaley have?

But he had spoken with the men she'd spurned, and heard the rumours that she planned to remain unmarried. What harm could it do to speak with her? When she laughed in his face, he would be in good company, for it seemed she had already rejected every unmarried nobleman in London.

So he had crossed the camp to talk to her, half imagining that he would say something to improve her opinion of him. But Val had gotten to her first. And when Stephano had reached her side and opened his mouth, he had behaved like a jealous idiot.

And then he had kissed her, in the middle of camp where anyone might have seen. He should thank her for the pain it had brought him, for it cooled his blood and spared him the shame of a public arousal. She smelled of meadow flowers. And he could not seem to get enough of the taste of her. If she had almost climaxed in his arms, just from the force of his kiss, what would it be like when they made love?

But then, he had finally remembered what he should have known all along: she was his hostage, not his lover. He wished to barter her innocence for Narborough's confession. The very nature of his plan, and his own sense of honour, required that he leave the girl untouched. He was a fool to have kissed her, and an even bigger fool to want more than that.

So he had pushed her away, and hurt her with his rejection. His hand throbbed as he remembered her parting words. But that was nothing more than a septic cut. He would go to Magda and get a poultice for it. His grandmother was not as good a healer as Nadya, but she should be able to manage something as simple as this. He went to his her tent, and held out his injured hand to her, as though he were a little boy.

She glanced in his direction and sniffed in disapproval. 'I wondered when you would come to me with this. It has been troubling you for some time, has it not?'

'Since Monday.'

'The first day that you brought the *gadji* to camp with you.'

'That was the day I cut myself.' He did not want to tell her how it had happened, for he was unsure whether she would congratulate him or berate him for his foolish pride.

'When you rid yourself of the girl, you will rid yourself of the injury.'

'I will return the girl when I get what I want from her father, and not before.'

Magda pulled back the bandage and gave him a hard look. 'Then for your sake, we must hope that you hear from George Carlow soon. You have a day. Two at most. After that?' She shrugged.

This was his grandmother at her most maddeningly cryptic. He had even less time and patience for her and her games than he did for the Carlow family. 'This is but a scratch. Give me a salve for it. Or a draught of herbs.'

'You know better than me, do you?' Magda gave a bitter laugh and uncurled his fingers. 'The cut is here—' she poked at his hand, knowing that it would cause him pain '—right across the life line which was already weakened by a split. We all heard her curse you on the first day. And again, just now. I heard what she said to you before she ran to the vardo.'

He glared back. 'That was no business of yours, Mami.'

She glared back. 'If you wish privacy, then make love to her in your vardo, and not by my cooking fire. You insulted her, and she cursed you. The cut let the words into your blood. Now, you will pay for it.'

'That is utter nonsense.'

'As your actions have been. You were mistaken when you took her, for she has no part in the curse.'

'Not true. For it is against the children of the men involved.'

Magda gave an indignant sniff. 'Look at the girl. For all her faults, is there a more innocent creature on the planet? You took her into your vardo, you treated her badly. Then you bound yourself tight to an angry woman by marrying her. I expected you to know better.'

'Very well, then. I should not have taken her.' *For so many reasons.* And now, it was even worse that he did not want to let her go. 'There is little I can do about that, now. If I return her to Carlow before he confesses, it will all be for naught.'

'Then you must prepare to pay the price for your stupidity. There is nothing I can do for the cut on your hand. Only she can heal it by lifting the curse she has placed upon you.'

He felt a twinge of doubt. For if the old woman was right, there was little hope for him. 'And why would she do that, after the way I have treated her?'

'That is a problem of your making, not mine. Go to her. Beg her if you must. But if she does not help you, there is nothing anyone else can do. The fever will come soon, and after it, death.'

He did not feel feverish yet, that was sure. He felt cold. But that was with fear, and fear could be controlled. He could not sicken now. She was the last, so she must be the key. She had to be, for if not to her, where else could he turn for justice? Carlow would weaken and confess, and the girl would be back with her family in no time. It would all be over soon. If it was not, then he did not need his life. For he could bear to go no further on the course that his mother had set for him.

He stomped back to his wagon for bed, and then softened his steps on the wooden stairs. She was already asleep within, or pretending to be so. If he was too loud, she would have to pretend to wake and he would have to speak to her. And then they would argue again, and neither would be able to sleep.

It was just as if they were married. He smiled at the thought. At some point, perhaps he would explain to her what had happened the night before when they had shared the salt and bread. And she would laugh at the trick he had played on her, putting her arms about his neck and lifting her face for a kiss.

He brushed his fingers against the cut on his hand, and let the wave of pain take the vision away, then pulled the shirt over his head and tossed it over a chair. It was perfectly normal to think of pulling off her kerchief and burying his face in the cloud of golden hair, touching his tongue to her ear and then whispering the sort of sweet things that would make her part her legs for an evening of dalliance.

But it was equally normal to imagine her leaving the next morning. What was he doing, thinking that she would stay, or that he would wish to keep her? Or that they would ever share pleasant memories about their first day together.

Of course, when she was not speaking to him, she did look surprisingly happy, for a prisoner. The way she had fought on the first day, he had imagined enduring a week of her company while she hurled invectives or furniture, weeping first for her mother and then for her maid. She would be little able to take care of her own hair, much less sleep upon a rush mattress in a vardo. She would turn up her nose at the simple fare, sneer at the other girls and sulk in the wagon.

But today, he had watched her help his grandmother with the supper, and talk and laugh with the rest of his people as though she were a part of the tribe. As soon as she had been sure of her personal safety, she had relaxed and treated the Rom around her as though they were her own people.

And when she smiled...

It seemed that very nearly everything made her smile. Even the company of Magda, who most times was the bane of his own existence. She had even smiled at him, on occasion, although she must understand that he was her sworn enemy. But when Val had walked past her, she had given him a special smile in acknowledgement, as though they shared a secret.

Val was a cocky devil, and Stephano guessed he had been trying to charm her for most of the day. Earlier, the children had been playing at conkers, and Val had scooped the nuts from the ground, juggling them nonchalantly and letting the strings stream behind them as they whirled in the air. Verity clapped her hands together in appreciation, and laughed as he caught them easily and made a deep bow before her.

She was clearly taken with Val and his tricks. Jealousy ate at him. He should have dragged her back to the wagon, just as he'd planned, if only to lecture her on propriety. For if she thought to parade herself before the men in the camp and gain a champion from them, he would teach her that the choice had been made on the first day. No one here would dare to challenge him, nor come between him and the woman he chose.

He shook his head. It was all nonsense. She might claim to be an innocent girl, but she used her feminine charms with the skill of a courtesan. She was driving him mad. Even in his own vardo, he was not safe from her. He could feel her watching him as he removed his clothes. But if he turned and looked at her, she would be feigning sleep with her golden lashes shading her green-and-brown eyes.

The heat in his hand seemed to flow up his arm to other parts of his body, pounding through him to the beat of his heart. Now he was imagining her naked in his bed, arms outstretched to lift the curves of her breasts, eager to please him, to show that Val and the others meant nothing to her. He reached out with his good hand to snuff the candle, for if he turned and she saw how hard it made him to think of her, she would surely be frightened. Or perhaps she would not. Had he just heard a faint sigh of disappointment from her side of the room?

Very deliberately, he closed his fist upon the cut in his hand until the pain was a blinding, deafening storm, drowning out all else. *She was not his woman*. She was a pawn, just as the others had been. Her youth and her beauty were immaterial. He'd have treated her just the same, had she been old and ugly. Their living arrangements were no more than an inconvenience to be borne until she returned to her family. Their marriage was a sham. She did not want him. And he did not want her. Anything else was a lie.

He lay down on the floor at her feet and stared up at the darkened ceiling. Then he said, since no matter what she might pretend, he was sure she was still awake to hear it, 'Tomorrow, I will go to London, to negotiate for your release.'

There was definitely a little gasp this time. 'You will see my family? Tell them I love them, and that I am all right and they needn't worry.'

Which proved that she did not understand the nature of things at all. No matter how safe she might be, it gave away his advantage to tell her family so.

And then she said, 'If they do not agree to your demands…' She paused to think, then said in a worried voice, 'Just what do you mean to do with me if they do not give you what you want?'

'They *will* give me what I want. To keep from losing you, I expect your family would be willing to do anything.' For he could see, after only a few days, how they must value her and how much it would hurt to lose her.

'But they should not lie to save me. And that is what they would have to do, to give you what you want.' In the darkness beside him, she sounded so sweet and innocent; he wished there were some way to shield her from the revelations that were coming.

'Even if they do not, no harm will come to you. Perhaps I will keep you with me, if only to bake my bread.' He meant it to be a joke. But it occurred to him, after he'd said the words, that he might as well have been threatening her with a life of drudgery. 'I am sure that we will reach agreement on the subject. You need not worry.'

'Do not worry, Verity. It will be all right, Verity.' She sighed again. 'You have no idea how I tire of hearing those words. Especially when there are great reasons to worry. And all around me, people pretend that there are not. Do you all think that my youth equates with stupidity?'

He smiled, despite himself. 'I suspect it comes from a desire to protect you.'

'A failed desire, at best. They did a poor job protecting me from you. And if you truly had my best interests at heart, then you would have left me where I was.' He could hear her shifting uneasily beneath the blankets. 'Sometimes I fear that none of you see me for who I am. There is not a one of you who care further than the end of your own noses about what my future is likely to be.'

Although it did not matter, he closed his own eyes in the darkness, to make it easier to see her in his mind. And the pain in his hand turned to an ache not unlike longing. 'Then I must prove to you that it is not true. Tomorrow, I shall go to your family. And if we cannot reach an agreement, then I shall plead my case to you, and you will decide what I am to do with you. Goodnight, Verity Carlow. Rest well.'

Chapter Eight

He rose before the sun, for the pain in his hand would not allow him to sleep longer, and set about the business of washing and dressing. It surprised him that Verity rose, as well. Apparently, she had given up on the idea of privacy, and went about her morning business much as he did, pulling on stockings and shrugging into her dress.

It took surprising effort to keep his back turned from her as she did so. And to keep his eyes focused on his own face as he shaved, rather than searching the reflection of the room behind him to catch a forbidden glimpse of her body. Down that path lay disaster. If he turned to look at her now, he would never let her go. And she must go home today, for her own sake and the sake of his aching hand.

He left the vardo and went to prepare Zor for the journey. She followed him in silence and stood by to watch, holding the horse's head and patting his neck as Stephano saddled him. When he had mounted, she stood back and looked up at him with a sombre expression. 'Travel safely,' she said.

He nodded, and spurred his horse out of the camp.

He went more quickly than he needed to, for despite the headache it caused him to leave her, it felt good to be doing what he knew was right. Whatever his business with her family might be, it could no longer involve Lady Verity Carlow.

When he arrived in London, he stopped first at his house on Bloomsbury Square. While he had no wish to put on airs and graces for the Carlow family, he was tired and sore. A clean shirt and a cup of tea would do much to restore him before the difficult meeting ahead.

As he always did when arriving from camp, he came into the house by the back door. Although the servants were used to his odd comings and goings and changes of name and costume, it was easier to avoid questions from the neighbours if Stephano Beshaley came in at the back and Stephen Hebden left from the front. But it meant that he was often well into the house before the butler noticed his presence.

And so it was today. He had walked several paces and thrown his coat upon a bench in the empty back hall, and had still not seen a soul. He called out to Akshat for his tea, and still there was no response. That was highly unusual. Even if the butler did not hear, the sound of his voice should have brought someone to welcome him.

And just for a moment, he saw the face of Jenny the parlour maid, popping out of the doorway to the study. She gave a quick shake of her head, before she disappeared again.

Something was wrong.

Before he could turn and leave again, Akshat appeared in the hallway ahead of him, walking stiffly, with none of his usual grace. Behind him stood Marcus Carlow, Lord Stanegate, with a pistol pointed into the butler's back. Slowly, as if in a dream, he saw Stanegate start in reaction to his appearance and push the butler aside. There was the hesitation of less than a second, as Marcus brought the pistol up and prepared to fire.

Stephano turned to retrace his steps and leave by the back door again. But Nathan Wardale stepped out into his path. The man still had muscles earned from several years in the Navy. But Stephano caught him unawares and lurched into him as he ran, pushing past him and knocking him to the floor.

The impact saved Stephano's life. There was a pistol shot as he careened off the opposite wall, and the woodwork splintered near the place where his head had just been. Stanegate gave a curse of frustration, and Wardale groaned from the floor. And from somewhere at the front of the house, there was the sound of others rushing to see what had happened.

It went against his nature to run. But run he did. He was out the back door without a second thought, sprinting to the place where he had left Zor. As he mounted and wheeled the great horse around, he saw Stanegate coming after him with the strength and speed of a great cat, and with as little mercy in mind. If they caught him, there would be no time for argument, threat or explanation. By the look on Marcus's face, death would come so quickly that it would be no different than extermination. As Stephano rode past him, he was struggling to reload the pistol, while his brother Hal shouted cautions from the house about being so foolhardy as to fire a gun in the middle of the city.

Stephano did not slow from a gallop until he was well into the country, and was sure that none had followed. As the horse ran, he had time to think, if not to relax. It gave him a feeling of violation to think of enemies camping in his home, lying in wait for his return.

And that they would keep his servants as hostages. He frowned and his eyes narrowed. At least there had been no signs of ill treatment. Jenny had looked pale, but stalwart. And there were no marks upon Akshat's face, other than the scar that had already been there.

Given his own recent actions, he supposed he was not entitled to mercy. Perhaps he had been naïve to expect Stanegate to act with civility. He'd thought that the young lord would hold onto the chivalrous rules of war for as long as he could, if only to protect his sister. There would be an air of diplomacy to the release of his hostage. A mutual hatred, of course. But that could not be helped.

At worst, he had expected to get a beating, accompanied by a series of ineffectual threats. The gentlemanly nature of his opponents would keep them from doing the savage things that might dislodge the secret location of the camp, and they would be forced to release him if they wished to see their sister again.

But this had been an ambush. There was nothing in their actions that implied a desire for capture or an opportunity for discussion. It was little better than a miracle that he was not dead. For though Marcus Carlow was not the soldier of the family, he would not usually have missed at such close range.

What had they been thinking to act in such a way? Had Stephano been a less-principled man, this unsuccessful attempt to kill him would have driven him to take his anger out on his hostage. Did they not realize that they placed their sister in jeopardy by their behaviour?

If they meant to see him gone for good, without taking the time to secure the safety of Verity? Then they were fools. Or driven mad with vengeance, just as he had been. Right now, she was hidden so well that they would never find her without his help.

Having met her, he could not imagine why they would behave so. Surely, she must be the jewel of the family, precious beyond measure. Did they seriously mean to place the fragile Carlow honour over her return? Suppose they had shot him before he had divulged the girl's location? They might have lost her for ever, in their eagerness to see him punished.

He was sure, after talking to her the previous day, that Magda would have released the girl as blameless if he had not returned to the tribe. Fairly sure, at least. But mightn't she also be seen as the cause of his demise? And if the tribe decided that a death for a death was fair payment?

The day turned cold for him at the thought. Or was that the only reason he was chilled? He felt unsteady in the saddle, and added another worry to his list. It was not fear for the girl or the narrowness of his own escape that bothered him. He was growing by turns hot and cold, sick and shaky. His fingers were stiff, and had begun to swell to the point that it was difficult to hold the reins. The wound on his hand was turning bad, just as Magda had predicted.

He balanced as best he could and spurred Zor, trusting the horse to know the way home, so that he could arrange for Lady Verity's return to her family. It no longer mattered what had passed between the Carlows and himself, in the past or present. If his condition worsened, he would not survive to find the truth of it.

Chapter Nine

When he came back to the camp, he found her sitting on the bed in the vardo, staring at a space on the floor in front of her as though it told more tales than a book.

As he looked at her, his injured hand began to throb anew. Verity would tell him that he was foolish. It was just a scratch, and not a curse even stronger than the one placed on him by his mother. It was no different than hundreds of other small injuries he'd survived. She already thought him a superstitious savage. There was no point in proving her right.

'You have returned.' Her voice was almost a sigh. She glanced at his clothes, and she saw he had not changed them, and noted the grubbiness of his appearance. She could tell that he had ridden hard, and that all had not gone as it should.

It made him feel even worse to see his own fatigue reflected in her eyes. 'Of course I have returned. I would not leave you here, if I did not mean to come back.'

'Am I to go home, then? Have you brought my brothers with you?'

She could not wait to leave him. Which was as it should be; he must not wish otherwise. 'It is not so simple.'

'Oh.' Her voice was so small, as though her hopes had been dashed by his answer. The pain twisted like a knife in the palm of his hand.

The irony of it almost made him smile. How had he ever thought himself capable of violence against her? If her disappointment could cause him such pain, then God help him if she cried. And if he truly hurt her—

At the thought, his own pain bit into him, with a ferocity that left him gasping for air. It had been so easy with the others. He had but to offer them the silk rope, and all events had followed naturally. And he had been so sure of his right to do so.

But it was clear that Verity Carlow was blameless in this, no matter what his mother's curse might say. At the thought, the blood pounded in the scratch on his hand, as if to prove her power over him. He could not hurt the poor little bird in front of him. Her pain was his pain. Perhaps to release her was to accept defeat and admit to the world that he could be bested by a girl. But if he forced himself to abide one more moment of her company, he would abandon all pride and beg her to ease his suffering.

He took a breath, and prepared his story. 'It is all settled between us. But I could not bring them to camp,' he lied. 'It would not be fair to the others, to disclose their location. I will find someone to escort you home.'

'And then?' she asked.

'And then, your life shall be as it was.'

'You can guarantee that, can you? If you mean to release me, it must mean that you have proven my father a murderer and a traitor to his country.' Her tone was dry, almost amused. 'You swore that you would not change your mind in this, for any reason.'

'Verity, that is not important now…'

'Not to you, perhaps. Are you freeing me that I might return to see him hanged? Will I have to spend the rest of my life in seclusion and disgrace?' She was gathering herself together again, letting her anger and frustration boil over against him. And as he watched, she showed the haughty Lady Verity that he had expected and not the sweet, vulnerable girl that he had grown to love.

He winced at the pain in his hand and the stupidity of that thought. He did not love her. He could not. It was lust that he felt, and the fever had addled his brain to make it seem like something more.

She gave him a bitter smile. 'Now that you are done with me, my future does not matter. You care for nothing and no one but your dead mother and her foul threats.'

He opened his mouth to argue with her that there was nothing wrong with his accusations. If her family would kill him before knowing she was safe, then they were not worthy of her affection. If she would but stay with him, then he would give her the loyalty she deserved. He would be Hebden or Beshaley, or any other man she wished, if she would only agree to stay. But that was just more foolishness, from the dull banging of his blood which grew with each passing moment. 'Not true,' he muttered, for it was all he could manage through his clenched teeth.

'I hope you are satisfied with your victory. And that your success chokes you. That you do not have a peaceful moment, from this point on. I hate you, Stephano Beshaley. As much as you hate my family.'

With her words, his head began to spin and another wave of weakness caught him. He reached out to steady himself, forgetting his injured hand. When the flesh made contact with the wall of the caravan, the pain was so sharp that it dropped him to his knees.

'What?' The girl stepped instinctively closer. She noticed the bandage. 'It is not your head that bothers you. It is your hand, where you cut yourself.'

He shook his head stubbornly. 'It is nothing.' He tried to pull himself upright with his other hand, and barely made it to his feet. He stood weaving before her, unable to disguise the severity of the injury.

'Show me.' She held out her hand to demand his. Her voice was free of the anger it had shown just moments before, but had the same sternness she might use on a child.

'I said, it is nothing.' He bit his lip, trying to gain mastery over the pain long enough to send her away.

'If it is nothing, then it will not matter if I see. Sit.' She had the audacity to gesture him to sit upon his own bed. When he did not comply, she stood up and put her hand on his shoulder, pushing him down upon the mattress.

He did not resist her, for he could feel the heat gathering in his blood. It was as though the fever were a fire, raging far upwind and growing ever closer.

She took his hand in hers, and he did not protest, fearing that a tug of war over the bandage would show her the extent of his distress more than a simple examination.

'Go to Val,' he said. 'He will see you safely back to London.'

'If you do not mean to hold me, then cease telling me what I must or mustn't do.' She unwrapped his hand, tsked disapprovingly, and threw the cloth upon the floor. 'No wonder the wound is septic, if this is how you treat it.'

'Because I am a dirty Gypsy,' he bit out.

'Because a silk scarf is no kind of bandage. Lovely, of course, but who knows what poisons were used to dye it. And you have wrapped your wound in them and let them into your blood. But never mind. I will help.'

'Don't.' He feared her help almost as much as the injury. For she owed him nothing, after the way he had treated her in the name of justice.

'I am not so useless as you think, sir. I have tended my brothers, when they were foolish enough to injure themselves. You will find I am quite a competent nurse.' She stood up quickly. 'But I have half a mind to let you suffer if you wish to be stubborn over it.' She crossed to the door of the wagon, and then turned back to him. 'Do not move from that spot.'

Once she was gone, he sank back onto the bed, closing his eyes for a moment. It would not hurt to rest. And if he was lucky, she would walk past the edge of camp, not stopping until she reached London.

But it would be better if, after he had collected himself, he took her at least as far as the inn on the main road. If she would not go with Val, perhaps Magda could escort her all the way back to Keddinton. The Carlows would not dare to hurt an old lady, should she be seen.

Verity returned a short while later, with a basin of water and a piece of strong soap.

He eyed her suspiciously, but said nothing.

In response, she gave him a stern look. 'I mean to clean the wound. If you know what is best for you, you will give me no trouble.' Then she sat beside him and took his hand in hers.

Her hands felt wonderfully cool where they were touching him, and he looked down for a moment. They were tiny compared to his; white against the dark of his skin. The contrast disturbed him, and he closed his eyes so that he would not have to see it.

She snorted. 'You are an infant over a little blood. But all men are.'

She thought him a coward, now? So be it. He wished he could stand and walk away from this. Then he would go to Magda and apologize for doubting her. Perhaps the intent to offer help had been enough to save him, and he would not have to endure the feel of those perfect little hands, as they took his injured arm, pushed back the sleeve and dipped his hand in the basin in her lap.

The pain was still there, but each touch brought a little more quiet to his blood, as though she could command the beating of his heart to slow—to a stop, if she so chose.

Verity shifted against him, and he felt her lean forward and place one hand on his calf as she slipped the other into his boot to touch the hilt of his knife. He opened his eyes quickly and gathered enough strength to cover her fingers with his good left hand.

'I need it to open the wound and to cut a fresh bandage.'

He stared into her eyes. Was that concern he saw, or some kind of trick? 'Why help me?'

'Because I would not let a dog suffer as you are.'

At least, she was honest. If she had couched her request in fine words, he might have feared a trap. He slowly removed his hand from hers, and let her draw the knife from the sheath. Quickly, before asking leave or giving warning, she slashed out with it and opened the wound, allowing it to drain.

Strangely, the pain was less than it had been, despite the fresh cut. It was as if he could feel the poison draining out of his hand, and from his spirit, as well, mixing with the blood in the basin. She was massaging the open cut, and it should have hurt like blazes. But instead, her touch was as gentle as it had been, and it made him feel peaceful, almost drowsy. 'You do not wish me to suffer. But you did not hesitate to cut me.'

There was strain in her voice as she answered, as though the act of cutting had hurt worse than the cut. 'Attempts at gentleness do little to help when there is a difficult task at hand. Nor would my whinging on, letting my fear affect you. Lift your arm, please.' She lifted the basin carefully out of her lap, took it to the door and threw the water onto the ground outside. Then she rinsed it with water from the pitcher and poured fresh, bidding him to soak his hand again. She wiped his blood from the knife and went to her clothing in the corner, reaching for a clean petticoat and slashing at the hem to remove the lowest ruffle. She came back to him and examined his wounded hand, removing it from the water, drying it against her skirt and wrapping it carefully with the white cotton cloth.

The petticoat of a woman was *mahrime*; very unclean. The contact would make him all but untouchable amongst the Rom, if any heard of it. But perhaps, because she was his wife, it was different.

He closed his eyes and opened them again, wishing he could clear his head. She was not truly his wife. Their marriage was nothing more than a jest to torment his superstitious grandmother. But he could feel his strength grow as the cloth that had been so close to her body touched his infected skin.

Damn Magda for pushing him to this. He did his best to ignore the Romany nonsense that the old woman fed him. And then it all proved true. Curses were real and words were dangerous, and the results of using them might have nothing to do with the intent. In forgetting that fact, he had gotten himself a *gadji* for a wife. He laughed.

'You find your current condition amusing?' she asked tartly.

He waved his good hand in dismissal. 'My life is a joke.'

'And now, the fever is talking. Rest.' Verity placed one of her small hands in the centre of his chest and pushed until he fell back on the bed, unable to resist her. 'You will feel better when you wake.'

'If I wake.' He glanced at the knife, still in her lap. His helplessness before her felt strange, as though it were possible for a thing to be both frightening and comforting at the same time.

'If I'd meant to hurt you, I would have let the cut kill

you slowly. If you do not do as I say, it still might.' She sighed and shook her head. 'Sometimes, I think I must be a great fool.'

'Not so great a fool as I am, Verity.' If she was his wife, then it could not be wrong to use her name. He managed a weak smile, and closed his eyes. She had been foolish. At one time, he would not have hesitated to use the knife on her, if she had given him reason. If she cured him of the weakness that had been overtaking him, perhaps his resolve to end the curse would return with his health. Maybe she was right, and it was the fever that affected him now.

But more likely, he would have much to explain to her when he awoke from his nap.

'And what am I to do with you now?'

Verity stared down at the Gypsy who had fallen into an uneasy sleep on his own bed. He needed rest, if he was to recover from the infection. There would likely be a fever, and all the symptoms accompanying it. Someone would need to redress the wound and see to it that he was bathed and fed, assuming he awoke to take any food at all.

And none of this was her problem. If she left him here, she could help herself to a horse and be gone before he awoke. It would not even technically be an escape, for he had promised to release her. But then he had lost consciousness. Perhaps he would not even remember what he had said, when he came back to himself.

He looked so helpless, lying there before her. It was not a normal state for him, and he would be mortified to know that she had seen it. The tribe had been all too clear in their admiration of him. To run from him now would be to display his weakness to them. It would embarrass him. And now that she could admire the proud cast of his face, she did not wish that for him. For some reason, the thought of him humbled in the eyes of his people pained her.

For a moment, his brow furrowed as though the pain of his wound still reached him in whatever dream he inhabited. No matter what he might wish people to think, he was sick and in need. She reached out a hand to smooth his forehead, which was warmer than it should be. Someone must tend him. And after two nights alone in the vardo with him, who knew him better than she did?

Removing his clothing would be less difficult if she did it now, before he was too deeply asleep. As she began to undo buttons and tug at boots, he seemed to understand what she was about, and he stirred himself sufficiently to help her, struggling with the garments like a sleepy child. When free of them, he drew himself together on the bed, huddling beneath the covers as though he felt a chill.

But his skin was still hot to the touch, and the water in the basin was foul. She went to Magda with an empty pitcher and explained the problem. The woman frowned for a moment, and then nodded in understanding, offering water and a selection of herbs that would make the fever pass more quickly.

Verity took them back to the vardo, and lit a candle against the growing darkness. Stephano's skin was even warmer, as though now that she was here to help him, he had given up fighting the sickness.

She pulled back his blanket, and took the basin and a sponge, using the water to cool his body and trying to ignore the dizzy way it made her feel to be so close to him. The body under her hands had been heavily marked by the life it had led. She touched his shoulder. The scar on it was small and rounded; it seemed to be from a bullet. In his elliptical descriptions of their family's recent troubles, her brother Marc had said something of gunfire and a man that would trouble them no more. Perhaps this mark was a gift from her family. She smoothed her hand over it, as though she could take the pain back from him.

But Marc had made no mention of a knife wound. Or the thin line of silver at the base of Stephano's throat where someone had cut him. Tracing back over his torso, she found a map of his past, the injuries smaller and not so fresh, the scars fading except for the burn on his hip. Pain, struggle and the anger of others were left recorded on his flesh.

From his treatment of her, she could guess how he might have earned the punishments written here. She knew the lengths he might go to achieve his ends. But when would it be enough?

The hours passed and she continued her work, changing his bedding, forcing water between his lips when he would allow it and dozing in a chair beside the bed when he was quiet. When the fever finally broke and he stilled at last, she was nearly as exhausted as he.

She could see that there was space enough for two on the bed, and the floor where he had slept was hard and uninviting. And while she knew it was terribly wrong of her to entertain the thoughts she was having, she was very tired and he was too far gone to know the difference. It would be innocent enough to lie beside him, she was sure.

And yet, it was not innocent at all. For she had never in her life done such a thing for anyone else she had nursed. But it seemed to help him to have her close. When she climbed into bed behind him, he leaned back against her as a remedy to the chill night air. It felt good to touch him and to lie beside him, feeling warm and protected. Without thinking, she laid her cheek against his back, trailing her fingers over the muscles of his arms, and tangling her legs with his.

It felt strange, and good in a way that was beyond comfort. There was an answering heat building low inside her. Was it the excessive warmth of his body that made her too hot to lie still, or was it something more? She could not seem to get comfortable, and her dress seemed to bind her like the ropes he had used when he'd brought her to the camp.

At last, she sat up and drew the gown over her head, casting it aside and lying down again in nothing but her chemise. He moved slightly, adjusting his body to hers, and his skin rubbing against her nipples through the cloth was a delicious thing. She wanted more of it, and moved against him to recreate the sensation, knowing that it was incredibly wrong of her, and incredibly foolish.

It was one thing to wish to remain unmarried, and quite another to be trapped as a spinster because one was a pariah. Poor Honoria had been forced into seclusion for sins much smaller than the ones she was committing right now. She was not sure exactly what had happened, for as usual, the family had kept the full truth from her as a protection. But she seriously doubted it was anything so scandalous as lying down with a man.

She suspected that even the Gypsies would be shocked at the fancies that crowded her mind, lying beside Stephano. As might he. In his own way, he had been a gentleman throughout this interlude. And he didn't seem to want her in the way she was growing to want him.

But tonight, she did not wish to think of that. Now that the fever had broken, she wished he would awaken and respond in exactly the way she had feared from the first, punishing her for her audacity with rough kisses, touching her body as though he possessed it, and then claiming her so thoroughly that she could never leave him. By day, she could live in the Gypsy camp, sitting by the fireside with the other women. And by night, she would nestle with her lover in the soft bed of his vardo.

It sounded very romantic and adventurous. And no doubt, it was nothing like that at all. There would be hardship and pain. He would uproot her at the slightest provocation, traipsing homeless around the country or the world.

And she would not be bored. While living in a Gypsy wagon might cause her to greet each new day with trepidation, it might be better than her current state. For before he had taken her, she had risen each morning with growing dread, convinced that today and tomorrow would be identical to yesterday and the day before that.

A brief acquaintance with the man lying beside her

was no reason to think that a lifetime with him would be something worth seeking. Nor did she have any indication that he wished her company. But in truth, whatever man she married was unlikely to know her better than this one. Although Stephano claimed to dislike the colour of her eyes, at least she was sure that he had noticed it. And when he kissed her... She smiled. If he did not like the way they kissed, then she would be pleased to learn another way, if he wished to be her teacher. But she could not imagine anything better.

The Gypsy rolled suddenly, turning to face her without waking. In his dreams, it did not seem to surprise him that there was a woman in his bed. He gave a contented sigh, and muttered something in Romany, burying his face against her neck. Then he threw an arm over her, dragging it down her back until he could cup her bottom with his hand, digging his fingers into the flesh and massaging it as though he were palming her breast. He pulled her tight against him, as if to facilitate their joining, and she felt the heaviness of his body stirring between her legs. And then, without releasing her, he settled back into sleep.

She should be shocked by his behaviour, but instead, she felt only envy. Whomever he thought he was holding, his affection for her was as natural to him as breathing. So she wrapped her arms around him, pressed close against him, and pretended, for tonight at least, that it was of her that he dreamed.

Chapter Ten

Stephano awoke with a start. He had not meant to doze at all. But he could tell by the light coming through the windows in the vardo that much time had passed. Shadows were growing, and he could see Verity moving around in the dim light of the cabin.

'How long?' His voice scratched, and he cleared his throat.

She turned to him, as though surprised. 'How long did you sleep? About a day and a half. You were very ill.'

He wanted to argue that it had been moments. But there was a fresh bandage upon his wound and a clean basin of water on a chair beside his bed. Leaves floated in it, and there was a white cloth resting on the side. Vague memories surfaced of small white hands holding the cloth to his temples, squeezing drips of water between his parched lips, and bathing him as though he was the infant she had accused him of being. His body felt suspiciously cool and clean, and the faint scent of herbs clung to his skin.

'You had a fever. But it has passed.'

He grew conscious of his nakedness beneath the blanket, and glanced at the knife resting on the table on the other side of the room. She had stayed with him, when it would have been a perfect opportunity to run. 'You should have left me when I was weak. No one would have stopped you. And yet, you did not.'

She turned her head and reached to straighten the cloth beside the basin, as though she wished to look anywhere but at him. 'You were trying to release me when you fell ill.'

'And you did not act on it?' He wished she would look at him. For if she did, he was sure he could read the truth in the depths of those fascinating eyes.

'I thought, if you had not already let me go, then perhaps there was still some hope that our families might reconcile peacefully. You are not foolish, nor is my father. He will not speak until he has me back. And if you had been fully satisfied with the results of your trip to London, I would have been gone already. If I am still here, then there is time.'

She raised her face to look at him, and in that moment, he knew he had lost his heart to her. She looked sad and yet hopeful, and totally trusting that he would do the right thing by her, if only she asked. How could he deny her? He was weak from the fever, but the ache in his hand had been reduced to the itching and prickling of a healing scratch. And his head was clearer than it had been for years.

So he propped himself up on his elbows and looked into her hazel eyes for what he feared would be the last time. And he said, 'I relinquish all claim against your family. If your father took a life, then you have given one back to me. If my mother is not satisfied with this, then she must come back from where ever she has gone and take her own vengeance. For I cannot.' He slumped back, wondering what the consequences of that speech would be for him. He doubted that the curse would release him as easily as he had released the girl. But it would be better if she were safely home when fate caught up to him.

'You will let me go? And my family?' There was such a look of blessed relief upon her face that he knew he had done the right thing.

He nodded. Even if it was brief, he could savour the memory of this moment, sure that he had been honourable. Her happiness would be enough reward. 'Send for Val. I will instruct him to drive you back. And you must take Magda or one of the other women as chaperone.'

And then, she seemed to hesitate. 'I would ask one more favour, if I could.'

'Anything.' And it was true. For he owed her his life.

'I would like you to take me yourself. And for my family to hear the words from your lips, that this is over. But you are not yet well. In a day. Maybe two. We can return to them then. Would you do that for me?'

It seemed his reprieve would be as brief as he expected. He would take her back to London, and her brothers would shoot him, as they almost had in his own home. And that would be the end of it. He laughed.

Her face fell.

And so he said, 'Of course. If you wish, I shall keep

you prisoner for another day. But it would be much more sensible of you to demand that I stop malingering and harness a horse.' He made to get out of bed and away from her, trying to resist the desire to prolong his illness for a few more days of her company.

She placed her hand against his chest again, to restrain him. 'Do not argue with me, Stephano Beshaley. I will not have you undoing two days of my hard work in nursing you. You will remain in this bed until I say otherwise. For now, I will get your supper and check your wound again. Then, *if* you are feeling well enough, you may get up. But rushing when you are still weak will undo the progress I have made.'

'I am not weak.' He glared at her, willing her to believe. Although in truth, he felt as weak as a kitten.

'Of course not,' she lied back to him, with a little smile that said she had no fear at all of his dark looks. 'Now, stay in bed while I get your supper.'

She left him alone in the vardo, and he settled back into the pillows she had arranged for him, feeling for a moment like the luckiest man in the world. His woman was tending to him, bringing him food and fussing over him because of a little cut that would never have affected him so, had things been different between them.

It did not matter that she did not know she was his. For a day, maybe two, he would pretend that there was more between them. It would hurt no one, if he allowed himself a little pleasure before giving himself over to his enemies.

Verity returned shortly with a bowl of stew and a thick slice of bread. She sat down on the edge of the bed and held it out to him, offering the fork.

He took the bowl in his left hand, and the fork in his right, then embarrassed himself by dropping it back into the bowl. He was weaker than he cared to admit. His fingers were stiff and could not grasp.

'Let me help you.' She took the bowl from him, and forked up a chunk of meat, offering it to him, as though she were feeding a child.

He took it, and ate. She was right. He needed to restore himself before they travelled. The food was good, and he was very hungry. If he had been able to feed himself, he'd have wolfed the meal. But instead, her ministering forced him to take nourishment slowly, and gave him the opportunity to enjoy the nearness of her as he ate. He leaned back into the pillows again, forcing her to scoot up the bed after him and to lean over him. It provided a tantalizing glimpse of her breasts as the neckline of her gown gaped in front of him. She fed him another bite, her hip brushing against his as she brought the next forkful to his mouth.

He smiled as he took the food from her, chewed and swallowed, then looked back at her and slowly licked his lips.

His response had been innocent enough, but he could see the way it affected her. Her eyes went dark as he looked into them, the pupils growing until the irises turned golden brown. Her skin flushed as though the fever from his infected hand had been contagious and she swayed closer to him as she dipped the fork to the bowl again and brought up another mouthful of food.

He reached out to steady her hand, his fingers closing around her wrist to bring the fork back to his mouth, enveloping the tines with his lips and drawing the meat off slowly, closing his eyes as he chewed and swallowed. He rubbed his thumb gently against the pulse point on her wrist, feeling the faint beat under the silk-smooth skin.

And then he guided her hand to her side, his meal forgotten. He stroked slowly up the outside of her arm to her shoulder, cupping his hand to the back of her neck and bringing her face to his.

He kept the kiss soft. After how he had behaved the last time he kissed her, he would not continue if she rejected him. But the way she had watched his mouth as he ate, he did not think she would mind. He teased with the tip of his tongue, and she opened for him. And this time, she kissed him back. Was the fever returning, he wondered? For the heat in him was building with each tentative stroke of her tongue into his mouth. And then, she pulled herself on top of his body, to be closer to him.

She knew. God's mercy, she felt what he felt. He did not have to hold her, to keep her near. She was free to leave, if she wished. She had stayed not just to nurse him or to secure the safety of her family. She had stayed because she wanted to be with him. She had stayed so that they might do this.

He let his arm slip to her waist to hold her against himself. His mouth created a gentle rhythm on hers, and as the sheet slipped low on his upper body, she laid her palms flat against his chest and pushed it further down so she could touch his bare skin as she must have when she'd washed him. But he was better now. He felt cool and dry, free of the fever that had plagued him. And he was awake to enjoy it. She seemed to feel no guilt or fear in tracing his nipples, letting her fingers sink into the muscles, massaging. He was overwhelmed with the sense that she knew him and wanted him, body and soul.

It was as if he had woken in a different world. This was a paradise, with a ministering angel who aroused him and welcomed his response. His hand slipped lower down her back, kneading the roundness of her hips, letting her feel how hard she made him, and waiting for any sign of fear from her. But there was none, for she let out a gratifying moan of longing at the contact.

He made no effort to hurry the kiss, brushing his fingers against her covered breasts until he could feel the nipples peaking beneath the fabric. She writhed under his hands and her hips gave an answering roll against his, as though she wished to excite him further. She gave a little gasp as she realized the pleasure that movement brought her. His body ached with anticipation as she began a tentative rocking against him, letting the desire grow between them. It would be like the last kiss they had shared. But better. For if he had released her from the curse, there was no reason to stop. Soon, when he was sure that she would not refuse, he would lift her skirts and push the sheet away. She would spread her legs to straddle him. And then… He squeezed her breast and thrust his tongue deep into her mouth, as he would thrust into her body.

The sudden realization of what she was doing hit her like a hammer. She went rigid against him, turned her head from his kiss and scrambled off of him, and away from the bed. She backed towards the door of the vardo, her hand to her mouth as though she did not know whether to cry for help or kiss him again.

And for a split second, he felt a disappointment so acute that he feared it must show on his face. Without thinking, he had raised a hand, to reassure her and coax her back to bed. Better to let her think that he was a wicked Rom who would feign weakness to seduce her, than to look like the lovesick fool he was. He smoothed the movement of his arm, folding it behind his head as a cushion from the wall. He changed his expression to cynical self-satisfaction, laughed and blew her a kiss.

With a look of utter disgust, she turned and hurried from the vardo.

Stephano closed his eyes so he would not have to watch her run from him, and listened to the sound of the slamming door. The crack was loud in his brain, and the pain in his skull came flooding back, as though the sound was the breaking of a dam.

He winced. If he was lucky, her brothers would take him the minute they were parted, and make a quick end to him. Even if they did not do the deed, he would not live long without her.

As she'd stretched out on top of him, it had become obvious that there was a much better way for two lives to become one than a benighted quest for vengeance. Loving her healed his head, just as her nursing had healed his hand. It did not matter if her father was guilty or not. His search was over. Verity Carlow was the only truth he would ever need.

And then she had realized what was happening, and

had run from him. What else could he do but laugh? For to do else would show her how deeply she had hurt him, and how easily she could control him.

Chapter Eleven

W hat had she done?

Verity patted at her dress and straightened her head scarf as though she was afraid that the bed play must be clear to all around her. But if there was any shaming evidence of what had happened, no-one commented on it as she went to the edge of camp and stepped out into the soothing greenness of the trees. She leaned against a beech, letting her skin cool and her pulse slow. It had been good. Wrong, of course. But very good. She could still feel it between her legs, a low trembling, a flame ready to re-ignite at the slightest touch of hand or body.

It was what she thought she had wanted. But with satisfaction scant moments away, she had grown frightened. Before he'd gone to London, he had claimed not to want her body. Had so much changed in just a few days? Or was he willing to use any girl who was foolish enough to crawl into his bed and offer herself? If the last rejection had hurt, it would be a hundred times worse if he took her maidenhead for sport, and then laughed and turned her out.

Magda called to her, and when she turned to look, the old woman gave a rare smile of welcome. She gestured to a place by the fire. 'You took the food to him? He is better?'

'Yes.' Verity tried to keep the breathlessness from out of her voice.

Magda eyed her appraisingly. 'And he is grateful to you for nursing him. That is good. I told the boy it would be all right. That only you could help him. But he did not believe.'

Verity shrugged. 'It was only an infected cut. It might have healed itself. Or you could have done the same for him.'

The old Gypsy shook her head. 'With time perhaps. But with a love such as yours, it takes very little time to put things right.'

'There is no love between us.' For what she had felt just now could not be called love, could it?

Magda made an odd huffing sound as if to dismiss her arguments. 'If it was not love, then why did you marry him?'

Verity laughed in response. 'I did no such thing.'

'You ate bread and salt with him. I was witness to it. And then you covered your hair with his scarf. You share his wagon. You are his woman.'

She was his woman. That was true enough. But if she could not even bring herself to tell Stephano, how did the rest of the camp know? 'I was brought to this camp as a prisoner. I ate with him of course. Because I was hungry. And with you, as well. He said the scarf was to protect my modesty.'

Magda smiled in triumph. 'It was to tell all who saw that you belonged to him. You broke bread that had been blessed with salt, and shared it between you. You are his wife, now. And to me? You are *bori*. Daughter-in-law.' The old woman leaned forward and put a hand on each shoulder, drawing her close to kiss her cheeks.

Verity looked around helplessly, for anyone who could help her explain that there had been a mistake. It was only a matter of language that kept Magda from understanding the situation.

And then, she remembered all the argued Romany conversations between Stephano and his grandmother. They must have spoken of this before now. Whatever his true intentions had been, he knew what the old woman thought. And he'd allowed her to think it since the first day, without correction.

The more she thought about it, the angrier it made her. He had paraded her through the camp as his wife and told her nothing. He'd kissed her when others were watching, but treated her as a stranger when they were alone.

Until today. Apparently, he meant to claim his rights as husband, before taking her home. And she had played right into his hands, crawling over him as though she could not get enough of his touch. He must have found it quite amusing to see her behave thus.

She turned and stormed back into the vardo. Stephano had moved very little from the position he was in when she'd left him. The bowl at his side was empty. Had he regained his strength? Or had the dropped fork been a trick to bring her closer?

He arched an eyebrow at her, waiting for her to speak.

'I talked to Magda when I was outside, just now,' she said. 'She was much more forthcoming than she has been.'

'I expect she is grateful to you for helping with me.'

'She called me *bori*. Daughter. And she says that we are married. How can that be, when I never consented to such a thing?'

He shrugged. 'Rom ways are not the same as the *gadje's*. It takes very little more than the consent of both parties, when it is time to marry. A clasp of hands in front of the tribe can be enough. The fact that you wear my scarf upon your head.'

She snatched it off and threw it to the ground.

He ignored her action and went on. 'Or the sharing of food, back and forth between us.'

'The bread and salt?'

'Yes.'

'My hunger was not the same as my consent. You cannot starve me into your bed.'

'I was not attempting to. I merely wished to offer you my protection.'

'Ha! You have a strange way of showing it, Mr Beshaley. I would not have needed protection, if you had not kidnapped me.'

'I meant to protect you from Magda. She was none too happy that I brought you here, and even less so that

I would share a wagon with a woman that I had not married.'

'So you forced me into a marriage.'

'Hardly, Lady Verity. You ate a bit of bread. That was all. It means nothing to you, does it? There will be no need for a formal annulment. There is no need to mention it at all, when you return to your family. You might just as well have dined with me, for all it means to them.'

And *they* were what really mattered. Because a pawn was not supposed to have feelings or to care what happened to it. 'You expect me to forget that we are married?'

He seemed mildly surprised by her anger. 'I did not expect you would find it out. But now that you have? *Yes.* Once you return home, I expect you will forget that it ever happened.'

Just as he would forget her. The least he could do was admit it. 'And what will you do, once I am gone? The curse is done. What are your plans?'

He opened his mouth, and then closed it again.

'Do you mean to divorce me? Marry again? Or does the ceremony you performed in front of Magda mean nothing to you, as well?'

He was going pink under the dark skin, as though she had shamed him to blush.

'You did not even think of it, did you? Because I am not even human to you. Just a piece of furniture to be moved from place to place.' She laughed in triumph at the baffled look on his face. 'Well then, it should not be difficult to come to a decision about something of so little importance. What will you do about our supposed marriage when I return home?'

She could see the change as she looked at him. There was a softening of his gaze as the cynical smile became sad. Then he said, 'You are free to do as you like. But I am caught in my own trap. I thought it was merely a ruse to please my grandmother. But searching my heart, I find that it is not. While I do not intend to hold you against your will, once my business with your family is through, I will not be able to marry again. I remain your husband, whether you are my wife or not. I cannot control my feelings towards you. And after this afternoon, I will not be able to control my actions, should I remain alone with you. The vardo is yours until tomorrow, when I will take you home. Tonight, I will sleep elsewhere.'

Chapter Twelve

The rain fell heavily upon the roof of the vardo, and Verity stared at the curved ceiling above her bed, wondering where Stephano had gone.

It was strange and foolish that she should even care. She had been very angry with him for tricking her. And angry with herself for giving in so easily as they had lain on the bed together.

When she had confronted him with the truth, she had expected him to laugh at her. To make some comment about how easy it had been to run rings about a silly *gadji*, very nearly tricking her out of her virtue. Or tell her that he meant to go to her father and announce, even after he had returned her safely, that he had taken her to wife and meant to ruin any further chances she might have to marry well.

But instead, he had looked so sad. She was sure that he had spoken the truth when he'd said he would let her go. And it was clear that he did not wish to.

It had taken a moment to collect herself, after he had

left her, to try and understand what he had told her. He had said he was her husband. He had not used the word *love*. But that must be the reason for his confession, mustn't it? If all he wanted was someone to bake his bread and sweep his wagon, there were Rom girls who could do better than she. Before the sickness, when he had called her a witch and complained about the odd colour of her eyes, he had done it because he was angry with himself for caring about her.

Val had been right after all. Stephano had feelings for her. And she knew what she felt for him. In her naïve and inexperienced way, she had wanted him from the first moment they'd met. Circumstances that should have rendered his attentions repellent had done nothing to change her mind. Despite the curse and the kidnapping, she felt safe when in his presence. And she was happier in this little wagon with him, than she had been wandering the many empty rooms of Stanegate Court.

She loved him. She knew it must be the truth, for even to think the words made her smile. He was her husband, and she loved him. And if they were married, then it would not be wrong of her to lie with him. The prospect made her shiver with delight. He would complete what he had started and give her what her body was craving. And she knew him to be an honourable man. Once they had been together, he would have to keep her, even if his original plan had been to send her home.

But now, he was avoiding her, convinced that it was for her own good. If she left the vardo to look for him, she wondered if she would find him at any of the fires or if anyone would tell her where he had gone. It was growing late, and it was raining. And he had gone to sleep elsewhere. Where could he mean? She had seen the looks in the eyes of other women in the camp when he had walked by. They would be quick to take him in, if he was not here.

Then she scolded herself. She was being unfair to the women, for they were bound by the rules, just as he was. Stephano could not say he had married her and then go to someone else. If he was not here, he was sleeping alone. She tried to imagine him swallowing his pride and admitting to his people that he had given her his wagon and she had given him nothing.

She got out of the bed, padded across the floor in her bare feet, and opened the door to look out into the rain-soaked camp. The cook fires were smouldering, and one or two of the tents glowed from within with lanterns or candles. But many of the families were already sleeping.

'Stephano,' she whispered, taking a step out of the wagon and shivering as the rain began to wet her shift. 'Stephano,' she said more loudly. 'Are you there?'

There was a rustle, and her husband rolled out from under the wagon, throwing off an oilcloth cloak and trying to avoid the puddles as he scrambled to his feet, his knife in his hand. 'What is it? Is there trouble?' No matter what had happened between them, he stayed close by, ready to protect her.

She sagged in relief. 'It is raining.'

'I am aware of that.'

'Come back in the vardo. You will catch your death.' She stepped aside so he could enter.

He did not move, glaring at her as though he still expected her to retreat in fear. She smiled back at him to remind him that it had been some days since that trick had worked on her.

At last, he sighed and then muttered as though defeated. 'I am cold and wet, and too tired to care what you think of my return. I will be gone before the sun rises, so that you might dress in private.'

He trudged past her, up the wooden steps, shaking the water from his dark hair. He put down the knife and went to his side of the wagon, removing his coat and boots, taking care with his clothing as he always did when he prepared for bed.

She closed the door behind her and went to sit upon the bed. Tonight, she made no effort to hide the fact that she wished to watch him, sighing a little as he stripped bare and towelled himself dry. The drops of water on his broad shoulders glistened like diamonds in the candle-light until he wiped them away. She marvelled at how beautiful he was, and how wonderful to touch. Then he reached for a' blanket, spreading his bed roll upon the floor.

She smiled into the darkness and thanked God for the fortuitous bad weather. It was a hard floor, and he must still be tired from his illness. He lowered himself to the floor, and as he turned his back to her, she heard a groan of pain suppressed in a sigh.

'Stephano?' she said, loud enough so that he could not pretend to be asleep.

'Yes?'

'It might be best if you reclaimed your bed this evening. You are still not well. You might take a chill from lying on the floor.'

There was a thoughtful silence from the floor. And then he said, 'I beg to differ.'

'I must insist. While I do not mind nursing you back to health, I should be most cross if I were forced to do it twice.'

The silence was even longer this time. And then he said, 'You are just as likely to catch cold, if you do not care for yourself. Your shift was soaked when you were foolish enough to go out in the rain to call for me.'

His comment came as a growl, and she smiled and wondered if it was because he was thinking of the way the cotton was clinging to her body. 'Do not fear that. I have sense enough to remove my clothing before lying down.' She pulled the garment over her head and let it fall with a wet slap on the floor beside him. Then, she scooted to the side of the bed to make room for him. 'And I am sure that there is enough room here on the mattress for both of us. I shared it comfortably with you last night.'

Now the silence from the floor had an unusual quality, as though he had not yet considered the fact, but was thinking most intently about it now. 'If that was intended to help me to an easy night's rest, I fear it will have quite the opposite effect. I might have been an easy companion while near death. But it will not be the case, tonight.'

'Is your hand bothering you, that you cannot sleep?' She prayed that it was not so.

'You might not think me in full health, Lady Verity. But I will find it difficult enough to sleep here, even if I remain on the floor. If you think I can lie peacefully in bed next to a desirable young woman, you would soon find that I am not so sick as all that.' He sounded exasperated with her, and faintly amused.

'You find me desirable?' She reached out a bare foot and poked him playfully in the back with her toe. 'I had assumed you found me to be a nuisance.'

'A man will put up with a surprising amount of bother, if the girl is pretty enough. And there was never any question of your desirability. Even from the first night.' His words were soft and sweet, and he said them as though he cherished the memory. 'But when the nuisance of a girl saves a man's life, even though that man has given her every reason to wish him dead and going straight to the devil?'

She smiled down at his back. 'Even if you were my worst enemy, I could not have let you die.'

'Am I not your worst enemy, then? Because the way I have treated you, I should be. No matter the quarrel I might have with your father and no matter how I might wish to see justice done, I should not have involved you in it. I will see to it that you are kept safe until I return you to your home, just as I promised.' He rolled to face her, and she watched his eyes go dark. He must have forgotten that she was bare, or assumed that she would have done something to cover herself instead of sitting naked on the edge of the bed above him.

'Stephano,' she whispered. 'Stephen? What is the Romany word for *husband*?'

He closed his eyes, to block out the sight of her. 'It is *rom*. The same as the word for *man*. And you are my *romni*. You are trying to destroy me, are you? To remove your clothes and ask that question? You make me wish that it were true.'

'You could make it so, if you want.' She felt herself tremble at the words. They were the most forward things she had ever said in her life.

'It would make me a liar. Did I not just promise that I would not hurt you? And how could my love not do that?'

'It hurts me more to know that you lie on the floor so near to me and yet you will not touch me.' She held out a hand to him, moving it as though she could touch his body from a distance.

And he seemed to feel the touch, for he moved on the floor before her, his breath hissing out from between his teeth, and his lips peeling back in a tortured smile. Then he rolled to a sitting position, as gracefully as a cat, and grabbed her hand, bringing it to his lips. 'Do you know what you are offering me? And what will happen when I come to your bed? There is no turning back, once the decision has been made.'

He would come into her. He would love her. He would give her his children. She smiled. 'Yes.'

Then he groaned against her skin and said, 'Then let me be damned for a liar and a thief and a breaker of promises. If you want me, I am yours. And I must make you mine. I should know better. But I have never met a woman like you, nor felt the way I feel.' He rose to his knees and leaned forward to cup the back of her neck, bringing her face down so he could claim her lips.

Any doubts she might have had vanished with the kiss. He was so gentle with her, it almost made her laugh to remember that she had once feared him. The touch of his lips on hers was worshipful, as though he were delivering the kiss in a church after saying his vows.

He whispered, 'I give you my word, as the Rom
Stephano Beshaley, and as Stephen Hebden, bastard
son of Christopher Hebden, Lord Framlingham, that I
lie with you tonight because you are, and always will
be, the wife of my heart. It is true in my world, and I
will make it true in yours, as well.'

'Yes, please.' It sounded so foolish, but she could
not find the pretty words in her heart that might match
his promise to her. It was all wrong-way round, to be
receiving and accepting the offer after the marriage—
and just before the bedding. Diana would have been
appalled. Her father and brothers would be livid. It was
all wrong. And yet, all right. For when she looked at
him, there was a feeling inside her that was like nothing she'd known. Nothing perhaps, except the feeling
she'd had in the ballroom when she'd first laid eyes on
him. Even then, she'd known that this was the man for
her and that if they could be together, the details would
work out all right.

His mouth crooked in a smile, and he wrapped his
arms around her waist as he knelt at her feet. 'Very well,
wife. Let us begin.' He released her and stood up, the
blanket falling away from his aroused body. 'Stand, so
that I might wash you.' His smile was almost sly, as he
waited for her to move.

'I am quite clean enough, I assure you.' It was a
strange request, and not at all what she had been expecting to hear.

'I am certain you are. But you have been tending to
me for several days. It would give me pleasure to return
the favour. Now, come and stand beside me, so that I
might touch and admire your body, as you have mine.'

And there was that tight, almost pained smile of his, as though it was only with supreme effort that kept him from devouring her.

She swallowed her nerves and stood up in front of him so that he could see her.

She turned back to face him; his gaze rested on her body like a hand, stroking over her breasts and belly to stop at her legs. And he grew in response, as she watched him. He was hard and erect. And her body grew wet with desire, ready to receive him.

He smiled. 'You see what you do to me?'

She nodded, a little frightened by his quick response.

'I must take care, for to look at you is to be ready for love. And you need time.' He turned from her and poured a fresh basin of water, gathering clean cloths and towels.

'I am ready,' she said, preparing her mind for what was to come.

'You are not. Let me show you.' He dampened a cloth in the basin, then ran it slowly over the skin of her face, letting it rest for a moment on her lips like a kiss. 'How can you be? For these lips know nothing, do they? I am the first man to kiss them.' He leaned forward, his own lips resting gently upon hers, before pulling away. 'And the first to see your body.' He was stroking along her neck and shoulders, up and down her arms. 'Lovely. So very lovely. The charms you reveal, when you grace the dance floor in a gown, and the charms you conceal from all but your lover.' His hands had settled on her breasts, the cool, wet cloth stroked lightly over her nipples. They drew tight in response. 'See? You grow hard, as well.'

His touch was stronger, as he rubbed her dry with a towel that seemed both soft and rough. 'Ripe like fruit.' He pinched them lightly, between his fingers. 'May I taste you?'

If he did not, she was sure she would die. All she could manage in response was to moan in frustration, and arch her back to him as though offering herself. So he caught her low about the waist, bent her back and buried his face in her breasts, sucking them deep into his mouth as though he could draw the soul from her body. She kissed the top of his head, and twined her fingers in his hair, satisfied and frustrated at the same time. And finally, she pushed him away so she could kiss clumsily into his open mouth.

She could feel him laughing against her, and he pulled away to whisper, 'So eager, my love?' before returning the kiss in the same languid fashion he did everything else. He did not part from her again until there was not a bit of her mouth unconquered.

Then he got up again, changing the water in the basin and choosing a fresh cloth. He knelt at her feet, taking each in turn and pouring the water over them in a thin stream, massaging the toes and the insteps, looking first into her eyes and then slowly dragging his gaze down her body to stop in the place she knew he meant to end. He took her hands and bade her stand before him, then washed her legs, his hands moving up and down them with long, smooth strokes, over her hips. Then he took the last cloth and squeezed a few drops of water from it into her navel as his hands settled between her legs. She almost collapsed at the first touch of his cloth-covered fingers, it was so good. But he knew there was more, and moved against her, varying the strength and the pace, before dropping the cloth and thrusting his fingers deep into her body.

She gripped him by the shoulders, revelling in the solid feel of his body under her hands and the shockingly possessive way he was touching her. Her body began to shake, and he laughed and leaned forward, licking the water from her belly. And then he thrust his tongue rhythmically into her navel as his fingers slid in and out of her, at last stilling, and curling, and drawing her body to his mouth for a kiss.

When his tongue touched her, she dissolved in a mass of contradictions, unsure whether to laugh or cry, gasp— or stop breathing altogether from the sheer pleasure of what was happening to her. The only thing she knew was that it would be even better if he were inside her.

She let her knees collapse under her, leaning against him as she slid down his body, cradling his hips between her thighs and settling her body against his as he guided himself into her. There was a perfect moment of pain-tinged pleasure as he claimed her. And then he began to thrust, his arms wrapped around her as she trembled with the after-effects of her release. 'Good,' he groaned, shaking with his own need. 'I could die happy, just from the feel of your body. You are so good.'

And she was. He pushed her back against the bed frame so that she could buck her hips to meet his thrusts, and she dug her fingers into his shoulders. His hands held her just as tight, until with a final thrust and a pos-sessive shout of her name, he came into her. Then he sagged, as weak against her as she was against him, and kissed her throat, her lips and her eyes. His head lolled against her shoulder for a moment, and then he looked up and whispered, 'This was not how I planned it. I meant to let you go. But in the dream where I kept you? There was nothing like this. To make love on the floor of a wagon? You deserve a true bed. And a real house. And a better man than the one you have chosen. I—'

She put a finger on his lips to stop his talking. 'It was wonderful,' she whispered back. 'Just what I wanted. And there is nothing wrong with the bed behind us. It is very comfortable.'

He put an arm around her waist and reached out a hand to pull them both up onto the mattress. But he had forgotten the injury to his palm; he drew back with a little hiss of pain.

She took him by the hand and shook her head, then climbed out of his lap, sat on the bed herself and reached for his good hand to pull him after. 'You must learn that it does no harm to ask for help when you need it. You are no longer alone, you know.'

'Not alone.' He smiled at the thought, and let her lead him to bed, curling his body close to hers and laying his face beside hers. 'Say it again.'

'You are not alone,' she whispered, and felt him relax as his eyes closed and sleep took him.

Chapter Thirteen

When she woke the next morning, she lay still and watched the shadows in the little room move and recede. Stephano was behind her on the bed, his arms wrapped about her waist to keep her close, his face pressed into the hair that fell down her back. She could feel his breath, warm and steady on her shoulder.

She moved and felt the breath change to a kiss on her skin. 'You are awake?' she whispered.

'I was watching you sleep. Does it bother you?'

She searched her mind, and smiled. 'It is several hours too late for me to be worried by your interest, I think.'

He hesitated. 'And do you feel in the sunlight as you did by moonlight?'

He held her so gently that she was sure, if she expressed outrage, he would release her and apologize, taking the blame for all upon himself. He would allow her to pretend that she had had no part in what had happened, if she wished it. So to answer him, she stretched and rolled in his arms until she faced him, taking his lips for the first kiss of the morning.

She could feel the moment of surprise, as she caught him unprepared. And then he began to kiss her in return. When they paused, she smiled and ran a finger along the smooth skin of his chest. 'Actually, I feel rather better than I did last night.' She thought for a moment, and was honest with him. 'Stiff. And a little sore. But so very happy that I think it does not matter.'

His hands moved over her body, stroking gently in reassurance. 'Happy.'

'Very happy,' she repeated.

He laughed. 'As am I.' He grew serious then, his eyes growing dark in a way that put the lie to what he had just said. He reached out and touched her hair, pushing it behind her ear so he could see her face again. 'There is much we will have to talk about. The situation has grown difficult. But not today, I think. One day is all I ask, where I do not have to think of the past or the future. I deserve that much, at least.' He sounded almost wistful at the idea.

It pained her that he should fear what was ahead, when to her it looked brighter than all the days in the past. But she pushed it from her mind and said, 'Then it is my wedding gift to you. Today, nothing matters but my love for you.'

'And mine for you.' Then he smiled again, sat up and reached a hand out to help her up.

They washed in the basin of cold water and helped each other to dress. It was strange being able to reach out and touch him, whenever she liked. And it made her laugh when he reached for her, as well, tugging at her hair and threatening to untie the kerchief as fast as she could tie it on.

When they were presentable, he started toward the door, then paused and looked back at her. 'You have given me my gift, but I gave nothing to you.' He thought for a moment, and then reached to his wrist and worked at the band of silver that he wore there. It was difficult, for his hand was still sore from the cut, and it was obvious that it had been a long time since he had removed the bracelet. He rubbed at his bare wrist as though unaccustomed to the feel of it, and the skin where the silver had been was much paler than the skin of his arm. And then, he held it out to her. 'It is little more than a trifle. And it will not fit you. But it is better than nothing.'

It was obviously much more to him than a trifle. As he removed it, he looked at it as though he were saying goodbye to an old friend. 'And you wish me to have it? Then I should love to wear it. Please.' She held out her wrist to him, and he slipped the thing on. It was heavy and still warm with the heat of his body. And she closed her eyes and imagined for a moment that it was him, reaching out to catch her by the wrist, his fingers smooth and gentle against her skin. She opened her eyes and smiled. 'Is it magic?'

'Magic?' He snorted. 'Hardly. But the man who gave it to me swore that it would keep me safe. And it has done its job well for many years. May it do the same for you.'

She gave a little frown. 'Then I will worry about you going without it.'

He smiled. 'Now that you are mine, I will be more careful. For I will always wish to come home safe to you.' Then he opened the door and jumped down, holding out his hands to catch her.

She stepped into his arms and he lifted her so that her feet never touched the stairs, and set her down gently on the ground beside him.

One of his friends called out to him from the other side of the camp, and Stephano gave a wink and walked away from her. Or rather, he sauntered. He moved in a way she had not seen before. Just as graceful, but with a lightness in his step. There was a cockiness about him that all but crowed his news to the world.

The other Rom noticed it, as well. She could see the slight tilt of the man's head, the quick shifting of his gaze to her and back, and then the broad smile and warm greeting. She could hear the men joking about something in Romany, and she wondered for a moment if they were speaking of her. But there was such warmth and joy in their voices that she was sure there was nothing mean-spirited in their talk.

She wondered if the women of the camp would see the same change in her that was so obvious in Stephano.

She walked to the fire in front of Magda's tent. The old woman was there, as she had been every morning, ready to add milk and sugar to the tea that was boiling strong and dark in a pot on the coals. Bread was baking in the pan beside it, and Verity's mouth began to water.

Without thinking, Verity dipped her head as she approached the woman, in apology that she must impose on her again. She reached for the chipped cup that sat

on the little bench beside the fire and waited patiently
for her turn.

Magda's head snapped up at her approach, and her
gaze seemed to pierce Verity. She looked across the
camp to her grandson, and then again at Verity, and
her eyes travelled down her arm to see the silver at her
wrist. Then she raised her eyebrows, pursed her lips and
nodded. She took the cup she had been filling for herself
and handed it to Verity, taking the chipped cup away.
She went back to the tent and reappeared with another
mug. It was undamaged, and a match to the one Verity
now held. She filled it for herself and then pulled the
bread from the fire and sliced it, offering Verity a large
plate and the pot of butter.

Magda watched her as she ate, and when she was
through, held out her hand and said, 'Show me your
palm.' Verity placed her hand gingerly in the old woman's grasp.

She examined the bracelet. 'It is loose. Foolish boy
should have fixed it for you, before giving it. He has the
skill to do it.'

Verity smiled at her wedding gift. 'I suspect he did
not think of it. It was an afterthought to give it to me.'

Magda shrugged and tapped her forehead. 'I have
seen the thing on your arm from the first day. That he
could not is no excuse for his carelessness.' She wagged
a finger in Verity's face. 'Do not lose it.'

Verity nodded obediently, and then said, 'He did not
tell me what it means. He seemed afraid that I would not
like it. But it is the most marvellous thing I have ever
worn. I think—' she bit her lip, searching for the word
'—I think it is powerful. Important.'

Magda nodded. 'My daughter's Rom husband, Thom the Silversmith, gave it to Stephano, when he first brought him to the camp. The boy was a scrawny thing, then. A pale nothing. Always hungry, angry and afraid. Always stealing. Pennies. Bread. He was trying to take Thom's purse when we found him.' She shook her head and smiled. 'Stupid boy, trying to steal from a Gypsy. Thom said the quickest way to break him of the habit was to make him rich. So he gave him the silver, told him he was a Rom prince, and brought him back to camp.' Magda smiled. 'And that is how he has behaved. Too proud, of course. But then, he has much reason.'

Magda turned the hand she was holding palm up, and studied it for a moment. 'Four children, and the first will be a boy.' She glanced up into Verity's eyes for a moment, then back down. 'All healthy. You, as well. You are very strong for a *gadji*.' She looked her body up and down. 'Wide hips make for easy birth. And you are as stubborn as my grandson. Stephano chose well.' She closed her fingers around Verity's, curling them into a fist, as though it was possible to grab the future and hold it tight. 'You will be happy. It will be all right.'

For a moment, she could see the future as clearly as Magda did. But to be happy would include a return to her family, and many explanations. No matter that they had promised she could marry whomever she liked, her father and brothers would be less than happy with her choice. And Stephano would have to renounce the curse, as he had promised. It all seemed helpless. 'But how?'

The old lady shrugged. 'I only know what I see.' She went back to prodding at the fire. 'What is your name, girl?'

She smiled. 'Verity.' She had been about to say Carlow. But was that her name, any more? She must learn to think of herself as Beshaley. Or perhaps Hebden would be easier. But was she entitled to either name?

'Truth.' The old woman nodded. 'It is a good name. Not Roma. But good. I shall call you—' she thought for a moment '—Tachiben. Because it is easier.'

For a moment, Verity thought to question why it would be easier to give her a new name than to learn the old one. But she suspected that there was no more reasoning with Magda on this than on anything else. 'Thank you.'

The old woman grinned at her. 'And now? We will have *patshiv*. A celebration. Val!' she shouted across the camp. 'Take yourself and your lazy brothers off to the woods. Bring us meat.'

There was laughter around the circle of tents, for she could hear the news, making its way. Men were setting aside their work, and taking up guns to hunt game or pulling out mugs and bottles to begin the party early. She could hear the sound of a fiddle being tuned, drum heads tightened, and saw penny whistles and wood flutes appearing out of pockets.

And the women had to work all the harder, although they did it with a light heart. By late afternoon, the cooking fires were bigger than usual, and large cast-iron pots had been gathered and filled with nettles, wild mushrooms and onions.

And everyone was happy. The children danced in circles around her. Men kissed her on the cheeks and slipped her gold coins. Women hugged her and offered her flowers or silk scarves, and took the coins that the men had given to her and embroidered them into the hem of her petticoat. Magda told her it was so she could keep her dower safe, 'In case her worthless Rom did not treat her well.' And she said it with a light tone that made the other women laugh, as though she were only teaching her new *bori* the correct way to stay ahead of a wild Gypsy husband.

And Stephano was on the other side of the camp, positively glowing with pride, gesturing in her direction and speaking in Romany. She could not understand a word of it, but could read the translation in his eyes. She was pretty, she was smart, and she was his. Were not the others envious of so perfect and wonderful a bride? Was he not the most fortunate man on the planet? When he was not bragging of her, he would come across the camp to take her hands in his, or to grab her by the waist and toss her into the air, then pull her close for another kiss.

And the other men laughed and kissed their wives, who pretended to be bothered by the distraction, all the while laughing and muttering, 'Later.'

And then, the feasting began. There was a stew made of wild hare, and something wonderful roasted on skewers that she was told was hedgehog. Everyone kept refilling their cups, and there were many toasts. Stephano was staring at her with a wicked smile and the somewhat unfocused look of a man who had drunk too much wine. She suspected that she must look the same to him. So they laughed, and danced until their heads cleared. Then he reached out to the fiddler and grabbed the instrument from him, playing a tune that was mad and fast and happy.

She covered her mouth in surprise, for she had not known he was so talented. He grinned back at her, and played all the faster, his fingers flying along the neck of the instrument, and his bow grinding away at the notes, making a sweet cacophony as it caught two and three strings at a time. She wondered if there was a way to play her harp that would sound so wild and free?

When he set down the instrument, he flexed the injured hand that had held the bow, and she reached out for it, turning it palm up to check the bandage.

'Do not fuss over me, woman. I can look after myself.' He grumbled the words, to put her in her place. But he was smiling as though it amused him to be bothered by her.

'You were looking after yourself when you got the injury. And then you had to come to me for help,' she retorted, and smiled back at him. For it was surprisingly fun to scold him.

He gave her another stern look, but spoiled it by laughing. And then he pulled her into his arms and kissed her until the party around them faded to unimportance. Finally, they wandered back to the wagon and made love in the big bed, falling into a bliss-filled sleep amongst the eiderdowns.

When she woke the next morning, he was watching her, stroking her hair.

She smiled at him, but he did not answer with a smile of his own. So she kissed him, hoping that his expression would change, and whispered, 'Are you still happy?'

'In all but one thing. Yesterday, your family was not at the feast.'

The thought made her frown, as well. And she struggled to find a response that would not sound as though she was ashamed of him and his family. 'I don't think that would have been wise. They would not have understood it.'

'I have given them no reason to like me. And you know I have no great love for them. But you?' He gave a puzzled shake of his head. 'I cannot truly hate them if they have given me you, even though they have done it unwilling and unknowing.'

'Have I spoiled your vendetta?' She did not laugh at him, for she knew how seriously he took the curse.

He shook his head. 'You still do not understand. Once started, a curse is not so easy to stop. When I said I would end it, my plan was to sacrifice myself to return you to your family.'

She wrapped her arms around him, tight so he could not shake her off. 'You will not. I forbid it.'

But his expression was as grim as ever. 'Then you must choose. If there is no way to prevent bloodshed, then who do you wish to lose? Your father, one of your brothers, or the man you barely know?'

'Why must I lose any of you? Surely, once I have talked to my brothers, they will understand.'

He laughed. 'At one time, I would have thought that true. But when I went to London, they proved me wrong. Your dear Marcus would have killed me in cold blood, had I not been fast and lucky.'

'Marcus?' She shook her head. 'I refuse to believe such a thing. It was obviously some misunderstanding. Once I have talked to him, I will prove it to you.'

'Just as you will prove to me that your father had

no hidden motive in accusing William Wardale of murder.'

She began to protest, and he laid a hand on her arm to still her. 'Let me tell you what I know, so that you might at least understand my actions in all this. When first I set out to settle with the families involved, I thought it was all quite clear, and avenging my family would be an easy thing for all were equally to blame.

'But the closer I looked, the more confusing it became. When my father was murdered, there was a traitor about. And all our fathers were set to catch him. But they suspected each other and were on the verge of a falling out. My father had discovered the spy and was ready to reveal his identity. But the night he died, his supposed murderer, Wardale, went first to our house, to the bed of my stepmother. If the scandal was about to break, why not rush to kill the man who was about to ruin him, and console the widow after?'

She shook her head in amazement. What he was saying was too scandalous. 'Could it have been a crime of passion?'

'Not likely. Wardale and Amanda made little attempt to hide the affair, and my father did not care a jot what they did. I have seen writings in their own hands to prove it true. Even your own father…'

Verity pulled away from him in surprise. 'The little journal that Diana Price stole from the study? She took it for you?'

'She did not know it at the time,' he said. 'But yes, I have read the journal. And a letter from Amanda Hebden. And other things, as well. And while I see much that proves Wardale was hanged unjustly, there is nothing to show that your father was not involved.'

'A lack of evidence is not the same thing as proof,' she argued.

'Nor is your oldest brother's recent attempt to murder me the behaviour of a man with nothing to hide.'

'He shot you before, did he not?' she said. 'How is it different now?'

'I had given him reason. I threatened his love.' He smiled. 'I fault him for his poor aim more than his actions for that day. He was in his rights to kill me. But recently?' And now, he looked truly puzzled. 'He attacked me in my own home, without a thought to your whereabouts or safety. Those are not the actions of a sane man.'

'And they are not those of my brother,' she assured him. 'There must be something terribly wrong.'

'All the more reason to send you home. I must see to your safety first, and then to my people. If the camp is discovered, your family will take revenge against me. There will be violence and more curses, and it will end in death for someone. If there is a way for us to be together at all, it will not be through fresh hatred between my people and yours.'

And where she would have wanted nothing more, only a few days ago, now the idea of returning to her family filled her with alarm. 'If I go home, then when will I see you?'

He was staring at the ceiling, not into her eyes. 'We must trust to fate that we will be together again.' But by his tone, it did not sound like he trusted fate at all. It sounded more like he had decided to give her up.

'Do you wish me to be a peacemaker? For I can tell you, without going home, that they will not accept you until you agree to end the feud. And that you will never find what you are seeking.' She hoped her confidence in her father would finally sink into him and change his heart. 'At least not in my family. My father loved Kit Hebden, despite all the troubles between them.'

Stephano gave her a stern look. 'I have reason to believe otherwise.'

'All rumour. You were not there to see it, so how can you know?'

He arched an eyebrow. 'As if you were? You were a babe in arms when it all happened. A squalling pink thing, as I remember.'

Verity started. 'You met me?'

'I played in your house, with your brothers and Nathan Wardale.' He paused for a moment, his face taking on a distant expression, and then he smiled. 'Things were quite different, back when I was to be raised as a gentleman.'

She wondered at how it must have been for him, to be cast out from all he knew and to have to start again in this strange life that was so very unlike the one he had been born to. She reached out and touched his hand. 'But you remember what it was like. Our families were friends, weren't they? When your father died, he was carrying a gift for me. It was a silver rattle. The same one I gave to Marc's first child.'

Stephano shrugged. 'Probably the one my mother gave to him.' He gave her an odd look. 'My true mother. It was meant as a gift for me.'

'For you?' She had gone her entire life, imagining

the beautiful thing as something special that Hebden had bought, just for her. But that he might have plucked it from his own son's cradle… 'Surely not. It was very expensive, as I remember it. With a coral handle, and tiny bells. Where could your Rom mother have gotten such a thing?'

His cheeks grew hot, and he looked away from her. 'She did not steal it, if that is what you are implying. When she was no longer with my father, she married a Rom silversmith. After I came to be with the tribe, Thom Argentari was more of a father to me than Hebden ever was. He took me in as a sign of his love for my mother. He taught me his trade.' He touched the silver cuff at her wrist. 'He made the bracelet you are wearing. Such a rattle would have been as nothing to him. There were vines etched into the handle, were there not? If you look closely at them, you will see an S. For Stephen.' He swallowed. 'I found the thing in my father's study, shortly before he died. He took it away from me. Said it was a bit of Gypsy foolishness, and not good enough for any son of his. But Thom told me otherwise.'

She swallowed hard, as well. It had been such a beautiful thing, and she'd felt beloved, knowing it was a final gift. 'Good enough for me, apparently. I should have expected as much. It was broken, you know.'

'It was most certainly not.' He seemed indignant beyond reason, and it was a moment before she realized that she had insulted his heritage by her comment.

'In all the time I had it, I could not make the whistle work,' she said.

'You must have broken it when you were a child. Jammed something in the hole, perhaps.'

'I never did. I was always most careful with my things, even as a child.' It occurred to her that it was most foolish to be having her first true fight of married life over the condition of a child's toy. But somehow, it seemed important that he not think her the useless, frivolous girl he had told her she was, on that first day. 'Nurse told me that it was broken from the time we got it. I always suspected that she had broken the whistle herself, just to keep me from annoying her with it. But mother said it was that way when she took it, the night…'

For a moment, Stephano grew distant, as though lost in his memories. 'Father took it from me because I was fooling with the thing, blowing into the end. He said the noise distracted him from his work. And he put it into his pocket.' He looked up at her, as though remembering where and when they were. 'I expect the damage happened during the struggle, the night of the crime. I will fix it for you, if you like.'

'Could you do that for me?'

He smiled for her, although it was not the brilliant grin of yesterday. 'I've made such toys myself, from Thom's patterns. I will take you back to your brother's house. If you can mend the differences between our families, then it will be no great feat for me to mend your rattle.'

Chapter Fourteen

They dressed in silence. And then he prepared his horse to take her home. He put her up on the saddle before him, wrapping his arms tight around her waist so that she did not fall. And as they rode slowly toward her home, he kissed her and whispered endearments.

She wondered what people would think, should they see her. She doubted even her closest friends would recognize her as Lady Verity Carlow. For when had Lady Verity gone out in public dressed in a plain stuff gown, with a scarf over her hair? And who would expect her to be riding in the arms of her Gypsy lover? But then, she doubted that they had ever seen Lady Verity look quite so happy, quite as content. Nor had she ever been as unsure of her future as she was today.

Stephano rode through parts of London that were well outside of her genteel acquaintance, to Suffolk Street in Covent Garden. There, he stopped and tied up his horse in front of a narrow red door. The sign above it had no writing, but was decorated with flames and a soul in torment.

She gave him a dubious look, but said nothing as he helped her down from the horse, opened the door and shepherded her inside. As her eyes adjusted to the dimness, she saw they were in a dingy tavern. A rotund man behind the bar greeted him with a wave and a shout of 'Well met, Gypsy!'

'Dante,' Stephano grunted in return, and made to pass the man without explanation.

'Will you not introduce me to your fine friend?'

Verity did not like the way the man grinned at her. It was too familiar, too knowing, and held too much amusement, which she feared was all at her expense. It made her want to pull the kerchief tighter over her hair and to shrink back into the protection of her shawl, as though to be smaller would prevent him from noticing her.

Stephano glared at him and seemed to grow larger in response to the threat. He nodded coldly in the direction of the man. 'Dante Jones is the proprietor of the Fourth Circle gaming hell. Dante, this is my wife. That is all you need to know in the matter.'

His face held such disdain that the man wiped his hands nervously on the rag at his waist, and muttered a hurried, 'No harm meant.' Then he gave a nod of the head that looked almost like a sincere bow before pulling back the curtain that led down a narrow hall. They walked for some ways, and came out in a large, smoke-filled room set with tables for faro, cards and hazard, and wheels for E and O.

At midday, the room was almost empty and Dante did

nothing to draw attention to his guests as he led them still further, to the back of the gaming room to a hanging on what appeared to be a blank wall. Behind it was an alcove. And at the back of that, a stairway. Stephano looked behind him, making sure one last time that no one had noticed them passing.

And she prayed they had not. For if it ever came to be known that she had come to such a place…

As though he could read her mind, he said, 'There is only one person I'm aware of that knows both this place, and you. And he has sworn to quit gambling. Should I find him here, he would have as much to explain as you do. And not even he knows of the rooms I keep above stairs. You will be safe here, and as comfortable as I can make you.' He tossed a coin to Dante, who retreated as he and Verity ascended.

Verity glanced around her, trying to assess what she was seeing. The stairs entered into a large parlour, obviously meant as some sort of public reception room, but done in the most garish taste imaginable. The walls were a lurid purple, with accents of gold on the plasterwork and an excessive number of mirrors which seemed to make up for the lack of windows in the room. The candles lit in the gold sconces reflected off glass after glass to light the whole room. It gave her the impression that it was already night, even though she had seen the bright sunlight of noon just a few moments before. It was quite horrible, and not at all what she had expected. But if her husband desired she stay here, then she would learn to make the best of it. She blinked at him and said politely, 'It is much larger than the vardo.'

He laughed. 'You do not think this is all I have to offer, I hope.'

'It does not matter. I do not need much, really. In any case, I mean to stay with you, even if I must live in a wagon.'

His smile was a little forced, as he said, 'I have a house in Bloomsbury Square that will be much more to your liking. Servants, as well. But it is currently unavailable to me. Your brothers have found it, and await me there.'

She smiled in relief. 'Then why do we not go to them immediately?'

'Because the reception will be less than welcoming. And I fear someone may be hurt before we have the chance to explain your return. It is better that I take you to your family's town house when it is dark, and then slip away quickly. I do not wish to force a confrontation before you have a chance to prove your safety.'

She did not like to think that her brothers would be a danger to Stephano, but if he said they were, then how could it not be true? Of course, they did not understand him as she did, and they must be thinking all manner of terrible things about her disappearance, no matter what messages he had relayed about her safety. But still, she looked around the room.

'It has not been changed since its previous use,' he muttered, embarrassed. 'My half sister, Imo, assures me that the Bloomsbury house is quite charmingly decorated. Nothing at all like this.'

She looked doubtfully at the walls. 'That is good to know.'

'I will get Molly to prepare a room for you.' He called

out to the thin, little girl who lurked in the periphery of her vision. The poor thing looked hardly old enough to do the job of a maid. 'Molly. Thank God you are here. The next few hours require a woman's touch. First, open the best room we have. For my wife.' Stephano said the last word with a small emphasis, as though he liked saying it as much as she liked hearing it.

There was a look of round-eyed amazement on the face of the girl before her.

He grinned to see her surprise. 'And you are the first to see her, so it can be your secret to tell the others. I will be taking her to her family soon. But she cannot go dressed as a Rom girl. Can you draw a bath for her and find a place for her to rest? Perhaps she would like a cup of tea. I will find her a gown for a lady of quality, stockings and slippers. But can you help to arrange her hair? I know you are not a lady's maid. But we must manage as best we can…'

'I am honoured, Mr Stephen.' The girl assured him, and hurried to one of several doors on the left wall.

Stephano turned back to Verity, taking her hand in his. 'I must go away for a bit. But I shall be back, soon. Is that all right?'

She gave him what she hoped was a brave smile, thinking how ludicrous it was to see him so concerned about her welfare in the hands of a trusted servant, after the way she had come to know his family. 'Of course. I will await your return.'

She followed Molly into the other room, which was every bit as garish as the salon. It was dominated by even more gilt and mirrors extending to the ceiling over the uncurtained bed. The maid hurried from candle to candle, trying to give light to the surroundings, and then she gave a small bob of a curtsy. 'I am sorry that the room was not aired, ma'am. I did not expect you. And it is difficult, since there are no windows.' She pulled back a screen in the corner to reveal a bathtub, and removed towels from a cupboard in the corner.

'That is most curious,' Verity admitted. 'What sort of a place, do you suppose, would have such few ways to get light and air?'

The maid gave a small giggle. 'I expect there are many places where the people in 'em would like privacy more than sunlight. But they are not the sort of places where gentlemen bring their wives. Before Mr Stephen let it, this was a bawdy house.'

Verity covered her mouth with her hand, unsure whether to laugh or be mortified. 'Stephano brought me to a bawdy house?'

'A former bawdy house,' the girl corrected. Then she gave a little shrug of embarrassment and said, 'It is quite clean. I've seen to that.'

'Thank you,' Verity said, not wishing to embarrass her husband or his servant. 'I hardly know how to behave. This is a most unusual circumstance. Of course, my husband is a most unusual man.'

Molly nodded in agreement. 'But a very good man, ma'am. If you knew even half of it…'

'Tell me.' For if the girl knew Stephano as Mr Stephen, Verity felt almost a hunger to know the details. 'Have you been to the other house that he speaks of?'

'Many times. But there has been a fire there recently. And there are some gentlemen—' the girl frowned

'—enemies of the master's, who are currently waiting there for him. He doesn't dare return now.'

Verity felt a quickening of her pulse at the idea that this girl thought of her brothers as villains. 'I am sure that it will all be straightened out soon.'

Molly nodded vigorously. 'And until then, you will be perfectly safe here. They will never find out about this place. Akshat, the butler, would die before telling. The master met him in India and says his name means *indestructible*, and that it suits him, for he can withstand hardship and torture without so much as blinking an eye. And then there is Munch, the valet. He is a big man with a face like a mastiff. I don't know what his past might be, but he is not the sort to stand any mischief. At first, they frightened me. But it is good to have them about the house, because of Mr Stephen's business.'

'He has a business?' The girl must think her foolish. But it had just occurred to her that her husband must have an occupation of some kind, since his family had disowned him.

But Molly prattled on, eager to tell all she knew. 'He is a jewel merchant, ma'am. And the safe is full of stones. Bags and bags of them, all loose like marbles.'

'Really! And his servants keep him safe from thieves?'

Molly giggled again. 'Set a thief to catch a thief. I am not so sure of some of them, for we all have stories in our past. But the parlour maid, Jenny, was a pick pocket before she came to Bloomsbury Square. She is ever so sly. She has been sneaking in and out of the house and bringing information to me. And the bad men have not caught her yet.'

'And these are his friends?' she asked doubtfully. If the servants were a parcel of rogues, then what did it say that her family were his enemies?

Molly nodded again. 'The master has done them all a good turn at one time or another, gotten them out of terrible trouble and brought them to Bloomsbury to work. Every last one would die before betraying him. And me, as well.' The girl gave a shy smile.

'And did he rescue you, too? What is your story, Molly?'

The girl gave her an odd look. 'I used to work here, ma'am. But I did not like it much,' she added hurriedly.

'And Stephano...my husband...' Verity swallowed.

The girl shook her head quickly. 'It was not as you might think. When he took this place and turned out the girls, some were content to find other employment and some he helped back to their families. But I had no one and nowhere to go. So he says, "You will come to work for me, Mol. And no funny business. A mop and broom are not easy companions, but better company than some you've met here, I am sure. Good, honest work, if you wish."' She grinned. 'Mr Stephen is not the least bit particular about a person's past, as long as they prove to him that they are good, honest folk to their friends and will stand up for their mates when it is important. But you must know that of him.'

Verity wondered if this was meant as an assurance that deficiencies in her own past would be overlooked, as well. And suspected that was the truth, for Mol went on to say, 'Now that he has married you, you can trust us all to be as loyal to you as we are to him. And woe be onto any that cross you.' The girl gave a surprisingly dark look for one so young and small. She looked ready to storm Bloomsbury and take on her master's enemies—single-handed, if necessary.

'That is good to know,' Verity said doubtfully.

'I'll just go and heat the water for your bath, shall I?'

'Thank you, Mol.'

When Stephano returned to the flat above the gaming hell, he found his wife sitting demurely on the edge of a bed in one of the guest rooms. She was dressed in a fresh chemise and stays, and her hair was piled high to reveal her smooth white throat. With her hands folded in her lap and her ankles crossed, she was a rare spot of innocence in an unexpected setting. 'I see you have begun to dress,' he said, setting the clothing he had brought for her on the end of the bed.

She stood up and gestured to her under things. 'Molly found these in a cupboard. She says they were left behind by one of the previous tenants. But she says I shouldn't mind that. They are brand new. For what use would a dollymop have with stays and proper undergarments?' She turned so that he could admire them. 'They are very fine, and almost pretty enough to wear outside the gown.' She toyed with the lace that covered the swell of her breast, and he watched with fascination.

'Really?' He silently cursed little Molly, for he feared she had been rather more informative than he would have wished. 'Then you know...'

'What sort of place this was?' She gave him a

strange smile. 'It was terribly wicked of you to bring me here.'

He swallowed. 'I would never have done it, had the circumstances not been most unusual.'

She was still smiling at him. 'But it has been very interesting.' She took him by the hand and led him to a table by the bed. 'I was looking for something to read, to pass the time. But the only books here are mostly pictures. She flipped a page so that he could see, and tipped her head from side to side, considering the illustration. 'I am not sure that this is even possible.'

'If it disturbs you, you need not concern yourself with it,' he said.

'But there is more.' She reached into a drawer. 'I found this, as well.' She was holding a length of silk rope very similar to that which he had used to bind her. 'Did you leave it here?'

Now, he could feel himself going quite pale, for he did not wish to explain to her what he understood of the tricks and toys one might find in such a place. 'No. No. That is quite different from the rope I had. I suspect that was left by a previous tenant, as well.'

'Well, it is a much more mysterious thing than ladies' undergarments.'

'Very mysterious, I am sure. You may put it aside, now.'

But she did not, running her fingers along the length of it. 'In case you wondered, I have quite forgiven you for binding me. No harm was done. The rope is quite soft. Feel.' She stepped forward and looped it about his wrists, tugging gently to pull them together in front of him. 'Perhaps next time, I shall be the one to tie you.'

She could have no idea what she was saying, nor the effect it would have upon him. But the sight of the rope was intoxicating against the white of her skin, and then on his own, as she tugged gently at his wrists. The knowing curve of her smile, the soft curve of her hip under the petticoat, and the soft bed beside her were almost too much to stand.

There was no time to dally, if he meant to get her home tonight. But his body was springing to life, and she was leading him back to the bed. Her smile grew as though she had known all along how completely she had tamed him. She sat down on the mattress and reached out to undo the buttons of his trousers, freeing him, stroking him with her hand, cupping and squeezing. There was no telling what his wife had learned in a few hours alone in this place, but she seemed eager to put it to use. It had built a curiosity in her, and a hunger that he was happy to appease.

He reached for her, and she batted his loosely tied hands away, and went back to her exploration. He held himself rigid, letting her have her way. He looked into the mirrors, watching the endless reflections of her fingers moving upon him. And the pleasure and excitement grew in him until he was sure that he would explode in her hands.

She must have realized how close he was, for she lay back upon the bed and let her legs fall open, slowly drawing up the lawn of the petticoat until he could see her knees, and then the rest of her, wet and ready.

He should not be allowing this, for every moment he kept her meant parting would be more difficult. But she gave a final flick on the end of the rope to draw him closer, and he lost all sense. How could he let her go, when it was she who possessed him? He could feel the tide rising in him as he gave himself over to her.

He pushed the rope off his hands and fell upon her, and into her, stroking deep, taking her roughly, biting at her throat and breasts, while she gave startling yelps of pleasure that dissolved into gasps of passion, and at last, a shuddered orgasm that drove him over the edge with her.

And after, they lay still upon the bed. And there came the feeling he had whenever he was with her. The strange, pleasure-drunk feeling. A lightness of head and body. And the still unfamiliar absence of pain. It reminded him of a day he'd spent swimming in the sea, where the waters were clear and deep. It was an afternoon free of care, wrapped in the warmth of the water, suspended as though weightless, carried with the waves and warmed by the sun, happy and at peace, wishing that he need never go back to the land.

But now, when he opened his eyes, there was his *romni*, his sweet truth, staring up at him, as gentle and warm as a sunbeam. 'Have I told you how beautiful your eyes are?' he asked.

She smiled. 'You told me they could not make up their mind what colour they wished to be. You seemed to think this changeableness was a deficiency in my nature.'

He smoothed the hair out of her face. 'I was a fool to let you believe that. I could stare for ever at them, looking for the place where the brown turns to green. It is as if they are caught between worlds.'

'As are you, Stephen Hebden,' she whispered. 'Tell me more.'

He touched her cheek, and wondered why he had held his compliments until it was almost too late. The sight of her and the feel of her loving him was perfection, and he had not told her. 'Your eyes are like Chinese jade.'

She smiled. 'Brown and green together. Is it rare?'

He shook his head. 'Not so much as a pure colour is. But it is still very beautiful. And to find a woman who can change as easily as the colour of jade, and be happy in a great house or a Gypsy camp…'

'Or a place like this?' she whispered.

He kissed her. 'You are rarer than diamonds. And I want to keep you. With me. Always. But no matter what happens, no matter where I am, I will never forget you.'

He could not say the words he was thinking, for he did not want her to hear his doubt. It seemed she could change for him, to be any woman he wanted. Once she was home, she would see how different they were. What would happen when she remembered who she had been and changed again?

I am afraid I will lose you.

Chapter Fifteen

Later, when the maid had dressed her, he came back to her. He looked as he had on the first night. The earring was gone from his ear, and his colourful shirt was replaced with a brown coat and buff breeches, unadorned except for the exceptional quality of the cut. Without thinking, she looked to his wrist, and then remembered that the silver cuff rested high on her own arm, hidden by the sleeve of her dress.

He smiled at her. But there was the same sombre tone to it that had been present that morning, as though someone had died and they were mourning the loss. 'You are very beautiful,' he said.

'Thank you. But with the look on your face, it hardly seems a compliment. Do you not like my dress?' She turned so that he might admire it.

'I do. Very much. But I liked you as you were before, as well. And I regret that you did not hear it from me every minute of every day that we were together. And I wish…' He shrugged. 'That there was more time.'

'We shall settle this. I doubt it will take more than a day or two. And then, we shall have all the time in the world.'

'Of course. A lifetime.' But it was clear that he said this only to humour her, and without any real belief.

She swallowed the sudden fear. 'Do you not want me any more? Is that why you are sending me back?'

He gave a small laugh and pulled her close, kissing her. 'I want you still. I am sending you back, because it is where you belong. I stole you.'

'Then you have no reason to be sad. Unless you think it is I who will no longer want you.' And looking at him, she was sure that it must be true. 'I am barely out of your bed, and you doubt my love? That is perfectly odious of you, Stephano.'

'You may call me Stephen, when we are in London. It will be easier.'

'I will call you whatever you like, as long as you mean to answer to it. Unless you continue to think me so false that I would…do the things we have done together…and then return to my family as though those things had never happened…' It had never occurred to her that he might not acknowledge her as wife, for he had promised. And the sudden feeling of loneliness that washed over her left her almost weak with sadness. But before the first sob could form, he had reached out to her and pulled her close.

'I did not. And I would never. You are my wife, my darling, my all. And I am yours, always and for ever, no matter what happens. But you do not yet understand what I have asked of you. And when you do…' It was as if the emotion went through him like a shudder, and he held her even closer, pressing his lips to hers. 'It will be difficult. More difficult than you know. But I will wait for you.

'But now, we must go.' He gained control of his emotions again, and busied himself with wrapping a cloak around her shoulders, tying it tightly to hide her gown. Then he offered her a bonnet and fixed a bit of veil over her features so even her closest friends would not be able to recognize her. He led her down the stairs and through the gamers gathered in the room. They gave no notice to the mysterious woman in their midst.

They rode in silence to Albemarle Street in a hired carriage. Although Nell and Marcus now had a separate home in nearby Bruton Street, apparently they had been staying at the Carlow town house since her disappearance. And when they arrived, Stephano paused with his hand on the door handle and looked at her. Now that it was time to let her go, he could not seem to find the nerve. 'If there were any other way…'

'Than sending me home?' She smiled. 'You do not think I am at risk on a visit to my brother, do you? Because that is quite an outlandish idea.'

He frowned. 'It is a dangerous world. Especially for the Rom.'

'But I am not truly Rom, am I?'

'No, you are not.' She could see it hurt him to say it.

She put her hand on his. 'I was born in that house. I hardly think you need be frightened of my returning to it. Once I have explained to my family, I will go to the Bloomsbury house, and send Jenny to find you. And we will be together again. Trust me.'

He turned his head to kiss her palm. 'Always.'

And then he helped her from the carriage. She turned back only once on her way into the house and saw Stephano, a dark silhouette inside the carriage. She could not see him clearly, but was sure he meant to watch until the door closed and removed her from his sight.

She was not truly leaving, she reminded herself. With each step, the time she had spent in the camp seemed stranger and more distant. But it was such a happy memory that she knew she would not forget, no matter how much she longed to see her family again.

So she turned from him and continued her walk to the house and knocked on the front door, waiting for Wellow the butler. When no one came to open for her, she let herself in. 'Hello?' she called out softly, surprised at the strange quiet that enveloped the front of the house. Perhaps she had spent too much time talking to Magda, and was now imagining portents where there had been none. But her old home felt like a place of mourning.

It got even stranger when a parlour maid wandered into the room to dust, took one look at her and ran screaming for the kitchen.

In response to the scream, she heard the thunder of footsteps in the upstairs hall, recognizing, even at a distance, the military cadence of her brother Hal's boots. 'Hal?' she called. It would be good to see him, but quite unexpected.

'Verity? Oh my God. Marc!' He was running towards her, yelling for their brother.

And suddenly the room was awash with confusion. People came from all directions. Nell sat down on the stairs, overcome with shock and near to fainting before even reaching her. Hal's wife, Julia, rushed to aid her. And Diana Price Wardale of all people, was back in the house and hurrying to Verity's side, openly weeping as she embraced her.

'What is the matter?' She reached out her hands to them all, the silver bracelet slipping on her wrist as she offered comfort.

'The matter?' The normally calm Diana let out a shrill laugh that bordered on hysteric.

'Verity.' Marc at least, was laughing in earnest as he reached out to hug her. But his grip was weak, as though the brief time they had been apart had aged him. And when he released her, she thought for a moment that she saw the sparkle of tears in his eyes.

'You are all being foolish,' she chided. 'I have not been gone a week. You all act as though I have returned from the dead.'

And there was a silence, as the people around her absorbed the statement. Finally, Diana spoke. 'You do not know what that monster sent to us? The horrible note. Of course we thought you dead. There was blood.'

'Probably his own…' Verity hastened to say. 'He cut his hand…'

'And on your chemise. We thought…' Diana ended on a watery gasp, 'And that after, he had disposed of the body. And that there could not even be a funeral, for we would never see more of you. We have kept it secret from your parents. Because what could we dare to tell your father? The truth would kill him.'

'Enough!' Marc's voice cut through the hubbub.

'Verity is returned to us. Safe and sound. She has nothing more to fear from the Gypsies, and we will not have to tell Father a thing. We will deal with the one who did this, quickly and quietly.' He cast a glance around the room to the gentlemen present, and there was a chorus of silent nods that made Verity pray that Stephano had gotten well away from the house.

'But you do not understand,' Verity said. 'None of you. It is all nothing more than a mistake. I can explain it all.'

'But not now, darling,' Hal said, putting a brotherly arm around her shoulders. 'There will be time, I am sure. For now, you must rest. And later, when you are ready, you may tell us anything you like. Or nothing at all, if you so prefer.' And for a moment, he seemed rather pale, as though he would just as soon not hear the story he was expecting from her.

'Hal is right. A rest in your room. A nice meal. A warm bath, if you wish…' Marcus was trying to guide her to the stairs, as though she could not find her own way to her room.

'I am quite clean enough, I assure you, and not the least bit hungry. I had a lovely dinner, just an hour ago. And a nap in the afternoon. There is nothing wrong with me, Marc. And yet, you sound ready to offer me a posset laced with laudanum.'

She had meant to joke him out of his fears. But her brothers looked past her, from one to the other. Her calm mood seemed to upset them more than it assured them. At the rate they were going, if she continued to resist help, she was liable to end the night in a doctor's care.

She shot a helpless look to Diana, who had the

presence of mind to reach out a hand to her. 'Maybe it is better, if I go to my room for a bit,' she said, signalling to Diana with a squeeze of her fingers that she wanted company. She gave the rest of them what she hoped was a reassuring smile, although properly frail so as not to arouse suspicion. 'But I promise. I am quite well. Totally unhurt. You have nothing to fear, and there is no need to go gallivanting off in search of justice. Not until after we have talked, at any rate. But for now?' She smiled at Diana, and Nell and Julia, as well, to include them in the retreat. 'My room, I think.'

Chapter Sixteen

'Maybe you can talk sense to her. For I despair of it.'
Marc closed Verity's bedroom door with a slam, leaving
her alone with Hal.

It was the middle of her first day at home, and it was
not going as smoothly as she had hoped. Diana and Nell
had been as understanding as possible, although rather
short tempered with her for defending Stephano—or as
they called him, 'that horrible Gypsy.' Eventually they
had given up trying to convince her, allowing that rest
was the solution to many things.

With the change of day, they had turned her over to
her brothers.

Now, Hal sat on the bed and stared at the closed door.
'I have never seen him so angry. And certainly not with
you. You never give him reason.'

'Not with Honoria, either. He did not make nearly so
much fuss, when she had to go to Aunt Foxe.'

'Because what she did was little fault of hers. But
you, Verity?' Hal shook his head and sighed. 'I know

you did not run away with the Gypsy. Do not think we blame you for your own kidnapping. But you do not understand how worried we were. Or the horrible message he sent.'

As they had lain together in the vardo after making love, Stephano had explained the reason for his injured hand, and the note he had sent. It had been wrong of him, of course. But her family seemed far too sensitive about it. 'What exactly did it say?'

'It involved a threat to your honour. The exact words are not fit for a lady's ears.'

'And so you will keep me in the dark about them, just as you have everything else. That is the root of all the troubles I have had, I think. People keep trying to protect me to a degree that makes it impossible for me to make up my own mind. At least, Stephano was open with me about what he was doing.'

'Stephano is it?' Hal gave her a sharp look. 'Do not give the man more credit than he deserves. He is as skilled a liar as he is a thief.'

'You assume, just because he is a Gypsy, that he is a liar and a thief. It is most unfair of you, Hal.'

'I assume he is a liar and thief, and a hundred other kinds of villain, because of the evidence of my own eyes. You should be the last one to defend him, Verity, after what he has done to you.'

'He did nothing to me, Hal, other than take me away from the party. While I was with him, he treated me with respect.'

'And did not lay a hand upon you? For if he touched you, Verity, I swear…' Hal was speaking gently enough to her, but she could see that he shook with rage.

She laid a hand on his arm. 'It is all right. Do not trouble yourself.'

Hal drew away from her and stared into her eyes in shock. 'Do not think yourself so sly, Verity. You did not answer my question. And I suspect there is a very good reason for it. It is because you cannot answer truthfully and get your way. I will not trouble you further about what happened, and neither of us will discuss this with Marc. But do not think that by hiding the truth, you will prevent us from taking action to prevent other young ladies from this…predator.'

She gripped his arm even tighter. 'You do not understand at all, Hal. Stephano would never do anything to hurt me. His ways are unusual, of course. But he is most gentle and kind.'

'I am sure it appeared as such while you were there. There are things that can be slipped into food or wine that make one behave in a way most unlike one's normal self. And he might have used such on you, to keep you docile while a prisoner.' She could see the lines of strain appearing around Hal's mouth, as though he were imagining her drug-induced submission. 'But now that you are home, the effects will pass, and you will see things clearly. Do not allow the truth to upset you, when it comes. Whatever occurred, you are not at fault.'

'How utterly ridiculous, Hal. I ate the same food as the others did, and my head was clear as a bell the whole time I was gone. If you are imagining some dramatic scenario of locked doors and drugged coercion, you must stop it immediately. The truth is very simple. I love Stephano, and he loves me in return. Once you get to know him…'

Hall looked as angry as Marc had been, and almost ill in his efforts to contain the rage. 'I have no intention of getting to know him, Verity. I know quite enough. As you would, if the man had not bewitched you. It is time someone explained to you the sort of man that has captured your heart. Then you will see why we are so angry and why we will not allow him to escape justice for what he has done.'

And he began, slowly at first, and with increasing speed, to list the offences of which her husband was guilty.

It was horrible. And she was sure that the stories were true. Because she had seen the contents of his heart and known him capable of it. Threats, lies, kidnapping and assault. And, although she'd known her sister's disgrace was at the hands of a rake, she had not known of Stephano's part in it.

'If you had seen her,' Hal shook his head. 'Marc told me her dress was torn. She was shaking with fear after having to fight for her honour. She was weeping and humiliated. It was only a fortuitous interruption that prevented her ravishment.'

'I am sure that he did not mean for it to come to that.' But how could she be sure, knowing how he spoke of the curse and how driven he had been to deliver it?

'Your precious Gypsy tricked her into straying off alone that night.' Hal gave a snort of disgust. 'I doubt he gave a thought to what would happen to her after. And it was not bad enough that he took you from us. Do you wish to know what was in the note we received?'

She could not speak to stop him. She could barely breathe. She had always hated the overprotection of her brothers, but now that it was gone, she felt vulnerable and frightened by what might come.

Hal stared at her with angry, hurt-filled eyes. 'He sent us your chemise, and said that it was stained with your virgin's blood. He described in detail how he had used you. And said that when he was finished, he strangled you with one of his damned silk ropes and left your body in the woods to be further defiled by scavengers.'

She knew her brother would not lie. Even if he did, he would not look as he did now. For speaking of this had so affected Hal that he was near to tears. But his version of the story was nothing like Stephano's. She reached out a hand to comfort her brother. 'There is a mistake, somehow. I am sure of it. Because the man I know…'

And Hal saw the confusion in her and seized upon it. 'You do not know him Verity. No one does. Ask Nathan Wardale if you do not believe me. At one time, they were as close as brothers. But when the Gypsy showed up with his silk rope, Nate made the mistake of helping the bastard, thinking their friendship would protect his sisters from that idiotic curse. And Stephen Hebden turned on him like a mad dog.'

'He betrayed a friend?' That was more damning than anything. For she'd have sworn, if she knew nothing else about the man she loved, that the bonds of affection once forged, were not easily cast off.

'He threatened Nathan's sisters,' Hal said, as though this explained it all. 'The man has no honour, and has attempted to abuse or seduce any woman he's had contact with. You are young, Verity. But we cannot protect you from this truth. Your Romany lover petted you and coddled you and filled you with sweet talk. And with each breath, he was lying. He tried to kill Father with worry. When he did not succeed at that, he sent you back to us, to be a traitor in our midst. It is the ultimate insult, to corrupt our most precious member and then watch us rot from the inside out.'

What could she say to relieve his anguish? The truth was inadequate. 'I did not know.'

'And now you do. Think on it, Verity. And if you cannot do it to save yourself, then for the good of your family. Forget Stephano Beshaley and the time you spent with him.'

The next days passed slowly, for they were empty and devoid of happiness. Everyone in the house, down to the lowest scullery maid, was watching her intently as though expecting some outburst of anger or tears that would prove she was ready to awaken from the nightmare of the previous week and come back to her old self.

But it seemed that her current life was as much a nightmare as the past they imagined for her. If the time in the Rom camp had been a lie, it had been a beautiful one. She had loved and thought she'd been loved in return. Even if it was nothing more than a cruel trick, she preferred it to the truth.

Here, everyone smiled and laughed and was careful not to speak of anything that might upset her. From the looks in their eyes, she could see that they were as close to cracking as she was. They were all desperate to return her to normal, even going so far as to send to the Veryans for her benighted harp.

And now, it seemed likely that Father would get out of his sick bed and would arrive in London along with it. He had heard rumours from Alexander Veryan of her mysterious absence, and insisted on travelling to see that she was well. The family was beside itself with the fear that an idle word might bring on the attack that would finish him for good.

She spent much time in the garden, hoping that it would clear the cold confusion of her heart. But the tailored nature of the plants and the perfect order of it all made her even more melancholy. Places that had seemed wild and natural before seemed full of artifice now that she had lived in a beech grove and slept under the stars.

She must learn to love her home again. She would play the harp and smile, if only to help calm Father. If her brothers were to be believed, Stephano was like a poisonous wine made with sweet fruit. Delicious, but deadly. He had used his charms on her, just as he had tried with Julia and others. But she had been the only one young and foolish enough to believe the things he had said to her. For the good of her family, she must accept the fact that this was home, and that the world she had known and loved was a betrayal of everything she had been raised to appreciate.

Stephano appeared out of the shadows, by the garden wall. Verity gave a start of fear, for a moment unsure that what she was seeing was real. But as he walked towards her, smiling and arms outstretched, her fear turned to anger. 'You.'

'Yes, me,' he said. 'You have not forgotten me, have you? Or your promise to send for me?'

She felt a moment's guilt, and a sudden desire to reassure him. *I have not forgotten. Never.*

Then, she remembered her brother's words. And she hardened her heart against the memories, for they were as false as the Gypsy. 'I made my promise before I heard how you treated my family.'

His smile disappeared, and his arms dropped to his sides. 'You knew how it stood between us. And you knew of the curse. I never claimed innocence to you. Nor can I now.'

'But you did not tell me the details, nor would anyone else. But now, I know what you did to Honoria.'

The man she thought she'd loved scoffed in disdain. 'I did nothing to Honoria.'

'Liar.' How could he be so blind to the pain he had caused?

He shrugged. 'I did not touch her, if that is what you fear. Any problems that she encountered were her own doing.'

The indignity bubbled fresh in her. 'She was very nearly raped.'

'I was hiding nearby. I would not have let it come to that. And after her escape, she went on to find love and a new life. As have they all.'

Which was true. But she remembered how lonely she had been, and how her brothers and parents had worried. 'She lives apart from her family. And apart from her honour, as well.'

'But she is happier for it,' he said. 'The loss of honour is not such a big thing. What is it, really? Naught but an idea. A myth.' He reached out to touch her arm.

She pulled away from him. 'A funny statement,

coming from the most proud man I have ever met. If you had no belief in honour, you would not work so hard to defend your own. What did I hear last week, other than the honour of your family and the catalogue of wrongs against you? You have devoted your life to punishing others. You are unhappy, but you think nothing of leaving a trail of misery wherever you go.'

She could see the hurt on his face, as though her betrayal meant something to him and was not just another vengeful plan gone slightly awry. 'You were happy with me. But now that you are back with your family, you are miserable? Whose fault is that?'

'Yours. For if you had not parted me from them...' *I would never have seen...I would never have felt...* She was too close to telling him the truth: lacking things that she had never known she wanted was leaving her almost sick with longing, in a place where she had known nothing but contentment, however bland it might have been. 'You tried the same with the others, did you not? Julia and Nell.'

His smile was triumphant, now. 'Is it jealousy, then, my sweet? They were nothing to me, and so it does not matter whether they succumbed to my charms or no.'

'It matters to me. For it seems I was the only one foolish enough to be dazzled by you, and to fall into your bed like a trollop, and let you...'

'Let me?' He gave a small laugh. 'Do you remember how it was when we parted? If anyone fell, it was not you. As I remember it, you did what you wished with me, with a great deal of enthusiasm.'

'Only to find that you laughed to my family about using me. And let them believe... You...horrible...disgusting...Gypsy.' She said it as though it were the worst thing in the world for him to be exactly what he was— and exactly what she loved about him. And it must have hurt him deeply. For otherwise, he would have no reason to pretend it didn't.

His eyes narrowed for but a moment. Then his smile returned brilliant as ever, and he nodded as though her response was exactly what he had expected to hear from a Carlow. 'After a few days of separation, you find you did not know me? And you are sickened by our association?' He gave a small, mocking bow. 'Then I shall consider our time together a complete success. I take full credit for the pain I caused you, and by extension, the anxiety it brought to the house of Narborough. It is no less than I wanted, after all. To see you humbled.' His forehead creased suddenly, as though another headache had come upon him, taking him unawares.

Without thinking, she reached out to soothe his brow, wishing she could press her lips to him until the pain relaxed from his face, as it had in the wagon.

He saw her response and laughed at her, but it seemed as though it caused him effort. He could not manage to make a sound of mirth or even mocking. The laugh came as a pain-choked gasp. 'I can see how glad you are, to return to your family. I have watched you for days. You sit here in the garden, crying for me. Even now, I could have you, if I wished. I have but to stretch out my hand and you will follow me back into the wilderness. Your family will never see you again. How amusing that would be...'

But the words sounded shaky, as though he'd said them to reassure himself, as much as to taunt her with them. 'How great a joke it would be, to take you right out of the bosom of your family. But I grow bored with your company, and am unwilling to saddle myself with a useless *gadji*, not even to satisfy my mother's spirit.' He waved his hand in a gesture that seemed an almost ceremonial dismissal. 'I release you. Run back to your brothers. And I hope your freedom brings you all that you deserve.'

Chapter Seventeen

As Stephano turned to leave, he could hear the sound of Verity sobbing as she ran toward the house. But it did not matter. Nothing mattered. The headache that had been gone for days had returned. It was a death knell in his skull. He did not care who saw him or who heard his muttered curses as he stumbled towards the garden gate. He was too angry to remember his object in coming here in the first place. But he was sure that he must have had a better reason to risk his life than the desperate and growing need to see his wife, if even for a moment.

His life, his health, his happiness were all there, inside the house. The love for her had come upon him so suddenly that he'd hardly believed it possible. Stronger than the fever, stronger than even the curse. He had been sure, for years, that there could be nothing stronger than the curse. But now he was Verity Carlow's puppet, just as he had been his mother's.

She had played him false, as he feared she would,

pretending that their time together was some common dalliance that he might have managed with the women who had married her foolish brothers. They had been quick enough to give her every detail of his time with them, probably embellishing to make it much worse than it had been.

Damn Verity Carlow, and all faithless women. Damn his mother, for her loose behaviour and her foolish curses. And damn Magda, as well, for forcing him to learn them. They had all claimed to care about him, yet they were willing to sacrifice him to get what they wanted. But once they were through, they did not care a jot if there was anything left of him.

And damn himself for not telling her every ugly detail of his past and then begging her forgiveness. He had behaved like a cad to every woman in her family, and then been stupid enough to forget that she would hear of it. For the first time in his life, he was truly ashamed. In his mind, he saw the faces of her friends and family, by turns frightened, pleading for mercy, or full of hatred at what he had done. This was his wedding gift to Verity. He was a coarse, bitter villain who tried to destroy everything he touched.

She was right to hate him. What he had done was wrong, no matter what his reasons. And if he had done wrong, he deserved to be punished, more than those he had persecuted. The only reason Verity had treated him kindly was her ignorance of the truth. For with a face as innocent as hers, he was sure that all around her worked to shield her from what had happened, just as he had wished to spare her any hardship when she had been his.

But now that she was home again, he doubted that her family had withheld any detail of his infamy. It was ironic that the very purpose of his life had lost him his love. But then, when had he ever been more than fortune's plaything?

The first blow came from behind, a strike across his shoulders that spun him around to face his attackers. Then a fist caught him in the jaw and brought him to his knees. He made no effort to rise. For there were several of them, and no point in fighting. He was limp on the ground with his eyes closed when the foot hit his ribs. Nothing broken, judging from other kicks he had taken in his long and unhappy life. But it was enough to take the wind out of him. The pains in his body combined with the pain in his head like a deafening noise, muting the conversation above him, setting him apart from the men who surrounded him and wrapping him in a blanket of agony.

He kept his eyes closed as he curled on the ground, giving them no reason to strike him again. If it was possible to make the feelings worse, he did not want to know. Nor did he care which blows had come from his brothers-in-law, and which from his oldest friend. Lord knew, he deserved what he got.

When he opened his eyes and looked up, Alexander Veryan had stepped from the protective shadow of the larger men around him, and Stephano was sure that the bruise in his ribs would match the pointed toe of the man's boot. He bared his teeth in a grimace of pain, and felt a moment's satisfaction as Veryan withdrew in fear, his gloating smile disappearing.

Then he was dragged to his knees, and his arms were

jerked behind him and bound. 'I thought that the shot would be enough. Or that perhaps you would drown. Or that you would die at the hand of another who you had wronged. How many times must we do this, Gypsy? What must we do to be rid of you?' Stanegate's voice was dispassionate, as though it mattered little to him what was about to happen.

'When I have destroyed the man who killed my father, you will see no more of me.' He gasped out the words around a knot of pain.

'And who do you think that is today, Stephen?' Nathan Wardale said, sounding more disappointed than angry. 'For it was not my father. Nor is it Carlow.'

'I do not know.'

'Then your tormenting of this family has all been for naught?' There was a bitter laugh. 'We will never be rid of him. For what happened to Honoria, and to Verity, for the insults to our wives, do we really need to involve the law?' It was Hal's voice, just as cold. Just as reasonable.

And here was where his old friend, Nathan, would plead for mercy or appeal to their better natures.

Or he could say nothing, as he was.

Stephano looked up into the angry eyes of Marcus Carlow and said, 'It is over. Do what you will.'

The men looked from one to another, as though discussing what was about to happen, though no words passed between them.

And then, he heard the scream from the house. *Dear God, no.* If the situation were different, he would have welcomed one last sight of his love. But no good could come of her seeing him humbled by her brothers. It would either poison her against them, or she would stand with them in approval and his heart would break before they could hang him.

'Marc! Hal! No!' She was running across the grass toward them. He could hear her panting breath. And then, she threw herself at him, her arms twining around his neck, her earlier anger forgotten. And even as she did it, he could feel the pain fading, as though it had never existed. It felt so good. She felt so good. It was all he could do not to turn his face into her body and nestle against her as though he were a child and not her lover.

And when she spoke again, there was nothing in her voice that reminded him of the sweet young girl that he had felt the need to protect. Hers was the voice of an avenging angel, and her arms tightened around him as though no force on earth would rip her away. 'Release him immediately.'

'Verity.' Stanegate's voice held a warning note, and Hal reached out a hand to her, trying to detach her arms from Stephano's neck.

She clung tighter, and he could feel her tears on his cheek. The pain of the beating subsided with the growing knowledge that she still cared for him, even if she could not forgive. 'Shh. Shh.' He murmured softly back to her, wishing that he could free his hands and give comfort to her, just as she was trying to give to him. 'It is all right. Go back to the house and let me talk to your brothers.'

'You are not talking to them.' She gave an incredulous laugh. 'They will kill you if I leave.'

'Verity.' Stanegate repeated his warning. 'Go back to

the house.' He acknowledged Stephano with the barest turn of his head. 'And you. Do not dare to speak to her. Not another word.' It was clear from his tone that once Verity went back to the house, Stephano would pay dearly for the few words they'd already shared.

Verity's head snapped around in response, and she glared at her brother. 'Do not treat me like a child, Marc. Nor you.' Now she was glaring at him, and he felt more threatened by that look than he had by the beating.

She stood, smoothed her skirts and pointed to her brothers. 'Release him at once.'

They did not move.

'Unbind his hands,' she said, her voice cold with fury. 'Whatever nonsense you have planned here will be impossible to accomplish, now. Unless you have the nerve to do it while I watch.'

'Verity, go back to the house.' But now, her brother sounded more exasperated than demanding.

'You will have to pick me up and carry me. And I will not make it easy for you.'

'She will not. I know from experience,' Stephano said. There was the faintest glimmer of amusement in Verity's eye. But her brother's anger seemed to double at the thought that Stephano had laid hands upon her.

'This man.' He waved a frustrated hand in Stephano's direction. 'Do you understand what he has done to your family? To your friends? What has he done to you, Verity, that you would plead for him now?'

'He married me.'

Marcus seemed near to apoplexy. He was incapable of speech. As he lunged forward, Hal grabbed his arm and gripped tightly, pulling him back.

Stephano closed his eyes again. It was certainly not that he regretted what he'd done. But he had hoped for a better time and place to present his suit to her family. As a fait accompli, when bound and on his knees before armed men, would not have been his choice.

After twenty-one years, Lady Verity had found her voice, and was having none of it. 'If you are going to take him to task for not seeking permission, I will remind you that you have already given it. You have told me often enough that I could marry whomever I liked, so long as it was done quickly, with no more fussing about.'

'But, Verity.' Stanegate's hand was at his temple, and for a moment, Stephano suspected he had found the location of his lost headache. 'I did not mean for you to marry this…this…criminal. You will come to your senses, and then we will seek an annulment, if that is even necessary.'

'An annulment?' His wife stood before them with hands on hips and a triumphant smile. 'Let me disabuse you of the notion, Marcus, that we are married in name only. It is every bit as you must suspect, though you insist on pretending it is not.'

'Verity.' Stephano muttered a warning that was as weak as he felt. If she kept on in this vein, he was dead the moment she left him alone. It was one thing to bed the man's sister. And quite another to come and rub the facts in his face.

She shot him a warning glare that was every bit as ferocious as Magda's. 'Be quiet, Stephano. This is a matter between my family and me.'

Her glare returned to her brother. 'There is no fraud

involved, nor was I forced to do what I did. I knew exactly what was happening, and I freely agreed to it.'

Which was not true at all. But when she was angry, she sounded very convincing.

'If you wish to part us, you will have to declare me mad and lock me away from him. And even if you do, I will scream to all around me exactly what went on between us, and I will never, ever be a fit wife for any other man.'

She took a breath and steadied herself, staring into the faces of her shocked brothers. And then she smiled sweetly at them. 'Or you can simply accept things as they are and wish us well. Would that not be easier?'

'Now, Verity.' Stanegate went white, and looked for a moment as though the girl in front of him had cowed him. 'There will be no more talk of madhouses, or screaming unpleasant truths. But surely you do not wish…'

'I do indeed. Most heartily.' For a moment, her expression softened, and then the glare returned. 'I am already married to Stephano, and happy to be so. There will be no more fighting. Not from either of you.' She stared at Stephano. 'We will sit down and reason this out like adults, with no more Gypsy curses or mad quests for vengeance.' Then she turned to her brothers. 'And there will be no debts of honour repaid by the bunch of you. Do you think to demonstrate your nobility by beating a lone man to the ground?'

Her brothers had the grace to hang their heads at this, apparently shamed by their behaviour.

Verity seemed to tower over them all, her soft hazel

eyes blazing. 'If, when we are through, Stephano deserves punishment for previous misdeeds and the unspeakable way in which he has treated my family, then I will be the one to give it, not you.'

Stephano felt a thrill go down his back at her words. She would punish him, would she? By the look in her eyes, she probably would. She was a formidable woman, his little *romni*. Then she bent her head to his and kissed him, open-mouthed, with the sort of demanding passion that he would expect from the wildest Gypsy wench. And bound and helpless as he was, he was incapable of doing anything but accepting it.

'We will discuss it later,' Stanegate announced, as though there was a way for him to control his little sister. But the look on his face told the truth: that the girl had become a force of nature, and he might just as well try to stop the wind.

'We will discuss it now,' she said, with a note of finality. 'Untie him. Or I shall.' When her brothers hesitated, she reached easily into his boot where she knew to find his knife, drew it and split the scarf that held him. Then she put the knife in her own pocket, leaving him defenceless in the midst of his enemies. She stared at her brothers. 'Back to the house, then?' She looked to him. 'And do you give me your word that you will behave?'

'Behave?' Stanegate almost exploded. 'His word?'

He bowed his head to her. 'I am at your disposal.' Then he looked at her brothers. 'For Verity's sake, I will do anything, including submit to your justice, should she wish it. But for now, she wishes us to talk.' He glanced around him at the men gathered there.

Stanegate gave a breath that almost seemed to shudder at the thought of allowing him across the threshold, and then said, 'For Verity's sake, we will talk. Whatever is done, it would be better in the house, than in the middle of the yard.'

'Where there are no witnesses?' He sneered at his host.

Stanegate caught the insult and sneered back. 'In the comfort of the salon, and not sitting on the grass like a bunch of damned travellers.'

'Stop it.' Verity's voice cut through the rancour, and once again Stanegate seemed startled to silence at this strange beast that inhabited the body of his normally content sister. 'We will go to the white salon. I will ring for tea. You will all drink it in peace if you know what is good for you. Then we will discuss the matter before us.'

And then, Stanegate smiled, as though he knew something about the situation that his sister did not. 'Very well, then. The white salon.'

'Do you think that's wise?' Hal asked, with a worried smile.

'I believe it is. Verity?' Stanegate gestured her forward, and they began their walk to the house. She had taken Stephano protectively by the arm, and he took the opportunity to rearrange her grip so that it was her arm that sat at the crook of his elbow. He would rather it at least appeared that it was he who escorted her. He noticed the other men had chosen positions to flank him, as though they suspected that he might run at any minute.

They entered the house and made their way to the

salon. And Verity, first across the threshold of the room, stopped dead in her tracks. Then she dropped his arm with a gasp, and ran to the man seated there.

'Father!'

Chapter Eighteen

It was the most uncomfortable tea party of Stephano's memory. Given that he had dined with a maharaja who held matched tigers on thin gold chains, while his own pockets were full of the man's stolen rubies, it said something to the amount of tension in the room.

The men around him stepped closer so that there could be no question of escape, as the Earl of Narborough hugged his daughter. 'You are well, Verity? Truly?' He held her back from him, as though to search for signs of damage.

'Of course, Father. Did you not read my letter?' She kissed him on the top of the head, which was greyer than Stephano remembered it. But Narborough did not appear as frail as his family had put about. 'And you?'

The earl sighed in relief. 'Much better, now that I can see you. Could you bring me a cup of tea, my dear?'

Verity started for the door. Then she recognized the ploy that would take her from the room, so that the men could talk in private. She gave him a pointed look, and lifted her chin. 'I will ring for a servant.'

He smiled. 'Very well.' He looked up at Stephano. 'So you are Hebden's bastard, that has given us so much trouble these last months?'

Confronted by the one who might very well be his father's killer, Stephano found he was momentarily humbled by the man's rank and the directness of his speech. Then, he stepped forward to greet his wife's father. 'I am.'

The old earl examined him. 'You are the spitting image of him. Darker, of course. But still. It was a bad business, all around, and we were all sorry to see your mother so ill treated. Both your mothers. But Kit was not an easy person to love. I expect you know that better than any of us.'

Of all the things he had thought to hear, when he finally came face to face with George Carlow, this was outside of his imagining. All he could do was nod.

And then, the old man turned to steel before his eyes. 'But it does not excuse your recent behaviour. What did you mean by ripping pages from my journal or taking my daughter and sending this note to my family?' He slapped a piece of paper on the table between them.

'Father, he did not…' Verity began. Stephano held a hand up to silence her. It would do no good to either of them for her to speak for him. Then he leaned forward to look at the paper, wondering if it would do any good to deny the thing. It was not in his hand, nor were these his words. He was not even sure where the blood had come from. While the trail of splotches he had left on the chemise he'd sent were vulgar, they were nothing like the amount of blood spilled here.

He could see where the vile boasts of the letter might have driven Stanegate to shoot at him, for the thought of someone hurting Verity, and then disposing of her so casually was anathema to him, as it was to her family.

But if he had not sent the note, then who?

And then, it all became quite clear to him. Of course, it proved he had been an idiot almost from the start, and had badly misjudged the situation and his level of control over it. But he would gladly sacrifice his pride, for the truth to be known. He hid his smile of success, for there was still the necessity of proving it to the others. 'The person who wrote this letter deserves punishment, for it was a most reprehensible trick.'

The earl nodded. 'I agree.'

'But the contents are all lies,' he amended. 'I kidnapped Lady Verity in an effort to force a meeting between us. But while she was with me, she was treated as a member of my own family.'

Narborough frowned at him. 'I can see that.' The windows behind him faced out onto the garden. He had likely witnessed all that passed between Stephano and his daughter, and must have been able to guess the details, easy enough.

'And I did not damage the journal that was removed from your library. It came to me in that condition, and I have no reason to think it had been tampered with after it left your house. Someone knew about that journal and defaced it at an earlier time.'

The earl nodded again, as though satisfied with his answer.

And here was where he would learn the truth of Narborough's character. 'If I may ask a question of my own, Your Lordship?'

There was a pause, as he considered. And then, the earl said, 'Despite your heinous behaviour toward my family, it was your father that died. You are more entitled to ask questions than any of us.'

'What had you written on those pages?'

'Apparently, something quite important. The person responsible for this must have learned of my penchant for record keeping and sought to obscure the details of the event. I can tell you that it contained my suspicions that I had done wrong by William Wardale, and made a grave error in testifying against him.' He looked to Nathan, his features etched in sorrow. 'There is no apology sufficient for what happened to your father. He was adamant of his innocence, to the last day. But I could find nothing to prove his claims. And to know him hanged—and the part I played in it?' Narborough shook his head. 'The guilt of it has weighed on my soul. And I fear I shall soon have to answer directly to William for the wrongs I did him.'

It was a touching story, but useless to Stephano. 'While I sympathize with the plight of the Wardale family, I must ask you to tell me the rest of it. You were there. I was not.' And he felt some of the old sadness and confusion returning, in the pure and innocent way he'd felt it when he was a child and known nothing of Romany curses. 'Please, Your Lordship. Tell me of the last moments of my father's life.'

The earl gestured him to take a chair. And as he sat, the rest of the people in the room gathered closer to hear the story. Stephano could feel Verity, just behind him, resting her hand upon his shoulder.

'You must understand, William and Kit and I were close friends, or had been, until the events surrounding that evening. But we feared there was a traitor amongst us. Coded messages had been passed to enemies of England, and no one was above suspicion. Tempers were short and blood ran hot. For my part, I said and wrote things that I did not mean. I was too quick to judge.' Narborough looked like he felt true regret. And having read the vitriolic entries that remained in his journals, Stephano felt he had good reason.

'But I thought our troubles were nearing an end. Your father was the one set to crack the code that the spy had been using. And he claimed to be successful. He was ready to turn the information over to the Home Office, and agreed to come to my house and show me before the thing was done.' He looked to Nathan. 'Your father was to meet us, as well. They were both late, of course.' He shook his head and smiled. 'I was accustomed to that. They were younger, and heedless of time. But perhaps that night, they had reason. It was raining, and travel was not easy.'

'And when they arrived?'

'I did not hear them come. If I had, perhaps I could have stopped what occurred. I had been called away to the Alien Office unexpectedly. When I returned, I went to my study to get a book. The doors to the garden were open. The rug was wet.' He stared off into the distance, as though he could see it all again. 'Perhaps that is it. For I remember wondering how it had gotten so muddy, if the struggle had happened outside. There was too much water. Perhaps there were too many footprints for only the two men I saw there.'

'There might have been more than one man in the room?' Nathan asked, eager to clear his own father.

Narborough nodded. 'But a perhaps is not the same as evidence. And the room got much worse, after Veryan and his lot arrived from the Home Office to take charge of things. The next morning, it was clean and dry. How could I be sure of my assumptions? But I swear, that night it was wet, and strewn with the broken needles from the rosemary bushes that used to be planted in the garden, just outside.'

Narborough made a face and paled, as though his illness was likely to return at any time. 'They had come in, not from the front, but through the garden doors, and crashed through the bushes. There must have been a struggle. The room stank of rosemary. To this day, I cannot abide the stuff.'

He shook his head, as though to clear it of the scent. 'And there lay Kit. Will Wardale was bending over him. My letter opener was still in Will's hand. His other hand was spread over Kit's ribs, as though he wished to stop the bleeding. But it was clear, by the way the stain grew, that he was doing no good. And there was a horrible bubbling noise when Kit tried to speak…'

'He was still alive?' Stephano's chest felt tight at the thought. It had been twenty years, but it was almost as if he could feel his father's last breath.

'For only a moment.' And in a gesture that shocked them both, Narborough leaned forward and laid a hand on his shoulder, just as Verity had done. 'I wish I could tell you he did not suffer. But for a brief time, he did. He tried to speak to us. In Latin, of all things.'

'My father spoke Latin?' Stephano almost laughed at the thought. 'He was well read, certainly. But with me, he did not rise to the poetic.'

Narborough looked confused, as well. 'It was broken Latin, at that. He was gasping for what little he could manage, and I am not even sure of what I heard. I thought perhaps it was some part of the code he tried to tell us. There are ciphers that are unbreakable, if you do not know the key. I have tried every Latin phrase I can think, that might suit. *Veritas omnia vincit. Magnas est Veritas et pervalebit.* Certainly not *In vino, Veritas.* Although if your father had a motto, that would have done well. But none of it means anything.'

'Father!' Verity's hand had tightened on his shoulder as the old man had spoke, until her grip was almost painful. 'You do not recognize your own daughter's name?'

'Of course, I do, my dear. But what would you have to do with this? You were a baby when it happened.'

'In a cradle. With my toys,' she said. 'One of them was a silver rattle, which was a gift from Stephano's father. He had it with him on the night he died.'

She came around from behind him, so that she could see into his face. 'You told me that you saw the thing in your father's study. You disturbed his work with the whistling, and he took it from you. But it was broken when I received it.'

He smiled into her marvellous hazel eyes, which were dancing with excitement. 'And you think that his last words…'

'Were "In Verity's rattle",' she finished, triumphantly. 'Could he have been solving the code, when you disturbed him? He probably pocketed the rattle without even thinking. And if he suspected he was followed to the house that night, perhaps he forced the cipher key down into the whistle so that no one would find it.'

He gripped her hand in his, and gave it a tight squeeze of gratitude. 'We must see.'

The earl made to rise. 'I will send to Stanegate Court…'

'No need,' Verity was grinning now. 'Marc, do you not know where it is?'

Her brother looked baffled. Verity gave an exasperated sigh. 'You are the nicest brother a girl could wish for, Marcus. And you, as well, Hal,' she added in afterthought. 'But sometimes, you are both quite useless. I gave you a gift, on the birth of your child. Honoria did, as well. But mine was a family keepsake. The very rattle that Christopher Hebden was carrying with him on the night he died was at the breakfast table this morning. You called it annoying and demanded it be taken back to the nursery. But it would be much more annoying if it whistled. And it cannot. Because someone put something down the hole. I will go and get it, and we will open it. If it holds the code key, then we will settle today what should have been done many years ago.' She turned and left for the nursery.

Stephano stood to watch her go, shaking his head in amazement. His Verity had been the key, after all. And his taking her, and everything surrounding it, had happened for a purpose. It had brought them to this day, where all could be revealed.

But her absence left the gentlemen alone. There was a moment of awkward silence, and he hoped that her faith in her brothers was well placed, and the truce was no sham.

'Tea, Marcus?' said Hal, smiling down the hall after his retreating sister.

'Something stronger, perhaps,' muttered Stanegate. 'It has been an eventful day.'

'Excuse me,' Alexander Veryan muttered, clearing his throat. 'A call of nature.' He shifted uneasily, looking like a man whose digestion could not be ignored, and made a hasty exit from the room. Stephano watched the slight narrowing of the eyes that the two Carlow brothers gave to each other, as though they liked the Veryan lad no better than he.

'It is his father that did the killing, you know,' Stephano said softly, and watched the men around him start.

'Keddinton? Certainly not.'

'What makes you think so?'

'The letter I sent to you? And the chemise?'

Hal muttered an oath under his breath, and it was Stanegate's turn to lay a cautioning hand on his father's shoulder, as the old earl paled in his chair.

Stephano continued. 'It was not that vile piece of rubbish on the desk.' He licked his lips, as though it were possible to ease the apology he must make. 'I have done many things for which I have no pride. But do you know me as a rapist or a murderer? The kidnapping was a threat to her honour, of course. But I took care that no one saw us depart. If you kept silent on her disappearance, and given me the confession I demanded, no one would have been the wiser. She'd have come to no physical harm while in my care. As you can see, she is very much alive and in good health and spirits.'

'You sent us the...' Stanegate paused as though he did not even wish to say the words. 'The bloody shift. What did you expect us to think?'

He held out his hand to them, showing the healing cut. 'The blood was mine.' As an afterthought, he added, 'And Verity was alone when she removed the chemise. I took it after. I was not there to see the results. There was no threat to your sister's modesty.' Then, at least. But now was not the time to discuss that.

'I meant to shock you, nothing more. I gave Keddinton a message and shed the blood in his presence. I expected him to tell the truth. He had helped me before, and swore he had more love of justice than he did for either of your families. I was an idiot to trust him. I thought I controlled him. But from the first moment, he played me for a fool, and used me as a tool against you all.'

'And we are to trust your word, are we?' Stanegate asked.

'I will provide a sample of my writing, if you wish to compare. But if the rattle contains an undiscovered message from my father, there will be proof enough, soon.'

For a moment, the men around him seemed to forget their hatred of him, and looked thoughtful at the information he had given them.

'And now I understand Robert's eagerness to tell me things that my own sons did not see fit to share with me.' The earl cast a disapproving eye on his children. 'There have been far too many attempts in my own household to shield me from unpleasantness for my own good. And far too few from the Veryans. Lately, they seem most eager to bear bad news, even when it comes to nothing.'

Hal looked to the door. 'How much do you suppose young Veryan knows of this, should it be true?'

'Enough so that I did not announce my suspicions in his presence,' Stephano said. 'But his behaviour in the next few minutes will tell us.'

'I almost hope he runs.' Hal shuddered. 'I never could stand the plaguey little beggar. And the idea that he was in mourning for Verity. That they'd have made a match of it...'

'It would have been most advantageous,' Stanegate argued. 'If only to get her to choose elsewhere. I expected a short time in his company would be enough to focus her attentions on someone else.' And remembering the result, he stared across the room at Stephano as though looking from the frying pan to the fire.

Hal remained fixed upon the door. 'Should we go after him, do you think? He's had more than enough time to take care of business. And if what the Gypsy says is true, we can't have him running off to warn his father.'

Stanegate gave a slight nod, and Hal exited the room. He returned a short time later, shaking his head. 'Too late, I'm afraid. He's piked off. How long to the Keddinton estate, do you think? Or is the old man in town?'

The brother's discussion of distances and coach

schedules faded into nothing as an apprehension took Stephano, growing in him like a wildfire.

'Never mind the *gaujo*. What has become of Verity?'

Chapter Nineteen

Just as she'd expected, Verity found the rattle in the nursery, in the damp hand of her nephew, William George. She smiled and held her own hand out for the thing. But the boy was unwilling to part with it without tears. If the mystery had waited this long, then surely it could wait the few minutes it would take to find a substitute plaything.

In an adjoining room, she found a similar rattle and gave it an experimental shake. The bells lacked the silvery jingle of her old toy, but when she put the whistle to her lips, it made the fierce tweet that had been lacking. Good enough for a distraction, she was sure.

When she turned to go back to the child, she bumped directly into the doughy torso of Alexander Veryan. He looked decidedly odd today, and seemed unwilling to yield. She gave him what she hoped was a friendly smile. 'Why, Alex. Have you come to look for me? I swear, I was gone for but a moment.'

It was even more odd to see the tiny gun he held in

his hand. Her smile froze in place as she thought of the baby in the room nearby and the danger of errant gunfire. 'Whatever do you mean to do with that? Not shoot me, surely.'

He seemed as nervous about the thing as she was, for his hand trembled a bit as he spoke. 'I will if I must, Verity.'

'Well, I shall give you no reason, I am sure.' She thought quickly and gave a moue of disappointment. 'But I thought we were such good friends. And that we were likely to be even closer. That was what our fathers intended for us, was it not?'

'But you have gone and married the Gypsy,' he said petulantly.

Whose knife she still had, in the pocket of her gown. 'That was but a ruse, to keep me safe from the wild men of his camp. No real marriage, certainly. The Romany customs are very strange, compared to ours. Nothing more passed between us than a shared slice of bread.'

A cloud of puzzlement passed behind the vacant eyes of Alexander. Her current story was nothing like what she had said in the garden. But she suspected it was what he wanted to hear. In the end, he could not seem to reconcile the facts, and he frowned. 'That is neither here nor there. Is that the rattle?'

She looked at the toy in her hand. 'Why would you want it?'

'Why would you?' he said, as though returning her question were anywhere near passing for wit.

'Well, that is neither here nor there, as well.' She smiled, deciding that for current circumstances, one rattle was as good as another. 'Perhaps I think it is interesting to solve a puzzle that is so old. Or perhaps there is nothing in it at all, and it will make Stephano Beshaley forget his nonsense and leave us alone.'

Alexander snatched the thing from her hand, and put it in the pocket of his coat without examining it further. 'We will take it to Father. He will know what is to be done with it.'

'We will, will we?' She gave a small laugh. 'You make it sound as if we are to be together.'

'And so we are. I cannot have you going back to explain to your brothers what I have done. You must come with me.'

'My brothers are bound to notice our absence, Alexander,' she explained patiently. 'There will be questions. And then they will follow. I expect they will be very angry with you for taking me.'

Alexander laughed. 'More likely, they will be relieved. At least this time you have not run off with a Gypsy. They will think it is an elopement—or that is what we shall tell them, when they come to fetch you. You will be mine, just as my father promised me. And your brothers will take care of Stephano Beshaley.'

Verity offered a silent curse to her dear uncle Robert, for showing so little concern as to her wishes in a choice of husband. 'Alexander, my brothers are not so crass as to *take care* of anyone. If justice is truly needed in this, they will take the matter to the courts.'

'That is not what they wished to do, when they saw the letter that we wrote.' Alexander's grin did nothing to make his face more attractive.

'You wrote that note?' For the first time, she felt alarm. She had seen the words of the letter, and the fate ascribed to her. And to realize that she was face to face with the person who had imagined it was both insulting and disturbing.

Alexander pulled back the sleeve of his coat, and she could see the beginnings of the deep scratch on his arm. 'And I sealed it with my own blood, just as the Gypsy did.'

She wanted to argue that he was nothing at all like Stephano. He was a hollow parody, and quite mad, to boot. But she remembered the gun, and said, 'How very resourceful of you.'

'And now, I shall take you away, just as he did. But I will be bringing you back to Warrenford, where you should have stayed all along. Once we are safely home, I shall give my father the rattle and there shall be an end to this nonsense.' He gestured again with his gun, and she walked ahead of him, down the stairs and toward the garden doors. Would he really shoot, she wondered? He held the gun as though he were afraid of it.

And in that fear was the greatest danger of all. Hal had assured her that it led to more accidents and loss of life in battle than anything else. 'You can't seriously think I would go away with you.' She said it louder than necessary, hoping someone might hear before they reached the door.

'I can and do.' He forced her outside, and then hesitated; she was sure that he had no real plans after this. He could not exactly take her to the stables and demand the grooms prepare a vehicle suitable for her kidnapping.

At least Stephano had been better prepared on the taking of her. And still was. For there, beneath a tree by the garden gate, was his great black stallion, saddled and ready to go. She felt the gun in her back again, urging her towards the beast. And for a moment, she felt like laughing. Zor looked ready to eat the interloper instead of letting him ride.

The horse reared as they got close, and she was sure there was no hope. But then, Alexander gestured her closer. 'Mount.'

'I do not think he will allow it.'

Alexander stood clear of the angry horse, but kept the gun trained upon her. 'He believes you both belong to his master. He will let you ride. Now, mount.'

She put a foot into the stirrup, which was low because of Stephano's long legs, and pulled herself uneasily onto the horse, riding astride. Once she was up and the horse was steady, Alexander pulled himself up behind her. He wrapped an arm around her waist and poked her in the back with the gun. 'Ride towards Warrenford.'

She let out a sigh of frustration, and tugged at the reins until the horse started at a walk.

Alexander took the reins from her hands and gave the beast a kick in the ribs, and their pace increased to a trot.

On the trip into the country, there was ample time to examine her emotions. She should be terrified. A man had kidnapped her and held a gun in her back, forcing her to who knew what fate.

But the man in question was Alexander Veryan. It was unusual for a girl of her age to have been kidnapped at all. But when it happened twice in a fortnight, one began to develop opinions on the subject. And while being taken from the Keddinton estate by the unarmed

Stephano had been a terrifying experience, being forced to return to it by the gun-wielding Alexander was more annoying than frightening.

It might have been different, had she truly believed him capable of shooting her. But since her death would render his final goal of marriage to be quite impossible, she suspected that she was in no real danger. Unless, of course, the gun went off accidentally.

And considering Alexander's difficulty in managing the gun, the horse and her, a stray shot seemed too likely to risk. If the poor boy had meant to leave her swooning with his commanding presence, the least he could have done was to learn the most direct route to his own home. In her critique of his actions, she had given him high marks for avoiding the main road to thwart pursuit, only to take them away again when they had to turn back not once, but twice on the way.

And now, she feared they were hopelessly lost again. At last, she gave vent to her frustration. 'At this rate, it is likely to be dark before we arrive. Do you, or do you not know the way home?'

His grip on the reins loosened, and she could feel the gun in her ribs again. 'If it grows too late, we will stop for the night.'

She suppressed a shudder of revulsion. 'Alex, I have no intention of camping in the wilderness with you on this night or any other. I demand that you take me back to the main road immediately so that we can be on our way to either your home or mine.'

'You did not seem to mind, when it was the Gypsy who took you. If your reputation is in ruins, there will be few as willing to offer for you as I am. You should not be so particular.'

And then, she felt him put the gun away, so that he could more freely demonstrate his intentions towards her.

'Alex, do not dare.'

Now, he was squeezing her waist, and planting a rather wet kiss on the back of her neck.

She leaned forward, trying to get away from him. 'Alex, this is your last warning. I mean it. You will be sorry.'

But he was fumbling with her bodice and licking her on the ear. He was ignoring her wishes, just as he always had. And she was so very tired of being ignored. So she reached into her pocket and took out the knife, giving a quick downward slash to his roving hands.

Alex yelped and reared back in pain. And then Zor begin to do likewise. So she grabbed the reins in one hand and the horse's mane in the other and hung on for dear life as the horse stood up and Alex slid off the back of the saddle and into a nearby hedge.

She settled the horse, patting him on the neck and adjusting her seat. Then she looked back at her would-be kidnapper, groaning in the greenery. 'I told you to cease bothering me, but you would not listen. Now, since you are so eager to sleep rough, I will not detain you from it.' She pulled on the reins and dug her heels into the horse's side. 'Zor, take me home. For I swear, you are the most sensible male I have seen today.'

Chapter Twenty

As the speeding carriage rocked from side to side, Stephano felt the pressure of the men's bodies around him. Without the mitigating presence of Verity, her brothers were being none too gentle in their treatment of him, allowing the occasional elbow to slip into his ribs as the coach jostled, or the accidental boot kick to the ankle. Nathan sat opposite, a neutral observer to the subtle aggression of the other two.

It was far better than the bullet he had expected when they'd first caught him. And considering how he had behaved about his own sister's lover, he supposed he had little grounds to complain. But their current behaviour was childish, considering what was at stake.

When they had first discovered Verity missing, there had been an initial air of panic, and much shouting of names and running about the house. The others had seemed surprised by his lack of response. They faulted him for being cold, and wondered aloud what it could mean about his feelings for his wife. It proved that they did not understand her at all.

If he had any regrets, it was that he had underestimated Keddinton from the first. It was galling to realize what a fool the man must think him. He had gone to the very heart of the problem and sought aid. He had befriended the one who had been responsible for the death of his father—and by association his mother and stepmother—and for all the terrible moments of his own youth. He had underestimated someone who made his living as a spy, who could lie, keep secrets and hide behind facades as a matter of course. He had fallen for it all, had thought the man an easily manipulated coward, and had proceeded to wrong the innocents around him, in a useless quest. All the while, Keddinton had pulled his strings like a damned puppet.

And now, his wife was paying the price for his stupidity. While he refused to believe she was in any real danger from young Veryan, she would be quite angry when next he saw her.

'There is no point in chasing after Alexander,' he assured her family. 'He is no real threat, and is too enamoured of your sister to do her any harm. But we must get to Robert Veryan before they arrive. He is the dangerous one.'

The Earl of Narborough was ready to ride with them. But it was clear that his travelling earlier in the day, followed by the difficult interview with Stephano, had taken much out of him. The latest shock had put him near to a relapse. Valuable time had to be spent convincing him to leave the rescue to younger men. But within the hour, a carriage had been prepared, and they were on their way.

Even now, the others doubted him. Hal stared out the window of the carriage. 'If he is taking her to Warrenford Park, we should have seen sign of them by now.'

Stephano repeated his assurances. 'If they kept to the roads, we will catch them. And even if they did not, we will not be far behind them.'

'You had best hope that you are right about this,' Stanegate said. 'If you have tricked us into haring cross country after Alex Veryan, while our sister is carried back to the Gypsies? Or if she suffers in any way from this misadventure? I swear, you will not live to see morning.'

Stephano smiled in pride, as he thought of her. 'If she were on her way to my camp, I would be at her side, not yours. As for the rest? I have seen the way she behaves when she fears the worst. Under pressure, she is quick and resourceful, and her nerves are as strong as any man's. And I have seen her abductor.' He sneered at the memory. 'She is more than a match for him. He does not realize that she pocketed my knife when she freed me.'

Stanegate blinked at him sceptically. 'So you suspect she has a knife in her pocket. What would she do with that, even if you are right?'

Again he laughed at how little the man knew his baby sister. 'She would stab him. Or cut him, more like. She has proven to me that she is not afraid to use the thing. If he touches her, he will be made more than sorry for it, even before I find him and finish with him.'

He glanced at the man across the carriage from him.

Stanegate was watching him intently. At last, the other man spoke with no preamble. 'This supposed marriage to my sister. Did it take place in a church?'

'No. It was a Rom ceremony. My people witnessed it, of course. And celebrated with us. But it was not a formal thing, with church records and rings. That is not our way.' He chose his next words carefully. 'To be legally binding in England, we will have to be married again. Which I am eager to do, so that there can be no question of her status.'

'But for now, she is free by law to marry elsewhere.'

'If she wishes.' He looked steadily back at his unwilling brother-in-law. 'If she prefers to forget me, and return to her old life, then I will not force her to remain. But neither will I stand by and watch you force her to do that which she does not wish.'

Stanegate was staring through him, trying to break him. 'And if you wished to forget her?'

'Marriage is not entered into lightly, in my people, nor in yours.' Perhaps that was not totally true in his case. But the truth did not support his argument. 'I would not have said the words, had I not meant them.' Somewhere in his heart, perhaps he had. 'I cannot go back to my tribe and tell them it was nothing, that I brought a *gadji* into their midst, called her wife, and shared my vardo with her. No woman would want a man so quick to cast off a wife who was no longer convenient.'

Stanegate frowned thoughtfully. 'But suppose you did not need to go back to your people. I understand that the Americas offer opportunity to a man of intelligence and resolve. Ten thousand pounds would go a long way, if one wished to begin a new life.'

So the man meant to bribe him? He scoffed. 'I have at least that in a year, and more.'

'Twenty then.' There was no desperation in Stanegate's voice. It was the calm tone of a man used to getting his way.

'Could you forget your wife, for twenty thousand pounds?'

He could see the question had struck home, for the man paused, and showed no sign of raising his bid.

Stephano pressed on. 'If it is a matter of money that worries you—or your sister's comfort or safety—let me remind you that I do not live in a wagon because I want for a house. You have seen Bloomsbury Square. Not as grand as the Carlow town house, of course. And there is some recent fire damage and a hole in the woodwork.'

His brothers-in-law both smiled at the memory of the damage.

'But there is ample space to raise a family. I have seventeen thousand a year. The original source of the money might not be to your liking, should I be forced to go back to my beginnings and account for every penny. But the business has been legal for a long time, and my investments are sound. Do not think I will need to pick pockets or tell fortunes, or that Verity will be wearing scarves and dancing in the street for pennies. Her life will be the same as any gentlewoman in England, with servants to tend her and enough money to outfit herself in the style she chooses.'

Stanegate's mouth quirked as though he had taken bitter medicine. Clearly, the news that Stephen was well able to care for a wife was not what he wished to hear. And while he might be in trade, a gem merchant was hardly the same as a green grocer.

While Stephen Hebden might have been willing to let the matter rest and trust the men he was with, Stephano knew he could not. 'I would be naïve not to realize that you are quite capable of sending me to America against my will, once this is settled. Your other sister married a ship's captain, did she not? If you wish to give the man knowledge of me, I suspect he would not hesitate to dispense justice. Considering my shameful behaviour in the matter of Verity's sister—' he paused significantly '—for which I am heartily sorry. Although I realize that no apology could be sufficient.'

He paused again, trying not to worry that he had given Stanegate an idea that had not already occurred. 'But if your thoughts lean in such a direction, I have a rather unusual request.'

'You request mercy from us?' This came from Hal, who sounded quite incredulous at the idea.

'On the contrary. I request that you show no mercy at all. Treat me as I treated you. If you cannot accept a truce, or my word that I will care for your sister, then I wish you to finish me quickly. Perhaps a ball to the back, should tonight's escapade come to gunfire, as I fear it might. An unfortunate accident, arranged between gentlemen, that will leave Verity with no ill feelings for her family and no doubt in her mind that her marriage is truly over. I left ample proof with my servants that I consider us wed and that my property and accounts should go to her on my death, should she wish to claim them. But I want her to be a widow, not an abandoned wife. Whatever happens, I beg you not to leave her with the impression that I willingly deserted her or forgot my vows. For I swore to her that I would not.' When he said it, it sounded foolish in his own ears. It hurt to think the woman he claimed as wife might not trust his word.

His new and unwilling brothers were looking at him in scepticism. 'You would turn down the money—and a chance at freedom—in favour of a quick death, to preserve Verity's feelings?' Stanegate said. 'You cared little for her feelings when you took her from us in the first place, and only for your own gain. Why should it be different now? What do you think to gain, should we kill you tonight?'

'I…' He gave a weak laugh, knowing that in speaking the next words, he left his true fear open before them. 'If I die tonight, as I suspect I shall, at least I will not have to continue in an empty life without Verity at my side. For as I examine my future, I find that it would be quite unbearable to be parted from her. If you allow me to go free, I will seek her out. But to be imprisoned, or transported, knowing that she was here, wondering what had become of her…if she was safe, if she had forgotten?' He shook his head. 'That is well beyond any punishment that I have meted out to you and your families.' He looked around him, at the faces in the carriage. 'For all the ill I have done, at the end of it, none of you were left loveless and alone.'

He could feel the stillness in the carriage, as the men around him considered their current state of happiness. He could see fleeting moments of softness in their eyes, as they thought of their wives. And then, Stanegate shifted in his seat. 'I hardly think your unfortunate demise will be necessary, although I will admit that the prospect had occurred to me. We will discuss the legality of your marriage and the state of Verity's future later, when the current affair is settled and we are safely home again.'

Stephen relaxed, and he felt a lessening of tension in the men on either side of him. Although nothing had been said, he suspected that, somehow, everything had been settled. 'If you would let me see the rattle in your pocket, now that we have time, I think I can shed some light on what happened. We must be sure, before we arrive, that we have the right man.'

Hal snorted. 'You have taken long enough to come to that conclusion, Stephen.'

He grimaced in response, but wondered if the use of his given name was evidence of a reconciliation. 'A point well taken. I have blundered badly while searching for the truth of this. It is too late to admit that I was wrong, I suppose. But it must be said. I was wrong. And I am sorry for it.' He looked them in the eye, one after the other. And there was not precisely forgiveness in their returned gazes. But there was something. A jot of understanding. And a twinkle that said they thought him to be a hot-blooded idiot. But hadn't they thought him that, as children? And he could not fault them for it, because it was so often true.

'Show us the rattle, then,' he said. 'If I am correct, it holds the truth.'

Stanegate reached into his pocket for the toy that he had rescued from his son, giving the thing an experimental shake and blowing the whistle, which gave not a shrill tweet, but a dry rattle. He stared down at it, then offered it to Stephano, who took it, turning it over and over in his hands and searching for the weak spots in the seam.

He smiled. 'It is the work of my Rom stepfather. A pity I must break it. Have one of you a knife that I might use to pry?'

Nathan reached into his pocket, and handed over his fob, complete with penknife. It made Stephano smile at the easy trust the man showed him. And then, he returned his attention to the rattle, searching for the point where the whistle had been hammered into the barrel. He was able to detach the thing with a single gouge into the metal, one that could be hammered out later, to preserve Thom's work.

And as the toy cracked in two, it exposed a tiny scrap of yellowed paper, rolled tightly and stuffed far down into the body. His hands shook as he set the pieces of the toy aside and unrolled the paper. 'My father's writing.' And he was sure it was, although it had been twenty years since last he'd seen it. On one side of the paper, the alphabet had been written top to bottom. Next to it was a column of numbers, and beneath a list of nulls and instruction for transposition of the coded information. At the bottom of the paper was a row of digits, and beneath it, in block letters:

VERYAN IS THE SPY

He handed the paper to Stanegate, who passed it around the carriage in silence. Then Nathan Wardale said, 'Veryan was looking for the code key that night. And he is still looking, after all these years. He told me so himself, last year. He thought my father must have taken it.' He shook his head. 'As though we would have kept it a secret, had we known.'

Hal spoke. 'He must have waylaid Framlingham that night, thinking he could kill him and make away with the key before he was discovered.' He glanced at Stephano. 'Your father was too clever; he had already hidden it. They struggled. Veryan grabbed a letter opener.' Hal gave a thrust with his empty hand, as though imagining the action. He glanced at Nathan. 'And your father arrived too late to help, but in time to see the end. As did our father. Veryan was forced to retreat empty handed, and arrive with the rest of the agents from the Home Office, acting as though he'd come when summoned. By that time, Christopher Hebden was dead, William Wardale was accused of murder, and the rattle was on its way to the nursery.'

Silence fell over them again, as if each could see the events of the night playing out in their minds. While the Carlows were affected by the information, Stephano doubted they felt the turmoil that he experienced from it. The painful vision of his father struggling and dying. And the frustration he felt knowing that with his last gasp, Christopher Hebden had wanted to be sure that someone would learn the truth. It was all followed by a rushing sensation in his soul, as though the earth had shifted, and all the disordered pieces of the story fell into place. Finally, over twenty years later, the truth was known and there could be justice.

He looked across the carriage, into the eyes of Nathan Wardale, who must be feeling something similar. But for Nate, it would be vindication. The single line scribbled on that paper brought his family out of disgrace. And if the crown saw fit, it would restore Nathan to his rightful title. The paper trembled in his hands. 'We have all seen it then?' He held it out, as though he still expected the words to dissolve to nonsense before his eyes. 'You are witnesses? Because I doubt anyone would believe it, if I brought it forth. Marc, you hold it.' He pushed the paper back to Stanegate. 'They will believe you, before the rest of us. You have precedence.'

Stanegate smiled. 'Today perhaps. But you hold the higher rank, Leybourne.'

Nathan shook his head. 'Too soon. Do not use it, until we are sure.'

Stephano laughed, as his old friend went pale at the mention of his title. 'He is afraid you will curse his luck.'

For some reason, they all found this funny and the tension in the carriage eased. It was just as well. He would rather see Nathan preoccupied with his future than with collecting a pound of flesh from Robert Veryan for all that the Wardale family had suffered.

Stephano feared he would not be so lucky. If he was forced to choose between his recent happiness with Verity and his destiny, there was little he could do to fight what was about to happen. His father's killer lived and prospered. Whether his mother had realized it or not, all the words she'd spoken were meant for Keddinton. And for years, he'd known he was to be the instrument of that curse. Now they would go to Warrenford Park to confront his father's murderer. He would gut Robert Veryan, and that would be an end to it.

And an end to him, as well. For it would not be possible to kill the man in cold blood, in front of witnesses, and walk away from the crime. He had no title to protect him, like Stanegate had. By removing Keddinton from the world, he had no doubt that he would be doing everyone a service and fulfilling the task that his mother had set for him. He would be doing his new brothers a service, as well. There was no quicker way for Stephano to end up on the gibbet than to kill a viscount. The Carlows would be rid of him, and their little sister could return safely home to marry the well-born *gaujo* of their choosing.

Once he was sure Verity was safe, he would be free to act. And if the opportunity was there, right in front of him, he would not be able to stop himself from acting. If fate was kind, he would find a way to serve his destiny and keep his life. But at the moment, he did not know what that would be.

Chapter Twenty-One

They arrived at Warrenford Park, having seen no trace of Verity or Alexander, or the big black stallion they had ridden. And since there was no reason to do otherwise, they entered through the front, led by Stanegate. The butler recognized Stephano and greeted him as Lord Salterton, which prompted some raised eyebrows from the men around him, but no comment. When the servant directed them to a drawing room to wait, Stanegate smiled and informed him that they were expected and wished to be shown directly to Keddinton.

Stephano supposed that, in a way, they had been expected. For Robert Veryan must have known that eventually this day would come. When they entered his study together and he first saw Hebden, Wardale and both Carlow sons, on his face there had been a fleeting…something. Disappointment? Anger? Resignation? Whatever it was, it had been a true indication of the man's feelings. But it had passed so quickly that it could not be recognized. And now, Stephano was sure that it had been filed away so that the man could return to scheming.

He smiled at them, cool and unruffled. 'And to what do I owe the pleasure of this visit, gentlemen?' He glanced to Stephano. 'Have you captured him at last? Do you wish me to see him properly disposed of, Stanegate?'

'I would like to see you attempt it,' Stephano said. 'I have told these gentlemen what you are guilty of, and they now stand beside me.'

'Guilty?' Veryan said in surprise. 'Am I a thief? Or a kidnapper, as you are?'

'You might as well be, for you were most helpful when it came to the snatching of Verity Carlow from your estate.' There was a stirring in the men next to him, as though the reminder of that crime drew fresh anger. And for a moment, they could not decide who was the enemy.

Stephano glanced at them. 'Had you not thought of that? You give me too much credit, if you think that I can waltz into the home of a spymaster and steal a girl out from under his very nose. He was my ally in that. He invited me to his house and left the way clear for my escape.'

Keddinton gave the men a sympathetic smile. 'He was invited to my house, of course. But he concealed his identity from me. I was surprised, as we all were, when Verity was taken. And now that she is returned and he is caught, he will say anything, just to save his skin. But is that not the way of his kind? Liars and thieves, all of them.'

'And yet, if we had a country to betray, we would not do it, nor do we murder our friends.'

'Murder and treason?' Keddinton gave a small shake of his head, and smiled as though he were correcting a minor mistake. 'You are talking nonsense and leading the others to the same.' He looked at the Carlows and at Nathan Wardale with the sympathy one would expect from an older, wiser man. 'He is nothing more than a lunatic, stirring up a matter that was settled long ago. The man responsible for the death of Lord Framlingham was hanged for the crime.' He spread his hands, as though he had encompassed the whole of the problem. And looking into his eyes, Stephano realized, again, how far he had underestimated him. For the man's lie was every bit as convincing as if he had been telling the whole truth.

Without another word, Stanegate reached into his pocket and withdrew the message they had found in the rattle. He held it out so that Keddinton could see, and withdrew it quickly, as the man reached for it.

Keddinton's expression was unchanged. 'It is so much gibberish, and could have come from anywhere. Do you expect me to believe that we were wrong, all those years ago, based on an accusation by this…this…Gypsy?'

Stephano stared at him and the men around him, wondering if they doubted. For to look into the face of Keddinton made him doubt himself, even though he knew the truth. And then, all the confusion burned away, leaving behind a certainty that was even older than his mother's curse. 'Gypsy I may be. But I am also the only living son of Christopher Hebden, Lord Framlingham.

Robert Veryan, you murdered my father, and let Ley-bourne hang for it.'

'It is over, Veryan,' Stanegate said. 'We found the code key in a place where only the murdered man could have hidden it. It has rested, undiscovered all this time. And it states your name as traitor. There is no doubt.'

As they waited for the man to respond, there was a silence that seemed eternal. And then, Keddinton gave a laugh that came near to a giggle of glee. 'Of all the refuse that has surfaced, in the last year...' He glared at Stephano. 'Bastards,' and then at Nathan. 'Waistrels. And all manner of nonsense cutting up my peace and changing the rightful order of things. You have come here to tell me it is a scrap of paper that will be my end?' He laughed again. 'Oh, gentlemen. That is rich. Too rich for me. I have spent all this time hiding files, burning journals and erasing every record of that time. And now a half sheet of foolscap and a little ink, and you have come to get me.'

Keddinton's laughter continued, and the men looked from one to another, unsure of what they were to do with a man so obviously mad.

He wiped his eyes, to clear the tears of mirth. 'But at least, if it is over, I will no longer have to put up with the Gypsy's pathetic attempts to manipulate me.' He stood up from his desk and snarled at Stephano. 'If you had not been so bloody incompetent, there would not be four of you to harass me now. I would think, in the months you have been at this, that there would have been significant mortality. But nothing. In the end, I had to hire someone to take action for you.' He glared at Hal. 'And even then, you did not have the sense to die.'

Hal broke his silence with an explosive oath. 'I was carved like a goose, you dirty bastard! What have I ever done to you?'

'You, and the rest of your family, are tiresome beyond belief. You and your all too perfect brother. George got you. And I got...' Keddinton shook his head. 'Alexander.'

He raved on. 'But then, George got everything handed to him along with his title. From the very first, when I was an underpaid junior, your father and the rest treated me as dogsbody and whipping boy. And until Hebden almost spoilt it, they never guessed what I was up to.'

He grinned at Stanegate. 'If you could see the look on your father's face, each time he sees a flower in my lapel. I had to do something, to explain the scent of rosemary on my coat that night, and tucked a sprig behind a rose in my buttonhole. I have made it a habit, because I know the smell annoys him.' He giggled. 'I serve lamb when he visits me, just to see him push away from the table. The mere sight of the rosemary makes him too green to finish his meal. If he would admit the weakness, I might spare him. Or perhaps he will someday have the brains to see that I am taunting him.'

'But what is the point of it, after all this time? If you had done nothing, you would have been safe,' Stanegate asked.

'Too many people asking too many questions. Someone was bound to stumble on the truth. When the Gypsy returned, I expected him to remove you, Wardale. Or that one of you would remove him. And in time, dear, weak George would die from the stress of it all. Then someone would kill the Gypsy, and there would be no one left to care. No one left but me.'

'But you must have known that it wouldn't succeed,' Stanegate said. 'There were too many variables. And to assume that we would remove Hebden, as casually as you did his father…'

Although it had been too close to the truth, for Stephano's taste.

'Do not tell me what will and won't succeed, boy,' Keddinton said. 'You are too stupid to know what men can be driven to with a little provocation.'

Stephano watched as the man's weight shifted in his chair, and before he saw a real movement, he knew that when next he saw Keddinton's right hand, it would be holding a pistol. An honourable man might shoot himself. But Robert Veryan had sacrificed what little honour he had, many years ago. If he had a gun, he would shoot the nearest man and use the confusion to run.

And Stanegate stood between Veryan and the window, with nothing but his honour to protect him. When he fell, his brother would go to him. Nathan was by the door, too far away to stop what was happening.

And apparently, Stephano had proven to Veryan that he was easily tricked, and therefore, no threat.

It was too late to stop what was about to happen without bloodshed. Veryan had begun to move. Stephano reached for his knife, secure in the knowledge that what he was doing would be in defence of himself or his friends, and not done from vengeance. But then he remembered. There was no point in reaching for something that resided in his wife's pocket. He had nothing to stop his father's killer from killing again.

The gun was out now, and he lunged forward, into the flash, feeling Veryan's throat under his fingers, and the searing pain in his side as he dragged them both to the floor. He was clinging, grasping, choking the struggling man, while the room grew dim around him. And from somewhere far away, there was the sound of voices. A man's shout. And a woman's cry of anguish.

'Stephano!'

Chapter Twenty-Two

He was in the beech grove again. The light filtering through the leaves was gold on bronze. He listened for the sounds of the camp so that he might know which way he must walk to go home. But there was nothing. Not even the sound of the wind.

Standing before him was a Gypsy girl, her fingers reaching out to pluck one of the leaves from the tree, turning it over slowly in her hand.

'Nadya.' He said it softly, but the girl did not answer. She turned slowly to him, looking up. And he realized he'd been mistaken.

'Jaelle. Mother.' He had never seen her, but it must be. And she did look like her daughter, hair rich and black, with the same almond-shaped dark eyes.

She smiled in response. 'Stephano. My son.'

He swallowed, for his throat tightened at the sight of her. 'Yes.' He stepped closer, and then froze, as she reached out a hand and signalled him to stop.

She dropped it to her side. 'You have grown strong, little one.'

'As you hoped.' He thought of Verity. And suddenly, he was full of doubt. 'But very tired. Do you have what you want? Is it enough?'

'Are you happy?'

He thought of Verity again. And he smiled. 'Yes.'

His mother smiled back at him. 'Then I have all I want.' She stepped close to him. 'Rest.' And he bent his head so that she could kiss him.

Chapter Twenty-Three

Stephano woke. He could still feel the kiss, cool on his forehead. And there was the headache again. But it was unlike the old pain. This was more akin to what he might get if some other man had tried to peg his skull. And there was the dull ache of a bullet wound. Deep, he suspected, because it was accompanied by the weakness from blood loss and the dry mouth of extended unconsciousness.

But there was also the feeling of cool sheets on his skin. And the gentle touch of a lover's hands.

'Verity.' The word came from his lips, hoarse and cracking, but he could feel the increase of pressure on the cold compress at his forehead and the brush of water against his dry lips.

'Here, darling.' She fed him carefully. The water trickling down his throat was cool and delicious and did much to restore him. He took the moment to gather his thoughts. He felt bad. But not so bad that he could not sit up and tend to himself. He had managed worse before, without a woman fussing over him.

But in a rush, it came to him that he did not wish to manage. He wanted to lie there for ever and allow Verity to do for him. Her hands, so gentle, made the pain fade. And they could do so much more.

He opened his eyes and smiled at her, safe and whole in front of him. 'Thank God. You are all right, then?'

'Of course, darling. But I fear Alexander is not. I had your knife. He got a nasty cut on his hand, and Zor threw him into the bushes and then took me back to camp. I made Val take me to the Veryans. I knew you would look for me there.'

He gave a dry chuckle of approval, but stopped short, for to laugh hurt very much.

She kissed him on the forehead again. 'You worried about me? You foolish man.'

It had been foolish of him, he remembered. To rush at a man with a gun, when you had no weapon, would land you in the position he currently occupied. Or worse, under six feet of earth with no more opportunity to regret the act. 'I could not help myself.' And he still could not. 'He meant to shoot.'

'At Marc. My brothers are both quite vexed at you. Hal especially, for he is so good at playing the hero in such situations. Although I think Marc is secretly impressed by the way you stepped into the line of fire. He said you were very fast in divining the way of things, and that even half unconscious, you were on the floor with your hands on Uncle Robert's throat, like a terrier worrying a rat. They had to pry you loose from the man before they could arrest him.'

'He would have killed your brother. I could not allow it.'

'Foolish. All of you are, for arguing over the right to be the one who was shot. But so very brave.' She was pressing her lips to his cheek now, and he relaxed and enjoyed it. If this was the reward that brave fools got, then it did not say much for choosing to be a wise coward.

'What happened to Veryan?'

'For now, Uncle Robert is still alive, and with much to explain. But he will have to do it in Newgate, for the world knows better than to trust him again.' She paused, watching carefully, as though she were afraid to see his reaction.

At one time, the thought that his true enemy lived would have been enough to send him reaching for his clothes. He would have ridden out to win the vengeance that he had been seeking for so long. But he remembered his mother. And he sank back into the pillows again. 'It is about time, for the sake of Wardales, Carlows and Hebdens alike, that the past gets a proper airing and all of his crimes are accounted for in court. Once the truth is known, the state can do what it likes with the man.'

'It is truly over for you, then?' She was relaxing against him, her arms stealing around him as though she would hold him back, should he show signs of changing his mind.

He placed his hands about her, as well. 'I have been released. You are the only woman, living or dead, with a claim upon my future.'

'I am so glad.' She kissed him on the lips. 'Thank you for saving my brothers, even if they do not think they needed it.' She kissed him again. 'And for preventing them from doing him harm before justice could settle the matter.'

And he sighed in gratitude that she did not know how close he'd come to that himself.

She smiled softly at him and stroked his hair. 'But I should much prefer it if you were more cautious in the future, should a similar circumstance arise. You lost a frightful amount of blood. And for a time, I quite feared...'

There was a little break in her voice, and he reached out and caught one of her hands in his, bringing it to his lips to reassure her. 'Do not think of it. It was a trifle, little more than that. I am still here, after all that has been attempted against me.'

'My brothers told me not to worry. They say that you are surprisingly hard to kill.' She frowned. 'But I told them that I had seen you near death from a tiny scratch. And that there was no telling what might happen in your weakened condition. They wished to hire a nurse for you, but I told them I would not be satisfied unless I was here myself to see that you were properly taken care of. But they would not allow me to stay with you in the Rom camp. So we are all at Stanegate Court.'

'Ahh.' That explained much. 'I am sure I owe my recovery to your skilful tending.' It would drive poor Narborough to another attack, if he caught his daughter in such a state, practically in the bed of a naked man. But Stephano had no wish to change his circumstances. So he made an effort to look as helpless as possible. 'But I am not out of the woods yet.' He sank back into the pillows, and she followed him, leaning her body against his, taking care not to disturb his wounded side.

Her hand brushed lightly against his temples as her lips tickled his ear. 'That is a shame. I am eager for your full return to vitality.' Her whisper had turned into a kiss, and the tempo of her breathing made his own pulse quicken and his body stir encouragingly.

He looked over her shoulder to see her brother standing in the doorway. The expression on Stanegate's face made it clear that, no matter his true state, he had best be too weak for any foolishness. The Carlow family would have no compunction against putting a fresh hole in him. He cleared his throat. 'I think I shall need six weeks at least, to be truly healthy.'

'Then I shall be at your side, the whole time, to make sure that you behave.' She was smiling down at him, and he could feel himself growing stronger. How strange. For he had not really believed that he would survive this mad quest his grandmother had set him to. And now? The future stretched forward, as far as his mind could reach. The path was clear, shining so brightly before him that he could hardly bear to look without his eyes becoming wet.

He reached out to touch her face. 'If you are intent on remaining with me, then it would be churlish of me to trouble you further.'

He arranged himself on the bed to leave some small space between them, and reached to take her hand, twining her fingers with his own. 'But if you would have me, and be Mrs Stephen Hebden, then my recovery shall give us more than enough time for a license and the reading of the banns.'

She pulled away and looked at him with startled delight. '*If* I mean to have you? Now you are being foolish. I thought it was all decided.'

'Between us, my love.' He glanced up at Stanegate. 'But I wish your family's blessing. If you would do me the honour to wed me in the eyes of the law, as well as the Lord, then both our families can celebrate the union.' He thought of the Carlows, the Beshaleys and the Hebdens, all in the same church, with the Wardales to stand witness. It made his head hurt again, but it was still nothing like the pain that he'd grown used to.

She kissed him again, making no effort to protect his wound, nor to hide her enthusiasm from her brother. 'You know I will have you.' She ran a hand under the sheet and down his bare chest. 'And you will have no opposition from my family.' She shot a glance over her shoulder, toward the doorway, her look as fierce as any Romany girl's. 'I mean to keep him, Marc. No matter what you and Father might have to say. And it will be better if we are properly wed, don't you think? So you must help me explain to the others.'

Stephen heard the exasperated sigh from the doorway. 'And I suppose if I try to exert some common sense, you will not give me a moment's peace.' He glared down at Stephano, but there was a touch of amusement in his eyes. 'If we give her to you, will you keep her in health and happiness?'

'She shall want for nothing.' He smiled at her. 'When I am a little better, we shall go to examine the contents of my safe. You shall have the pick of the stones there for your ring. Do you fancy a diamond? I have emeralds, as well, and rubies of unusual clarity. Or all three. I will cover you from head to toe with jewels, if you wish.'

She put her hands to her lips to hide her smile. 'That will not be necessary. For my ring, I should like jade.' She whispered, 'The colour of my eyes.'

He smiled. 'Not as precious as a diamond. But it is just as beautiful, if you have a discerning taste. And although gold is more valuable, I think the setting must be silver, to honour my family. It will be a most singular piece. Like no other in the world, just as you are like no other woman. Once I can retrieve Thom's tools and clean the workshop in Bloomsbury Square, I will make it for you myself.'

Her eyes grew wide with surprise. And he remembered why they reminded him of jade, for he could lose himself for ever in them. 'You could do that for me? It would be most wonderful. I knew you were talented, of course. And the way you played the violin was most exciting. But that you could make me a ring, as well...'

It almost made him blush to see her so excited about such small displays of skills. To be good with one's hands was a virtue demanded of any Rom. But he hadn't thought that an earl's daughter would be so intrigued by the very things that had shamed his own father. He brought her hand to his lips. 'Of course, my darling.'

She closed her eyes and smiled as though a simple kiss was near to paradise. She was still smiling, when she opened them again, and her eyes brightened as though it were a surprise to find him still there, close to her body. 'I never imagined...' And her eyes were so full of love and amazement that he felt he could stare into them for the rest of his life.

'Nor did I.' And he kissed her on the lips, not caring about the disapproving harrumphs from her brother, letting himself sink slowly into the happiness that was to be his future.

Epilogue

V erity walked down the aisle towards the man waiting at the front. Her father gave her arm an encouraging squeeze, and she turned and smiled at him. It was good, after his long illness, to feel him offering support to her as they walked, and not the other way around.

Of course, he had been less than pleased with her choice, at first. But Stephano could be charming when he wished to be, and quite hard to resist. And he wished to be, most heartily in the case of her family.

There he was, staring back at her from the front of the church. And could it be? He appeared to be nervous. The man who was never out of composure had unravelled at the prospect of marrying her. He wore a trim grey coat and spotless white trousers. His linen was immaculate, the cravat tied in something that looked as uncomfortable as it was complicated. He was elegant but conservative, and deserved the snickers and mutters of *'gaujo'* she heard from the Rom.

Magda looked to her and nodded in approval. For

before the ceremony, she had shown the old woman the petticoat that the Beshaleys had made for her, raising the skirt of her jade-green dress a few inches so that one of the coins was visible, and slipping the bracelet down her arm so that it would show beneath her puffed sleeve. While her beloved might look every bit an English gentleman, she did her best to carry a bit of their Rom life to the altar with her.

She tried not to smile at the sight of Stephano fidgeting. He gave a faint shrug of relief as she drew near, and it was clear that he would have her, just as planned. There would be no sudden hitch to spoil the proceedings.

He relaxed even further after the ceremony had passed the critical moment when one might object. Though she had assured him that none would, he swore he would not be at peace until the ring was safely on her hand. She was sure that he must have given Nathan no end of bother over the ring itself. As witness, he had been left in charge of it. And while Diana had assured Stephano that there was nothing to fear, Nathan had grinned, examined the thing and announced that it would make an excellent starter for a game of hazard.

Diana had reached out to Verity, pretending to straighten her dress, and kissed her on the cheek and whispered that he was only joking. The new Earl of Leybourne had no reason to gamble. Even if he did, he would certainly not do it with Verity's wedding ring. But Stephen had been wicked to them. And it served him right if they gave him reason to worry.

And it seemed that each couple took some small pleasure in seeing the man suffer. But she could hardly blame them. He had been odious to almost everyone in the church, which made for a most interesting guest list. But he was making an effort to reform. He had gone from family to family, offering apology and redress, and making a silver rattle for each of the wives, as a remembrance of the events. Of course, the revelation of Keddinton as murderer had done much to restore their relationships and had gained him the enthusiastic support of all the Wardale family.

And her own brothers had seen him pay in blood. Will Wolversley, who had married Nate's sister, Rosalind, was of the opinion that a man who had managed to give Robert Veryan his just deserts could be forgiven very nearly anything. Rosalind heartily agreed, and she kissed Verity's cheek in congratulations.

If only Honoria could be here with them, Verity would know for sure that things would go right. She hoped that Stephano's letter of apology had reached her safely, and that his inclusion of a magnificent rope of pearls along with a silver rattle would soften any remaining hard feelings.

He had assured her that it was an excellent gift, for a newly married couple. While having met Gabe Hawksworth, he did not doubt that the man would land on his feet anywhere he chose to settle, there was nothing wrong with the insurance of jewellery. And pearls were an easily shared dower, should Honoria be blessed with daughters. They were a gift for the future.

It was sweet of him to think so. And in Verity's heart, it felt good to know that she would be his bride. For now that he had pledged himself to her, he was just as loyal to her family as he was to his own.

There, on the other side of the church, was Stephano's own family, dressed in their Gypsy best, packed into pews, nudging each other with good humour at the curiosity of Stephano's *gadje* wedding. Her own parents looked on them with a kind of horror. Marcus laid a hand on Father's shoulder in a gesture of reassurance, and Hal looked at her, as if to say, 'Is this what you truly want?'

She gave him a nod, and he seemed to relax in his seat.

Stephano's sister Nadya sat side by side with Magda, who turned to the rest of her tribe and offered a glare that silenced them easily into respectability. And at Nadya's side was her own *gaujo* husband, Rhys, who looked at the chaos, and gave Verity a conspiratorial smile and a wink.

And there, mixed in with the Gypsies, sat Stephano's other sister, Imogen, and her husband Monty, Viscount Mildenhall. Imo had nearly overwhelmed her, with her easy affection, and excitement at having another sister. Verity had assured her that she would be equally excited to see the new niece or nephew that would be a part of the Claremont household in a few short months.

She glanced behind her, at the packed church, and smiled. Had it really been just a few weeks ago that she had been missing the company of her family, and considering a lonely future as spinster? Now that she was marrying, Nell and Julia felt more like sisters to her. Diana was again her confidante. And an entire tribe of Gypsies claimed her as one of their own.

And in a few minutes, she would gather them all together for a wedding breakfast at Bloomsbury Square.

They would be served by all manner of rogues and scoundrels, and at least one fallen woman. But it did not worry her. For the band of retired miscreants had welcomed her both as lady of the house and comrade in arms.

Everywhere she turned, people loved her and wanted her company. Not a one of them cared that she was the Earl of Narborough's daughter. And the man beside her loved her most of all.

She turned back to the altar and sighed in satisfaction, as she married Mr Stephen Hebden. Again.

* * * * *

COMING NEXT MONTH FROM

HARLEQUIN®
HISTORICAL

Available January 25, 2011.

- **LADY LAVENDER**
  by **Lynna Banning**
  (Western)

- **SOCIETY'S MOST DISREPUTABLE GENTLEMAN**
  by **Julia Justiss**
  (Regency)

- **MARRIED: THE VIRGIN WIDOW**
  by **Deborah Hale**
  (Regency)
  Gentlemen of Fortune

- **A THOROUGHLY COMPROMISED LADY**
  by **Bronwyn Scott**
  (Regency)

REQUEST YOUR FREE BOOKS!

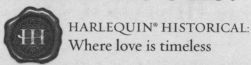

HARLEQUIN® HISTORICAL:
Where love is timeless

2 FREE NOVELS PLUS 2 FREE GIFTS!

YES! Please send me 2 FREE Harlequin® Historical novels and my 2 FREE gifts (gifts are worth about $10). After receiving them, if I don't wish to receive any more books, I can return the shipping statement marked "cancel." If I don't cancel, I will receive 6 brand-new novels every month and be billed just $4.94 per book in the U.S. or $5.49 per book in Canada. That's a saving of 20% off the cover price! It's quite a bargain! Shipping and handling is just 50¢ per book.* I understand that accepting the 2 free books and gifts places me under no obligation to buy anything. I can always return a shipment and cancel at any time. Even if I never buy another book from Harlequin, the two free books and gifts are mine to keep forever.

246/349 HDN E5L4

Name	(PLEASE PRINT)	
Address		Apt. #
City	State/Prov.	Zip/Postal Code

Signature (if under 18, a parent or guardian must sign)

Mail to the **Harlequin Reader Service:**
IN U.S.A.: P.O. Box 1867, Buffalo, NY 14240-1867
IN CANADA: P.O. Box 609, Fort Erie, Ontario L2A 5X3

Not valid for current subscribers to Harlequin Historical books.

Want to try two free books from another line?
Call 1-800-873-8635 or visit www.morefreebooks.com.

* Terms and prices subject to change without notice. Prices do not include applicable taxes. N.Y. residents add applicable sales tax. Canadian residents will be charged applicable provincial taxes and GST. Offer not valid in Quebec. This offer is limited to one order per household. All orders subject to approval. Credit or debit balances in a customer's account(s) may be offset by any other outstanding balance owed by or to the customer. Please allow 4 to 6 weeks for delivery. Offer available while quantities last.

Your Privacy: Harlequin Books is committed to protecting your privacy. Our Privacy Policy is available online at www.eHarlequin.com or upon request from the Reader Service. From time to time we make our lists of customers available to reputable third parties who may have a product or service of interest to you. If you would prefer we not share your name and address, please check here. ☐

Help us get it right—We strive for accurate, respectful and relevant communications. To clarify or modify your communication preferences, visit us at www.ReaderService.com/consumerchoice.

HH10R

*Harlequin Romance author Donna Alward is loved
for her gorgeous rancher heroes.*

*Meet Wyatt as he's confronted by both a precious
little pink bundle left on his doorstep and his neighbor Elli
who's going to show him the ropes....*

Introducing
PROUD RANCHER, PRECIOUS BUNDLE

THE SQUAWKING QUIETED as Elli picked the baby up, and
Wyatt turned around, trying hard to ignore the feelings of
inadequacy as Darcy immediately stopped fussing.

"Maybe she's uncomfortable. What do you think, sweet-
heart?" Elli turned her conversation to the baby.

"What do you think is wrong?" Wyatt asked, putting the
coffee pot back on the burner.

A strange look passed over Elli's face, one that looked
like guilt and panic. But it was gone quickly. "I couldn't
say," she replied.

"But you were so good with her this afternoon." Wyatt
put his hands on his hips.

"Lucky, that's all. I just…remembered a few things."
The same strange look flitted over her features once more.

Wyatt took the coffee to the table. "You fooled me. You
looked like you knew exactly what you were doing." So
much so that Wyatt had felt completely inept. A feeling he
despised. He was used to being the one in control.

Elli and Darcy walked the length of the kitchen and
back. After a few moments, she admitted, "I haven't really
cared for a baby before. The things I thought of were simply
things I'd heard about. Not from experience, Mr. Black."

Her chin jutted up, closing the subject but making him

want to ask the questions now pulsing through his mind. But then he remembered the old saying—*Don't look a gift horse in the mouth.* He'd benefit from whatever insight she had and be glad of it.

"I don't really know what babies need," he said. "I fed her, patted her back like you did, walked her to sleep, but every time I put her down…"

Wyatt almost groaned. Of course. He'd forgotten one important thing. He'd been so focused on getting the formula the right temperature that he'd forgotten to check her diaper. Not that he had any clue what to do there either.

Pulling calves and shoveling out stalls was far less intimidating than one tiny newborn.

"She's probably due for a diaper change, isn't she." He tried to sound nonchalant. This was a perfect opportunity. Elli must know how to change a diaper. He could simply watch her so he'd know better for the next time.

Instead, Elli came around the corner of the counter and placed Darcy back in his arms. "Here you go, Uncle Wyatt," she said lightly. "You get diaper duty. I'll fix the coffee. Cream and sugar?"

Oh boy, Wyatt thought, looking down into Darcy's pursed face, his smug plan blown to smithereens. He was in for it now.

Will sparks fly between Elli and Wyatt?

Find out in
PROUD RANCHER, PRECIOUS BUNDLE
Available February 2011 from Harlequin Romance

Copyright © 2011 by Donna Alward

HREXP0211

Try these Healthy and Delicious Spring Rolls!

INGREDIENTS

2 packages rice-paper spring roll wrappers (20 wrappers)

1 cup grated carrot

¼ cup bean sprouts

1 cucumber, julienned

1 red bell pepper, without stem and seeds, julienned

4 green onions finely chopped— use only the green part

DIRECTIONS

1. Soak one rice-paper wrapper in a large bowl of hot water until softened.

2. Place a pinch each of carrots, sprouts, cucumber, bell pepper and green onion on the wrapper toward the bottom third of the rice paper.

3. Fold ends in and roll tightly to enclose filling.

4. Repeat with remaining wrappers. Chill before serving.

Find this and many more delectable recipes including the perfect dipping sauce in

YOUR BEST BODY NOW
by
TOSCA RENO

WITH STACY BAKER

Bestselling Author of THE EAT-CLEAN DIET®

Available wherever books are sold!

NTRSERIESJAN

HARLEQUIN Presents

USA TODAY bestselling author

Sharon Kendrick

introduces

HIS MAJESTY'S CHILD

The king's baby of shame!

King Casimiro harbors a secret—no one in the kingdom
of Zaffirinthos knows that a devastating accident has left
his memory clouded in darkness. And Casimiro himself
cannot answer why Melissa Maguire, an enigmatic English
rose, stirs such feelings in him…. Questioning his ability
to rule, Casimiro decides he will renounce the throne.
But Melissa has news she knows will rock the palace
to its core—*Casimiro has an heir!*

Law dictates Casimiro cannot abdicate, so he must find a
way to reacquaint himself with Melissa—his new queen!

Available from Harlequin Presents
February 2011

www.eHarlequin.com

HP12972

Silhouette Desire

USA TODAY bestselling author

ELIZABETH BEVARLY

is back with a steamy and powerful story.

Gavin Mason is furious and vows revenge on high-price, high-society girl Violet Tandy. Her novel is said to be fiction, but everyone *knows* she's referring to Gavin as a client in her memoir. The tension builds when they learn not to judge a book by its cover.

THE BILLIONAIRE GETS HIS WAY

Available February
wherever books are sold.

Always Powerful, Passionate and Provocative.

Visit Silhouette Books at www.eHarlequin.com

SD73078